THE CANDY MAN

A CHARLES BLOOM MURDER MYSTERY

MARK SUBLETTE

JUST ME PUBLISHING

Published by Just Me Publishing, LLC.

Library of Congress Control Number: 2020912531
The Candy Man / Mark Sublette
ISBN 978-0-9998176-4-3
1. Fiction I. Title

Quantity Purchases
Companies, professional groups, clubs, and other organizations may qualify for special terms when ordering quantities of this title. For more information, contact us through www.marksublette.com.

Cover design: Patrick Travers
Layout and production: Jaime Gould
Author photo: Dan Budnik

Printed in the USA by Bookmasters
Ashland, OH • www.bookmasters.com

AUTHOR'S NOTE

The Bloom murder mystery series and the characters that populate the books are all works of fiction. *The Candy Man* takes place in New Mexico; the settings represent areas I have visited, with the exception of the Mesilla cartel location, which exists only in my imagination. This book's focus is on the power of politics outside of any given party affiliation.

All the characters are fictional, including, but not limited to, the police officers, politicians, state and trading post employees, cartel organizations, art galleries, candy companies, and art dealers. The Native Americans in my book are also fictional and any resemblance to real people by name, clan, or physical description is pure coincidence.

The T.C. Cannon painting that features prominently in this book's plot line does not exist. Cannon was an exceptional artist for whom I have immense admiration. He was a true Vietnam War hero whose tragic death is accurately depicted, as are the facts about the artist's New York gallery and his love of Bob Dylan's music.

The Historic Toadlena Trading Post, a central component of all the Bloom books, is a real working trading post that exists as described on Navajoland. This historic post specializes in Toadlena/Two Grey Hills weavings and is well worth the effort to visit. I would like to thank its proprietor, author Mark Winter, and his wife, Linda, for their invaluable insight and their editing prowess. Thanks, too, to the Brown family that lives in the Toadlena basin for their insightful comments with regards to Navajo traditions.

No book is complete without a great cover, and I'm most appreciative to Josh Elliott for so graciously allowing me to use THE BLUE CHAIR to capture the essence of the Navajo Nation and to serve as a central component of the plot line as well. Thanks, too, to Patrick Travers and Jaime Gould for their graphic design skills, to Patricia West-Barker for her editing and sage fact-checking, and to Peter Miller, whose detailed eye in editing helped immensely.

All the photographs of Santa Fe, Mesilla (Las Cruces), and Navajoland that appear in the book were taken by me, and serve as points of reference that correlate to the chapters in which they appear. Hopefully, they will help give the reader the sense of place and moment in time that I experienced when I took them.

CHAPTER 1

MA

The mule's new F-10 pickup was a modified vehicle made for Mexican-U.S. border crossings. The side panels—constructed to secure loaves of uncut cocaine—were special-ordered from the factory for a select clientele. A pile of freshly harvested watermelons in the truck bed completed the ruse: five watermelons near the bottom were stuffed with bags of blow. The watermelon load was worth the risk. Mules by definition were expendable, and oblivious cops, often on the cartel's payroll, meant more money flowing into the borderland.

The hidden door compartments were expertly constructed. A modified truck had once been confiscated after border agents found fruit stuffed with sacks of cocaine in the bed, but the bounty-filled door compartments went undiscovered, the drug-sniffing canines unable to detect the load. The confiscated cocaine-laden truck was later repurchased by the cartel at a Las Cruces police auction at a bargain price—no risky border crossing was necessary.

Mules based in Mexico passed through minimally staffed entry points, the regular guards on both sides being friendly to the cartel's cash contributions. A favorite crossing was located not far from Mesilla, New Mexico—no invasive I-94 forms required. The newly constructed concrete barriers gracing the checkpoint were a Trojan horse, suggesting more security, more payouts, and the false appearance of safety. When the cartel was involved, no one was safe.

In the early 1990s, the cocaine hauls were substantial. Business flourished as white dust covered America's landscape, a booming economy making cocaine the drug of choice. Once cut for the market, the average load brought in $2.5 million; the mule was paid a handsome $5,000 for his efforts. After five border crossings in six months, a mule would likely be reevaluated and discarded at year's end: longevity was not a part of the job requirement.

Angel Molina Veracruz had been running transportation logistics for the cartel for the last five years. Under her guidance, the cartel's productivity and inventory had steadily increased. Products, once limited to drugs, had expanded to include such money-laundering goods as pre-Columbian artifacts, fruits, vegetables, electronics, counterfeit luxury purses—occasionally, even human chattel—all collected and sold in the name of the Veracruz family.

Angel was a graduate of New Mexico State University. Her degree, at her father's insistence, was in business. The major was not her choice; she leaned more toward the creative side of academia. But she understood her role well. Third in command in the family's male-dominated hierarchy, her ambitious nature and immense drive would never allow her to attain the top position: a woman's role was to coordinate the business, not control it.

Juan Gabriel Veracruz—a vicious man and her beloved father—had ascended to the number one position of the El Paso-Las Cruces drug cartel with the support of his wife. Descended from a family of well-heeled Colombians, she had provided Juan Gabriel access to the Medellin Cartel's cocaine production elites, a critical component of his rise as a drug lord. Connections, brutality, and intelligence provided the secret sauce for long-term success—and Juan Gabriel had equal portions of all three.

Converting the raw drugs into cash fell to the second-in-command, Angel's older brother Federico, whose lack of empathy and sadistic propensities were legendary.

Arriving cocaine bricks were unloaded into an unassuming adobe building with a nondescript flattop roof, speckled gray by the mourning doves and pigeons that gathered for the grain Juan Gabriel provided—a touch of local color. Located off a cottonwood-lined dirt road not far from the central Mesilla Plaza, the unassuming compound was now a center of commerce in the drug trade.

The old Hispanic home, constructed during the period of the Gadsden Purchase—a potential jewel for archaeologists—was now lost to time and corruption. It sat next to an enormous metal building, once a farm-machine hangar, whose spacious interior and electric doors offered easy access to vehicles delivering product.

The occasional tractor made guest appearances from the multitude of fields that surrounded the area, but for those who cared to look, the steady flow of dark Cadillacs told the real backstory. The Veracruzes were an old New Mexican family, generous to the community and church, which meant few questions were asked. In the community's eyes, they were simply *chile*, cotton, and pecan farmers—even if their crop production was sub-average year after year.

Through expert pharmacological manipulation, a single 4- x 6- x 12-inch block of pure cocaine quickly became four blocks judiciously doled out by Federico to a series of boots-on-the-ground dealers in Phoenix, El Paso, Tucson, and as far north as Albuquerque. Successful dealers were given more bricks, while those who reduced the guaranteed Veracruz buzz by stepping on the product, skimming profits, or missing their sale quotas, soon found themselves in a tragic combine accident on one of the Veracruz fields.

All monies generated by the sale of the cocaine went into the Veracruz family financial pool, destined for investment after laundering. Finding a bank to clean the money would have been the quickest route, but that had proved to be the riskiest. Juan Gabriel believed bankers were greedy by nature, and vast amounts of cash would tempt their so-called righteousness, so he preferred laundering his money himself. Cash-heavy enterprises proved to be the best way to do the job: half a dozen laundromats scattered throughout poor towns in southern New Mexico, topless bars, old Route 66 motels, cafés, and a marina at Elephant Butte, near Truth or Consequences, New Mexico, provided the bulk of outlets. Vehicles, cheap rental properties, and leased farmland were also desired assets: helping troubled sellers in need of cash was a Veracruz specialty.

Angel, who loved art and as a child dreamed of becoming an artist, not a drug dealer, had recently come up with another avenue for disposing of huge amounts of cash by investing in an appreciating asset—fine art—and convinced her dominating father to let her enroll at the University of Arizona for a fine art degree.

It wasn't the school's curriculum or professors that had piqued her interest: it was the story of the U. of A. museum's stolen Willem de Kooning painting.

In 1985, a middle-aged couple strolled into the University of Arizona Museum of Art, and, as the woman distracted the lone guard, her male accomplice neatly cut the masterpiece from its frame. The multimillion-dollar de Kooning painting was rolled up and smuggled out hastily under a rain jacket. By the time the empty frame was discovered, the thieves were long gone. With scant information, no video cameras, and a guard's shaky description, there was little to go on. Two decades passed with no sign of the painting or the culprits. All that remained in the museum was an empty frame with the canvas remnants of the once-spectacular painting left hanging on the museum wall, a reminder of the despicable act and a beacon of hope for its safe return.

The story of corruption, art, and millions of dollars tied up in one easily stolen painting was Angel's ticket to both garner her father's attention and cooperation, and to get back to her true love—art—by enrolling in the Master of Arts degree in Art History (MA). Juan Gabriel could relate to the well-executed heist, and realized that by learning more about art, Angel might be able to discover the whereabouts of the valuable painting and make a deal for it—an educational pursuit he could support. The business of art looked to be an excellent medium to launder big money or to use stolen masterpieces as a form of credit for the cartel.

Trading drug money for art was coming into fashion among the cartels, especially in Miami. In 1990, robbers dressed as police strolled into Boston's Isabella Stewart Gardner Museum and walked out with thirteen masterpieces worth hundreds of millions of dollars, and Angel was convinced these works were headed to the East Coast drug trade. Understanding the art market would allow her to advance from a dead-end transportation lackey to the head of a very lucrative trade in stolen art, where she could hopefully extricate herself from the world of drug kingpins and make her own mark. But the first step to success was to understand the foundation and nuances of this niche market.

Juan Gabriel gave his blessing, and Angel was off to get her second degree: Art History with a minor in painting. The one-time transportation expert who specialized in cocaine and human flesh would transform herself into an art expert. Her areas of interest—Western, Native American, and Hispanic art—were considered an old boy's club that excluded women, but those who crossed Angel would soon learn her name was a misnomer. Ruthless, and blessed with ample capital, she would become a force in the white-glove art profession. She wanted to be the boss of her own domain—and anyone who got in her crosshairs would feel her bullets' searing pain.

CHAPTER 2

END OF A BARREL

Tucson's culture and climate were agreeable to Angel, and gave the young woman on a mission a new perspective. Her age, twenty-seven, belied a much older soul. She had seen human beings disposed of in piecemeal fashion and towers of blood-soaked Benjamins stacked in Tinker-Toy fashion against a red-tinged sink waiting to be cleansed of their human stain. Unlike her sadistic brother, these things neither disturbed her nor gave her pleasure.

A veteran of the cartel's inner sanctum, Angel was the most unusual student in the fine arts department. Her business degree had been for her father; this diploma was for her. Studying had a purpose this time, and she decided she would focus on classes and avoid horny young men. She was no longer a college kid, but a woman. Dating was only acceptable to accomplish a goal: finding a suitable mate who was as driven for wealth and power as she was. There would be few possibilities in the university setting; college professors were a dead-end. Successful businessmen or well-placed politicians were more in line with her financial and status goals.

Angel vowed to never again work on the front lines of the Veracruz organization—and would not consider men in the cartel's line of work as partners. She planned to carve out her own niche at arm's length from her father's organization, using her new profession to accumulate wealth through the acquisition and sale of art and artifacts. She would focus on becoming a different type of money cleaner for the cartel—a new life, and one not dependent on the Veracruz family.

Angel concluded that a part-time sales job at a local art gallery was a necessary training tool. To learn the new business, she needed practical experience—the kind she had gotten at her father's knee—even more than an academic degree. She honed in on the best gallery in town, whose owner, Clarke Walden, was near the end of his career. Walden had dealt in Western art and Indian artifacts for nearly fifty years and witnessed Tucson's change from a town of twenty-five thousand to over five-hundred thousand. He had purchased art directly from some of Tucson's most celebrated artists, including Maynard Dixon, Edith Hamlin, Ross Stefan, Ted DeGrazia and Pete Martinez. Walden had both knowledge and connections; he was the perfect first step up the ladder for Angel. Her stunning looks and mature disposition were no match for the old man: she was hired on the spot, no references required.

Walden put Angel directly into sales, eye-candy for the collector. Men dominated the market so her sexuality was not a problem. She was used to being objectified and could handle any man. Her new job title might as well have been gopher/secretary. After running a multimillion-dollar operation, the demotion to a glorified bottle washer should have provoked her ego, but it didn't; it was freeing. With no real responsibility, she could soak up the old dealer's knowledge and, most importantly, steal his client list. Computerization was making inroads in all businesses, but Walden was an old-fashioned art dealer with a Rolodex and no website.

Angel, however, realized the future was in developing an internet market, and she bought a few key URLs that related to her future endeavors. She almost purchased Money.com—a joke about her money-laundering intentions—but decided to focus only on her field. Tunnel vision was hard to shake, even for Angel, so she purchased website names that might have significance for an art dealer. AngelArt.com, FineArt.com, and AmericanPaintings.com were her favorites, but she also bought her employer's gallery name, BuffaloTrails.com, in case the job led to a future buyout opportunity. Obtaining the company name gave her great satisfaction, and made her feel that she was more the owner of the gallery than its founder. Walden would never see this side of Angel. If he knew her true nature, he would have been terrified.

Walden told Angel that knowledge of three key components made for a successful gallery: how to buy, know your clients, and how to execute a sale. Since he mostly dealt in work by deceased artists and antique Native material, he taught her that you couldn't just order new stock: you needed estates, divorces, and tax burdens to cough up new inventory. Fifty years in business at Buffalo Trails Art Gallery had made it the default place to go when people had to sell their art.

Walden was an honest man for the most part—too honest in Angel's eyes. She saw that his greatest weakness was on the buying side: he would never ask what the seller wanted for a piece. Instead, he would offer the price he would pay. Angel realized the old man was leaving money on the table, as many of the sellers wouldn't have a clue about the value of the work, and would simply blurt out some number they had in mind for grandma's old Navajo blanket.

"Wouldn't it be better to have the sellers tell you what they want before you make an offer?" she asked Walden.

He seemed perturbed by Angel's question. "That would be stealing, Angel. I try to play fair so both parties win. You have great power as an art dealer; many of these people's only asset is their art, which they often sell in times of great need."

Angel agreed with her boss's ethical reasoning, at least to his face. But she knew this kind of honesty was a significant defect for success as a businessman—a flaw that would get you killed in the drug trade. Maybe in the art world these ethics resonated, but in the world she envisioned, they would be seen as a sign of terrible weakness.

Walden's clients were listed by their name, phone, address, past purchases, and possible interests. This data was the heart of Buffalo Trails' success, its Holy Grail. Angel offered to make the Rolodex list more searchable by putting it in a spreadsheet on her new Mac computer. Walden didn't understand the nuances of the spreadsheet, but if it created more sales, he was agreeable. Within four months of going to work for Walden, Angel had his entire client list and past purchase history, effectively stealing the content of his gallery. If she chose to open a gallery of her own and compete, she had everything she needed.

The gallerist was thrilled with the long computer sheets of data, the information now safely stored on a drive at Angel's home.

Sales were Walden's forte. His ability to tell stories about the history of the art and artist, embellished with his wonderful gift of gab, made selling effortless. He understood the human psyche, recognizing the appropriate moment to close a sale and how to add more pieces to the sale, building a strong relationship with the buyer through trust.

Angel knew her social-bonding skills were weak; her natural tendency was to not trust anyone, get to the point of the transaction, and move on. This was the opposite of Walden's approach, which was based in finesse rather than brute force.

She watched the old dealer's eyes brighten as an old customer walked through the gallery doors and observed his immediate engagement in idle banter. These abilities were not in her arrow quiver yet, but, with effort, she could learn how to act the part. The next three years were spent understanding sales on a personal level, not at the end of a semiautomatic—her natural predilection.

Angel was determined to be a force to reckon with in the art world, and she would let no one would stop her ascent.

CHAPTER 3

BUFFALO TRAILS II

Graduation day was bittersweet for Angel. In college, she had excelled in the academic interests of the art department, and even enjoyed creating three-dimensional sculptures. But she realized that while her discerning eye could recognize fine art, she wasn't cut from the same cloth as artists who produce the works. Angel had mastered art history and found a deep passion for Western and Native art, which were on the upswing value-wise. It was not uncommon for Buffalo Trails to buy and sell paintings in the $15,000 to $25,000 range. In Santa Fe, the same works sold for double those amounts, and galleries were popping up everywhere. "Santa Fe Style" was all the rage.

Angel's next stop was Northern New Mexico. She knew her father would pressure her to come home and help run the family business; when that failed, he would make a play for her to develop a Veracruz branch of the cartel in the Santa Fe market and beyond.

The Martinez family, whose lineage could be traced back twelve generations, controlled the drug trade in Northern New Mexico and Southern Colorado. Taking on Martinez would be a risky undertaking as the family had strong allies and was equally ruthless. Still, Juan Gabriel Veracruz reasoned that if he could merge with Martinez—or eliminate the competition if Martinez wouldn't join forces—his daughter could run that portion of the distribution system.

Angel opposed a turf war. She had a better idea: forget selling drugs and focus instead on laundering cash and making huge profits by investing in art. With her father's help she would have the money to be taken seriously in the largest market for Western art in the world: Santa Fe. She would keep the gallery low-key and off the beaten path, not to raise suspicions but to let the other dealers know she was a woman of means. Her education and intelligence would come into play. She could buy paintings by the Taos Society of Artists, Maynard Dixon, and Western modernists like Georgia O'Keeffe, perhaps even branch out to more minimalist territory with Taos artist Agnes Martin, who was now bringing in big money.

Angel had an affinity for early Navajo blankets with their simple lines of blue, red, brown, and white. She could envision her small but tasteful gallery juxtaposing magnificent weavings against some early New Mexico modernists, connecting the painters with what she saw as the primary source of their inspiration.

It was a simple plan. The cartel could spend $100,000 cash for a painting that was worth $75,000. The painting could then be banked as an asset while waiting for it to appreciate in value, or sold at a loss at an auction, or traded toward another asset, cleaning the money spent to acquire it. Even if the piece lost half its value, there was now $50,000 in legal money that could be used for more traditional investments, with all future proceeds from the initial investment now clean.

Paintings were easy to transport and hard to value as each one could vary widely in price depending on the dealer, subject matter, date, and condition. There were few experts in Western or Native art in the world, and none in the FBI or IRS. The law had no way to understand the art market: a painting was a painting was a painting.

Because Angel had experience with the drug cartels, she would be able to recognize a sting operation if the Feds caught onto her gallery's laundering activities. The best part was that Angel could also create a legitimate business: she could sell art just like any other Santa Fe dealer—and business was good. She didn't want a high-profile space on the plaza or Canyon Road; the risk was too great there. Instead, she found a quaint adobe home with a long driveway off Palace Avenue. Clients would find her by word of mouth and walk-ins would be rare—just what she needed to build her reputation as a person with great taste and even better art.

Angel loved the fact that the art she was selling to the cartel was of high quality and should appreciate over time. She would also have the opportunity to resell the same pieces on consignment in the future—and make a nice profit with the now legitimate money. Who else would the cartels trust with their paintings? She was one of the few ex-drug dealers turned gallerists in town.

Her gallery—Buffalo Trails Art Gallery–Santa Fe—was an immediate success. She appropriated her former boss's gallery name, adding "Santa Fe" as a minor modification. After all, she had his client list and his domain name, and had trademarked "Buffalo Trails" under her own name a few years earlier. If the real owner, Clarke Walden, objected, she would close him down for infringing on her trademark.

For now, Angel would let Walden sell art in Tucson. If business got too good and she needed to expand, southern Arizona might be the logical place for a second gallery, taking over Walden's business on his home turf. For now, time was on her side. The aging gentleman would retire soon, and, if any one tried to buy his gallery, she wouldn't allow them to use the Buffalo Trails name. Essentially, Walden was already out of business; all she wanted from him now was his stellar reputation.

Inventory appropriation was simple: a letter was sent to Walden's old clients letting them know that the gallery's new management in Santa Fe was actively buying notable artists at top-dollar prices. Within two months, Angel had spent nearly a million dollars—and the Santa Fe art market took notice.

A few of the lower-rung dealers nuzzled up to Angel, offering her secondary works. The bottom-feeders quickly realized that she was no novice when it came to understanding quality and switched their tactics: they would go to the better galleries in town and borrow art "on the arm," offering the pieces to Angel for 10 to 20 percent more than the consignment price—which meant she would pay retail or retail plus. Angel needed to clean money, but she didn't have to throw away capital. A portion of this cash pot was hers and she figured out the ropes very quickly.

One gallery selling art to another is a delicate operation. First, you needed the trust of a high-end gallery to give you a short consignment for an expensive painting—usually no longer than a week. Seasoned dealers realize extreme care is required when it comes to peddling a precious painting. The golden rule is that a consigner can show only to clients, never to other dealers, and to no more than two clients at a time to avoid overexposing, or "burning," the work.

A gallery owner's worst fear is that a consigned painting would disappear, along with the dealer who had the piece on the arm—which can and does happen. A typical scam involves offering a hungry art dealer more than the retail value of a piece if the gallerist would give you the painting for a couple of days. The inflated retail values prove too tempting for the greedy, who end up losing their art as the adroit grifter moves on to the next location, painting in tow, selling it to the first sucker they find. Greed is a constant problem for most art dealers.

Angel knew better, but hadn't yet learned about art on the arm. She made it clear to anyone bringing art to her for purchase that she wouldn't take kindly to buying a neighbor's art unless it was priced at huge discount from retail and all parties were paid. Her heavy spending in a short period of time kept the secondary dealers' antennae tuned to her. If they had understood how ruthless she could be if poked, they wouldn't have dared to try to sell another Santa Fe gallery's paintings to her.

Angel flexed her enforcement muscle on a must-need basis. Her mantra was "business is business." She had both the makings of greatness in the art world and her family's resources if she ever needed to emphasize the finer points of "Don't screw with the Angel."

CHAPTER 4

BUSINESS IS BUSINESS

Ten years had passed since Buffalo Trails Art Gallery-Santa Fe had morphed into AFA (Angel Fine Art) now in its fifth year of operation. Like a molting snake, Angel had shed her primarily Western gallery's skin and created a new, larger concept for her business.

Tastes among the rich are an ever-evolving process, now focusing on expensive electric sports cars, smaller homes filled with technology, and art with a more contemporary bent. AFA's selection followed the trends and diversified to include a strong collection of modern masters. The gallery was no longer limited to Western or Native art. Focusing instead on major pieces in a multitude of disciplines, Angel now worked by appointment only with a select group of collectors, the best material hanging on the walls of her home.

With the help of a well-crafted Castilian past whose roots went back many generations, Angel had found her niche in Santa Fe's upper social circles. Her home was a palatial white-washed adobe nestled along a small acequia on the back part of three generous lots in Santa Fe's exclusive East side. A walking path through a copse of aspens connected the house to the small but well-heeled building she designated as a gallery—no signage required.

Her father's and brother's lives had taken a different turn. They found their demise at the end of a gun barrel—many gun barrels to be exact. Juan's instincts to conquer the Northern New Mexico drug territory while his gang was at the height of its power had been correct. But the Martinez family syndicate turned out to be the more aggressive. Veracruz offered to combine the two family cartels into one operation, but Martinez wanted to maintain control. Juan and Federico Veracruz should have taken the deal, but they misjudged their place in the syndicate's hierarchy. Yes, they had Colombian connections and the required alpha-dog mentality, but Juan saw himself as the Godfather—a stance not appreciated by the Medellin cartel.

Father and son made a desperate attempt to depose Victor Chacon Martinez in a failed coup in the small Northern New Mexico town of Ojo Caliente, but the Martinez cartel had been tipped-off and was waiting. The two men died in a hail of bullets that rivaled the May 23, 1934 event. But, unlike Bonnie and Clyde, whose shredded bodies went on public display to be witnessed by thousands, the Veracruz men's bullet-riddled corpses were unceremoniously deposited in their black Escalante at the Mesilla complex for a private burial.

A simple bloodstained note was pinned to each man's chest: "Surrender" and "Or Die." Returning the bodies to the family was as close to an olive branch that Angel would receive from Martinez: the usual disposal method for snitches, coyotes or other mortal enemies was burial in small crypts throughout the borderlands, where they would never be seen again—a well-known end for rival cartel members and unsympathetic ranchers alike.

Angel, who recognized her precarious position as the Veracruz heir apparent, met alone with Victor Martinez. A low-cut black dress and ruby-red necklace were her calling cards: the process was the same whether she was selling art or brokering a drug deal. She agreed to transfer her family's drug inventory and connections for a lump sum—$3 million cash—a bargain considering the stacks of uncut cocaine and the good graces of her mother's critical Colombian contacts. It was a practical and necessary arrangement, and Angel understood its ramifications. Retribution would only get her killed and she had already moved on. Drug dealing was no longer her profession: art ruled.

Martinez's thugs would leave the remaining Veracruz family alone. They could return to growing pecans and cotton and distributing stolen goods locally, a part of the business that had been expanding as El Paso grew. But there would be no more human trafficking or drug distribution. Those became part of the Martinez's domain, and that was fine with Angel.

Her mother, first cousin, and their loyal henchmen could handle the properties and the flow of hijacked merchandise. Angel was out, making her name in art rather than stolen goods. For once, being a woman had worked in her favor: the macho Martinez wasn't worried about a female heir—though he should have been.

Angel's art business had been brisk and, for the most part, legitimate. A fresh source of capital—her $1 million cut from the sale of the organization—and her skills as a dealer now allowed her time to focus on other pursuits, and finding a suitable mate appeared on her radar screen for the first time. Her childbearing years were coming to a close, which was no big loss in Angel's mind: children were a burden that limited a woman. Money was her true love.

She was an attractive woman with thick black hair so straight it never tangled, reaching halfway down her back. Her sharp, unwrinkled features belied her middle age. Powerful men were her aphrodisiac, but even that had its limits. Angel ruled out being Victor Martinez's mistress: that was just a boat too far. She could live with the man's murderous side—after all, it was simply business—but not with his influence, which was local and limited. Angel's sights were set higher. She would not stop until she found the perfect mate, no matter how long it took.

CHAPTER 5

TO THE NEXT WORLD

A sharp wind and a single loose shingle slapping methodically atop the roof had worked their way into Rachael's dream. Each beat was transformed into a stab from a vicious knife's blade, each stab at her swollen abdomen threatening her unborn child. She was now three months pregnant.

A familiar voice percolated through Rachael's subconscious, reproducing the melodic timbre of a long-gone time: "All will be fine, my daughter. This is not your last child. Be strong for others and yourself."

Rachael awoke from her mother's words drenched in sweat, her husband, Charles Bloom, shaking her shoulder.

"Hun! Are you OK, Rachael?"

Rachael was not OK. Something was terribly wrong with her pregnancy, which she realized as she began crying.

"NO! Something's wrong with the baby!"

As she spoke, a sharp pain pierced her and she understood what was happening in the moment. She was miscarrying their third child and there was nothing she could do to stop the loss.

"Charles, I'm losing our baby...."

"No, Rachael. It's a bad dream, that's all. You're fine," Charles reassured her, his own concern mounting.

Rachael reflexively felt her underwear; it was sticky wet. Her hand trembled as she pulled it from underneath the sheets and they both stared at the bright blood in disbelief.

"Let's go. NOW!" Bloom shouted, realizing the situation was dire.

Bloom had been happily anticipating his wife's pregnancy. Rachael had always wanted three children, and this would have been their last child, a perfect family. Now their world was in turmoil.

"Here's a robe. Put on your socks and shoes. It's cold tonight and we're heading to Gallup right now!"

Bloom was frantically trying to help Rachael put on her socks.

"The kids, what about the kids?" Rachael asked, her voice trembling.

"They will come with us. There's no time, and it's too late to wake the neighbors. They have to come with us, Rachael."

"Go get the truck, Charles. I'll find a towel and get our babies up. Try not to freak out, Bloom. I need you to be strong for all of us," Rachael said, looking into her husband's blue eyes, her own streaming with tears.

"I'm trying, Rachael, but we need to go. Maybe there is some drug the doctors can give you. I'll get the kids. I don't want you to lift anything. Just get in the truck."

As Bloom dashed out of the house barefoot, a hard wind hit him in the face, the cold sending a reflexive shiver down his spine. He pulled Rachael's Ford pickup to within a few feet of the front door, opened the passenger doors, and ran back into the hogan to scoop up his two children.

Rachael's cramps were coming steadily and hard now, outpacing the loose shingle's heartbeat. It was clear that the newborn would escape the Fourth World and was heading to another plane. She would follow Bloom's wishes, but in her heart Rachael knew this child was not to be.

Bloom's blue-tinged toes matched the hospital slippers the nurse had given him, the cold ER floor seeping through the flimsy cotton material. The cavernous waiting room was empty except for a thirty-something drunk slumped over in one corner. A stream of dark blood oozed from the man's forehead, followed the contour of his high cheekbones, and formed a small puddle on his dirt-tinged pants. The pink square of gauze crudely taped to his head was not staunching most of the jagged cut's blood flow.

The drunk's baritone moans bounced off the stark, sterile walls, a macabre scene that was now permanently etched in Bloom's memory. His mind skipped to his friend Marvin Manycoats, who remembered everything.

"What a terrible burden he must endure," Bloom thought before his mind returned to his own circumstances.

Willy and Sam were asleep in a heap, their bed an old padded green chair whose large stiff arms were stained in a variety of sienna colors. Covered in Bloom's winter coat, they were oblivious to the surrounding mayhem. He was thankful it was late at night—maybe they wouldn't remember any of this.

Bloom paced the floor, remembering how his wife had been rolled down a long hallway on a metal gurney, one out-of-balance wheel producing a high, squeaky noise, the bilagáana doctor by her side talking to the nurse who trailed him, her white uniform popping against her chocolate skin. His mind raced, replaying the numerous times he had wondered whether having a third child was reasonable, but when Rachael had broken the news that she was pregnant all doubt was vanquished by her tender words of joy.

Another life was a gift, one that was now being ripped from their family's bosom. Guilt washed over Bloom as he sat in a single blue plastic chair, his children at his side. As he stroked their sleeping heads, occasional tears gently streamed down his face as he prayed to some higher being for his wife and their unborn child. Bloom leaned forward and watched the teardrops of his pain as they hit the worn linoleum and disappeared into a crack.

The trance broke when he heard his name: "Mr. Charles Bloom?"

He wiped his face and searched for the source. The young doctor had returned, no nurse this time. Their eyes met and the news was not good.

"Mr. Bloom, I'm Doctor Breedlove. I've just examined your wife Rachael, and I'm sorry to tell you she has had a miscarriage."

Bloom tried to comprehend the doctor's message. "How's my wife… is she going to be OK?"

"Your wife is a strong, healthy woman and will be fine. This shouldn't stop you from having another child in the future. It appears she has expelled all the fetal material and her bleeding has stopped for the most part. We will watch her for a couple of more hours and replace her fluids. Once we are sure there is no additional hemorrhage or unexpected sequel, she will be free to go home."

Bloom wondered how doctors could be trained with so little empathy for their patients. His child was "fetal material" and he had no idea what "sequel" meant. "Hemorrhage" sounded ominous, too.

"Doctor, what do you mean by sequel?"

"Sorry. If she doesn't have any other complications and her uterine bleeding subsides, then she can go home. You're welcome to go see her. The nurse can watch your children for a couple of minutes."

"Will she need anything special over the next couple of weeks?"

"Assuming there are no sequelae—I mean complications like fever, abdominal pain, or bleeding—then nothing else will be needed. If she does have problems, she might need a D and C to clean out the uterus. It's unlikely, and it's an outpatient procedure.

"It appears your wife was three months along. Eighty percent of miscarriages occur during the first trimester: it's the body's way of protecting the fetus and family from a bad outcome. I know it's a horrible night for you and your family, but it could be a blessing in disguise. Often, when these events occur, it means there may have been a serious genetic or metabolic issue."

Bloom ignored the comment about the miscarriage being a blessing. If this was a blessing, it was from a very evil god. He must be strong for Rachael.

"Assuming no other problems, then, she will be fine?"

"There can be mild and occasionally severe depression from the significant change in hormones, and often there are feelings of guilt. Many women believe the bad outcome was somehow their fault. I can assure you there was nothing that you or Rachael could have done to prevent the miscarriage. If your wife becomes depressed, bring her to your family doctor, who can order some tests and medications to help. I'll give you a list of symptoms to watch for."

"Thank you, Dr. Breedlove. Would you please ask the nurse to keep a close eye on my children in case they wake up while I'm gone? I don't want to traumatize them any more than I already have." Bloom cast his eyes toward the sleeping drunk to make his point.

Bloom followed the doctor through the E.R. doors to a bed in the rear of the unit. He was thankful it was a slow night." The white-sheeted beds were empty while waiting for the next car crash or bar fight—both possible outcomes in Gallup.

Rachael was sitting upright, buried in a sedimentary layer of brown woolen blankets, both arms poking out of their warm embrace. On one wrist was a purple bracelet with her name and blood type in large bold type. The other arm had an I.V. line dripping a saline solution, the machine blinking numbers and occasional mechanical beeps. The overhead fluorescent lights amplified Rachael's ashen face. She smiled weakly before bursting into tears as Bloom gingerly stroked her hand, squeezing his hand in return as they shared their unbridled grief.

Bloom consoled his wife as best he could, but understood that even the brave Rachael Yellowhorse would not be unscathed from a life lost, her child. This cold winter night was a low point in their life's journey, one Bloom hoped would be the bottom, but Rachael's pain would not end here.

A dark cloud of despair was building on the horizon of the Navajo Nation as the unimaginable consequences of another child's lost life would soon resurface. A long-forgotten child killer had come home to roost, and the entire Bloom family was in grave danger.

CHAPTER 6

IF YOU HAVE THE MUSCLE

Two weeks had passed since Rachael's miscarriage. Charles had religiously monitored the doctor's symptom sheet. As best as he could tell, Rachael's mood swings mirrored the northwestern New Mexico March weather: it changed daily, but gradually she improved.

Bloom cooked, cleaned, and ferried their two children to and from school. He had been scheduled to work for Sal Lito, the owner of the Historic Toadlena Trading Post, on the weekends—but after Rachael's unexpected medical emergency his days were dedicated to his wife.

On Bloom's recommendation, Marvin Manycoats—a longtime customer and Toadlena resident—filled the trading post position. Lito was impressed with Marvin's abilities and wondered why he hadn't hired him years ago. Marvin's memory was legendary; he was never late; was bilingual; rarely drank (and never to excess); and seemed to know everyone in the valley. After two weekends, Lito realized he had found a new long-term employee.

Bloom was leaving for Santa Fe in a few months anyway, so Lito figured the loss of income was not going to be much of a financial hardship for him and Rachael. The fact that his replacement was Marvin it would make the loss even more palatable. Both Bloom and Rachael adored Marvin.

The March winds never stopped on the rez, and Bloom was looking forward to escaping their home's atavistic stove that demanded round-the-clock fuel and monitoring—and still leaked heat. Soon they would be leaving Toadlena for La Cienega, just south of Santa Fe, where a large house surrounded by grand cottonwoods would be waiting for them once the kids' school let out for summer break.

This was the same house they had rented and enjoyed in the past, and Bloom was ready for the impending move. The adobe in La Cienega was drafty, but never like Rachael's hogan; it also had central gas heat so there would be no chopping firewood or stoking the stove each night and morning. Another plus: the thick adobe walls in an adjoining room kept rambunctious kids' disagreements to a dull roar.

Charles was ready for a change of scenery. Rachael, on the other hand, was content with her Toadlena surroundings: in winter, she enjoyed the smell of burning piñon, the cold mornings, and the deafening sound of children roughhousing. But she did realize that Bloom needed a purpose other than nursemaid. A phone call from his father in Las Cruces was the excuse Rachael needed to get her husband temporarily off to a warmer climate. She wanted to force herself to be self-sufficient and productive, which she knew would help heal the traumatic loss. And she knew how to work Bloom's vulnerable spots to accomplish her goal.

"How's your dad, Charles?"

"Charles is it?"

"Bloom, give me a break," Rachael snapped.

"That's more like my Rach.... Well, since you asked so nicely, he just turned eighty years old, and I feel bad that I didn't visit him on such an important birthday."

"That happened during Indian Market, so you can forgive yourself. Your dad understands."

"I know, but the added twist of the knife is that it means I'm getting old too," Bloom said, avoiding the real question.

"We're all getting old, my love. But that's not what I asked. You're avoiding the question: how's your dad doing?"

"He's amazing. That man is working harder than me. He just secured a contract to evaluate a collection of pre-Columbian pottery, and he says it's enormous."

"That money will come in handy, I'm sure." Rachael saw her opportunity; her husband relished professional work of any kind.

"No doubt. A professor's retirement can't be that great and his Social Security is probably paltry. I've asked him about his finances, but you know Dad—he's squeamish when it comes to discussing money. 'It's not appropriate dinner talk.'"

"Not like his son, for sure. Have you taken that 23andMe DNA test? Maybe he's not your real father...." Rachael teased, knowing Bloom enjoyed discussing family finances, even with his young children.

"You've seen our Bloom Roman noses, right? No test needed!" Bloom retorted, turning sideways to show off his prominent proboscis.

"That's true. Lucky for Samantha and Willy that they inherited their mother's Yellowhorse profile—a strong yet reasonably sized Navajo nose." Rachael giggled as she, too, turned to the side to compare noses.

"Are you sure? Maybe you'd better take that genetic test to make sure you are truly Navajo. That nose looks more Greek to me."

“True, this olive skin might be Mediterranean. After all, my dad was in Italy during the Second World War.”

“You’re in a good mood. Getting back to normal?” Bloom asked, seeing his wife’s humor returning.

“Well, I must admit I’m feeling much better. In fact, do you see that lonely, large loom gathering dust in the corner? I’ve decided to start weaving again in earnest.”

“Wow, that’s fantastic. But are you sure you’re up to it? Maybe you could start by working on the smaller rug you started last month rather than tackling a major work?”

“I doubt that I will ever finish that rug. I told you this in passing, Bloom, and I’m sure you don’t remember it, but many Navajo women won’t weave a rug when they are pregnant because they’re afraid the warp threads will cause their unborn baby to strangle on its umbilical cord.”

“I had no idea, Rachael. I’m so sorry,” Bloom said, his concern showing.

“Nothing to be sorry about. It was my decision and only mine. I asked Violet Brown and she reminded me that my mom wove during both her pregnancies. She even asked a few of the other grandmothers on my behalf, and they all said it was fine to weave, as long as I said my chants before I wove—which I did. The grandmothers told Mrs. Brown to tell me that if we women didn’t weave when we were with babies, then how were we supposed to pay for all them baby clothes. I took that to heart.”

“Rachael, are you sure you are ready to start again?”

“I can handle weaving, that’s in my DNA—but not that small rug I was working on, at least not yet. I’ll start another, bigger one. I’m no longer pregnant, so it’s the best therapy I can imagine.

"On the other hand, you, Mr. Charles James Bloom, are unemployed for the moment, so why don't you go visit your dad for a week or so? You could celebrate his birthday and help him catalog that collection. I'm sure he would love his son's help, and it would make up for last August's misstep."

"No, I couldn't do that. You might need me and I have to keep checking the symptom sheet."

"That's ridiculous!"

Rachael slid past Bloom, brushing her hand on his bare leg. Then, with a dramatic flare, she picked up the doctor's sheet lying on the table, crumpled it into a ball and deposited it into the nearby kitchen stove.

"Why destroy that, Rachael? The doctor specifically asked me to watch for those symptoms," Bloom asked in dismay.

"Charles James Bloom, I'm fine. I need you to take a break from me and the kids and go visit your father. It will do you a great deal of good. Your hózhó is out of balance, my love," Rachael said as she put her arm around his neck and sat in his lap, her bare leg touching his.

Bloom considered Rachael's words; she was incredibly intuitive when it came to harmonic balance, more than Bloom could ever be.

"You're sure that you don't need me? The kids are a handful, and the doctor said for you to take it easy and not lift over 20 pounds."

"It's been fifteen days. I haven't had any bleeding for ten days, my color has returned and so has my stamina. Go to Las Cruces. It will be good for both of us, and maybe your dad will pay you to help him."

Bloom ignored her teasing.

"All right. I'll call Dad and see if he's up to having me stay for a week. He did mention he needed help with this collection and I do owe him a visit. But you have to let me warp the big loom before I go...."

"That you can do, if you have the muscle," Rachael parried, knowing it took strength to prepare a loom for weaving, and she wasn't supposed to strain herself.

"You know, Rachael," Bloom realized with excitement, "by August you could get a major tapestry finished for Indian Market. That Scottsdale client has been waiting for something special."

"You're right, Bloom, and I'm going to fill that order. The timing is perfect; we will have extra money for the kids' fall school clothes."

Rachael smiled to herself, knowing she was back in charge of her family's welfare. Though the thought of not shopping for baby clothes still stung, the doctor was right: there was plenty of time for another child. She needed to get mentally prepared and stop blaming herself for the miscarriage. Taking charge of her life was a perfect start.

CHAPTER 7

FANG

The six-and-a-half-hour drive to Las Cruces gave Bloom time to consider his life. He didn't want to admit that Rachael's miscarriage had hurt deeply. In his mind, they were already a family of five, but now that picture had been shattered and it wasn't clear if that dream would ever circle back. Rachael's biological clock was ticking hard, and the math didn't favor him seeing a new baby mature once he was past fifty.

His own father was a strong, vibrant man at eighty, but in the last year Bloom had noticed small changes, occasional memory lapses on the phone. His father's driving years also would expire soon. Bloom had no siblings and his mother had passed; at some point soon, he would need to become his father's father figure. Maybe an aging parent would fill that wish for another child.

Bloom wanted to take his children to school before heading out. He would get a late start to Cruces, but he didn't care. Rachael was at her loom, lost in the wool, when he returned home. She turned her head, winking her right eye lovingly toward her husband, while never missing a batten maneuver. Bloom felt a twinge of disappointment that she hadn't run over for a hug, so he took the initiative, walked behind her, reached down, and gave her a bear hug and a kiss on the cheek.

"I love you Rachael. Please call me if you feel blue or need me to come home. You remember the symptoms to watch for, right?"

"Yes I do, Charles Bloom. I'm fine. See—I've nearly got a weft row in place. Weaving helps me as much having you nurse me. It keeps my mind occupied and my creative juices flowing. Call me when you get to Cruces."

"I'll text you when I reach Gallup. I'm going to stop to pick up a quick Lotaburger to take on the road for lunch," Bloom teased, knowing Rachael never understood his unreasonable attraction to the hamburgers from his favorite restaurant.

"This trip isn't about eating double-cheese and green-chile Lotaburgers," Rachael said. "Go spend some time with your dad."

"That's a double-meat-green-chile-and-cheese burger, not a double-cheese," Bloom teased, hugging her more tightly, not wanting to leave.

"Go now. The roads will be warmed up, and you'll have smooth sailing. Text me...."

Bloom relaxed his grip on her and headed out the door. If he had walked around to see Rachael's face, he would have seen two tears making their way down her flushed cheeks.

The outside temperature was 20 degrees as Bloom pulled away from their hogan, and fresh snow graced the pines on the adjacent Chuska Mountains.

New Mexico's landscape is as varied as its cultures—and its charms never fail to surprise those visiting the Land of Enchantment. As Bloom turned his Ford truck off of I-40 to head south on New Mexico State Road 6, the temperature had risen perceptibly, hovering near 45 degrees. The topography shifted from stark white snow and blood-red bluffs to gray volcanic tabletop mesas. The lack of moisture was palpable; the promised abundant El Niño rains were as yet a no-show.

The region known as Mesa Redonda in Valencia County was once lush with vegetation, an ancient seabed filled with grazing mammoths. Bloom had recently begun studying the earth's early inhabitants, with a specific interest in the fossils of the Southwest. He was able to recognize different geologic formations and the animals that inhabited them. He had no desire to collect fossils, understanding that, much as in his own art world, there was an underbelly of unscrupulous dealers trading nefariously; the learning curve to outwit them would be great. He had had the misfortune to meet one such black-hat dealer and his skull still bore a scar from that encounter.*

Bloom's father was a retired Eastern New Mexico University professor of archaeology. He had left Portales and was living out his retirement years in Las Cruces, where the much warmer climate and wider array of intellectual types were a good fit for a solitary man. Dr. James Bloom, a widower for close to ten years, had found an uncomfortable rhythm to life as a bachelor. He played a regular Wednesday golf game with retired professors from New Mexico State University—a real bargain at the college course. The rest of the week he worked as an independent consultant in his primary area of expertise, identifying prehistoric Southwest art. The consultation fees and occasional grant money kept him busy and his mind active. He missed fieldwork—the taste of the dirt and the thrill of an

*See *Guardian of the Cornfields*, the seventh book in the Charles Bloom Murder Mystery Series for the full story.

unexpected find—but those activities were physically demanding, a younger man's game. His finds were now mainly limited to the dusty shelves of museums, libraries, and universities.

Dr. Bloom was thrilled to have Charles, his only child, help him catalog a monstrous private collection of pre-Columbian art housed in a large, secluded compound in Mesilla. He needed his son's help but hadn't wanted to ask for it, knowing it would interrupt his son's family's school and work routines. Dr. Bloom didn't want to admit it, but climbing ladders had become daunting.

Bloom's job on the project would be to measure the objects and take photos of them with his father's iPhone for documentation, while the professor wrote descriptions and overall condition reports. It was unusual for his father to take a contract to document a private collection, but Bloom figured the pay must either be good or the older man needed the money. His father was, for the most part, in the camp that believed pre-Columbian material should only be in museums, not bought and sold.

Pulling into his dad's midcentury red brick house, Bloom recognized his father would soon need help with more than cataloging. The brown grass hadn't been cut since fall and the bushes were in desperate need of trimming. Bloom wondered why a man who loved the desert and was ecologically minded would have grass surrounding his home.

Bloom started to put his key into the front-door lock, then decided to try the handle first. The door was unlocked: "another warning sign of trouble," he thought.

"Hey, Dad—it's me," Bloom yelled, knowing his father probably wasn't wearing his hearing aids.

"I hear you. I'm not deaf. I'm in the back," Dr. Bloom replied.

Bloom scanned the house, looking for any signs that his father was having difficulty taking care of his home. The floor was clean, there were no dirty dishes, and the air had yet to acquire the musky aroma of aged occupants. The inside temperature was hovering at 80 degrees, but other than thermal regulation issues, all looked copacetic.

The art hanging randomly on the faded eggshell-white walls was limited to over-framed works Bloom had created in high school, none of which was very good—relics of a time when he dreamed of attending art school and becoming a famous painter. Given the dearth of artistic stimulation in his boyhood, Bloom sometimes wondered how he had managed to become an accomplished art dealer. He attributed his creative bent to his mother, whose needlepoint was the only other art form gracing the walls.

"Charles, my boy, it's great to see you… glad you could make it down. As you know, I've hit the big eight-o and I can tell you your help is a godsend. I'm overwhelmed with the magnitude of this collection."

Charles had not shared the news of the new pregnancy with his father. He and Rachael were planning to tell the relatives and friends at the start of the fourth month, and they were still a week shy of that marker. Charles gulped as tears started to fill his eyes, then quickly blinked to clear away any residual sadness.

"I'm glad I could find the time, Dad. I'm sorry I missed your eightieth birthday."

"Not a problem, Son. You were in your busy time and what's important is that you're here now, when I can really use your help."

"I'm glad it worked out for both of us—and I must say the place looks as good as the last time I was here."

"I know the yard is a mess, but I'm going to get rid of that water-sucking grass this year and put in some local desert plants. It was stupid to have a lawn in the first place, but the green reminded me of your mom. She always had a front yard in Portales…." His father's voice trailed off. Ten years clearly wasn't enough time to recover from his mother's death, and Bloom wondered how long this miscarriage would haunt him.

"Good idea, Dad. That will save you money and, in my opinion, lawns are incongruent with the desert. Maybe you can fill the ground with jumping cholla; it would make a nice security fence and you are very close to the border." Bloom enjoyed teasing his left-leaning father.

"How about a wall instead?" the professor shot back, knowing his son's political views were more centrist.

"So tell me about Rachael and the grandchildren I never see. How come you didn't bring them along?"

"School's in session and Rachael needs time to weave. August will be here soon and since I'm not working, so to speak, I guess I've been invading her 'me' time."

"Oh, believe me I understand that. If your mother were still around, I would have never retired—that would have been the end to her needlepoint and probably our marriage," Dr. Bloom joked.

"Looks to me like you haven't retired anyway," Bloom smiled.

"True enough, I do enjoy working. It keeps my brain active and money coming in. I don't want to be a burden to you in the future. I know I will need help someday, so I'm planting the seeds now and looking for solid returns. You ever heard of FANG stocks?"

"No, what's that? A rattlesnake anti-venom company?"

"No, Son, not quite. FANG is the acronym for Facebook, Apple, Netflix, and Google, though Google is now called Alphabet. I started buying those stocks five years ago and have been pretty successful with it. I never sell—just keep adding to my portfolio with these consulting jobs."

"How did you know what to invest in?"

"I didn't. I watched a show on TV and everyone kept saying FANG this, FANG that, so I figured I'd give it a go. As you know I'm not the best when it comes to business. Anyway, it's worked out pretty darn well. I'm surprised at what compounding can accomplish."

"Dad, I'm very proud of you. Can I ask how much you've made?"

"Well, I don't like to talk money; it's not really appropriate. Let's just say that I'm closing in on seven figures in the stock market."

"WHAT?"

"Yeah, the old man is a FANG expert," Dr. Bloom laughed, baring his teeth like a lion and clawing at the air with his hands.

"Father, I'm proud of you. But, as you pointed out, you're eighty and you might want to pare down some of those profits. That's what I do in my world: pigs get fat, hogs get slaughtered. You might have some unexpected medical bills, and it would be good to have some cash socked away."

"I'll take it under advisement, though I hate paying the capital-gains tax."

Both men chuckled at the absurdity of his father's new business acumen. What they didn't know was that Charles' words were more prophetic than either man could imagine.

CHAPTER 8

EWMN (Evil, Wicked, Mean, Nasty)

Breakfast was at James Bloom's favorite restaurant in Mesilla, Josefina's Old Gate Cafe. Their huevos rancheros, served Christmas style, were as good as any in Santa Fe—at a fraction of the cost. Smothered with a thick red sauce and Hatch green chiles and served with a stack of fresh corn tortillas, the delicious take on a Southwestern classic was one Bloom planned to recreate in the future.

"Dad, you're right; this place is the bomb!"

"What's a bomb?"

"That's slang for the best." Bloom laughed to himself, having incorporated a new word his son had brought home from school.

"I guess the world continues to revolve, Son. I remember when everything you said was 'cool' this and 'man' that. It drove your mother crazy."

"I remember 'man'...." Bloom smiled at his father.

"Did you know that the word 'hello' was an invention for use on the telephone in 1898?"

"You never cease to amaze me, Dad."

Bloom loved his quirky father's factoids. Professor Bloom bobbed his head in approval as he put the first of the steaming fresh tortillas in his open mouth.

"So tell me, Dad, what's the story on this huge collection? How did you end up getting called in? Is it prehistoric pottery?"

"Actually, its pre-Columbian."

"Really? I didn't know you knew about that stuff."

"It's not what I'm known for, of course, but I have a good enough working knowledge of the material to be dangerous."

"Wow, Dad. I wish I had known that a few years ago," Bloom said, thinking back to a collection of pre-Columbian artifacts he had uncovered in Santa Fe.

"Well, all you had to do was ask, Son. I'm also quite literate in Inuit material. But to answer your question, I'm not exactly sure how they got my name to evaluate this collection. I'm guessing the university gave it to them—they're good about referrals.

"As far as the collection goes, it's so massive that it looks to me like a generational project. There are so many pieces, and the information on the collection goes back as far as fifty years. They've asked for dating and classification of the ceramics and stone pieces as best as possible without carbon analysis, which, of course, is somewhat limiting. I explained I have no knowledge with regards to valuation, and that it would be better to call in an appraiser, but they seem fine with what I can provide."

"Why don't they want carbon dating?"

"I believe it is a time issue; they were quite insistent on getting the collection evaluated quickly."

"I guess that's a legitimate reason, but doesn't it seem odd not to have an appraiser on the team? What do they want to do with the collection? Donate it?"

"I'm not sure. I asked a few of those questions, but Jorge, the individual I'm working with, just shrugged and said, 'That's above my pay grade. I just do as I'm told; seems you might want to do the same.' I left it at that. I'm getting paid one hundred dollars an hour, which is amazing, and they said I can bill for your services at a similar price. It's really none of my business how the material I provide is used. I'm simply providing the best contextual information I can under the circumstances is how I see it."

Bloom considered his father's words before speaking.

"Is it possible, Dad, that this report you're providing is for something that's not on the up-and-up?"

"That seems highly unlikely, but anything is possible, Son. I didn't get that impression. Seems more like rich people wanting to protect an asset in case of damage. Lots of fires going around these days and, as you say, hogs get slaughtered and pigs get fat. Maybe they're simply risk-averse."

Bloom was amazed at how his father was sounding more like a stockbroker than the archaeologist who raised him. He was clearly spending all too much time listening to the talking heads on CNBC.

"OK, Dad, but I'll reserve my opinion until I see the place and meet Jorge. It never hurts to be cautious. I've dealt with shady people in the past, and I always listen to my inner voice."

"Well, Son, my inner voice is saying I need another glass of water! This red chile is extra hot."

The Bloom boys finished breakfast and headed to work—a place where no inner voice could scream loudly enough to be adequately heard.

Bloom's antenna was at full alert when his father's Pontiac station wagon pulled up to the compound entrance and two burly guards strapped with side arms approached the vehicle as it rolled to a stop.

"James Bloom and Charles Bloom here. We are doing the inventory assessment of the pre-Columbian art in the rear house."

"Hello, Dr. Bloom. Is this your son?" A large, well-groomed German Shepherd at the man's side was barking menacingly.

"Sorry, I couldn't hear what you said. My ears aren't what they use to be...."

"I'm sorry for the noise. These dogs have minds of their own today."

The large man pulled at the dog's choke chain and the animal ceased barking and squatted down next to the open window on the driver's side.

"I asked if this is your son?"

"Yes, I told Mr. Gutierrez he would be helping me categorize the collection. It's larger than one old man can expect to work through in any reasonable amount of time."

The security guard talked into a mike attached to his ear as another man slid a long stick with an attached mirror under the car.

"Yes, Charles Bloom, Professor Bloom's son. Yes, I see. Roger that.

"I will need to make a copy of your son's driver's license before you can enter."

Bloom had been in many expensive homes, including those of a few celebrities, and this seemed like overkill. But he complied, retrieved his hand-tooled Navajo wallet, and fished out his driver's license. Then he leaned over his father and presented it to the guard. An enormous hand—each knuckle tattooed with the letters E-W-M-N—took the license from him. The crudely made letters must represent a transgression from an earlier life, Charles thought, as this man appeared professional and well dressed.

"Thank you, Mr. Bloom. If you would pull over to the side there, I'll be right back." The guard disappeared into the adobe guard shack.

"Dad, what is all this?"

"Just routine. I check in each day when I arrive and when I leave. It's no big deal, Son."

"Well, I'm not a fan of my driver's license leaving my hands and going who knows where. And how about that tattoo?"

"They're running the license through some database to make sure you are who you say you are. I think those letters probably refer to a university like ENMU or NMSU—a frat thing."

"No, father, that's gang stuff, not academia. And who has access to that kind of database besides the police or the FBI? Are you sure this isn't some kind of weird FBI sting?"

"Son, you have been watching too many shows on Netflix. This isn't *Ozark*. These guys are nice, just doing their job, so relax. It's all routine."

The large man returned, bent down, and took an intense look at Charles Bloom, comparing him to the photo before handing back the driver's license.

"Thank you, Dr. and Mr. Bloom. As you know, Dr. Bloom, photographs of the collection are limited to those made on your phone's camera. They are not be reproduced or shared, and only the pre-Columbian collection is to be documented, as specified by your contract."

"Yes, we understand the rules. It's not a problem."

"Well, have a nice day."

The burly man turned and headed back to his guard shack, his stride showing him to be a confident man who was not to be messed with.

"Dad, I got to tell you this is some weird stuff. Why all the cloak-and-dagger?"

"I don't know and I don't ask. I'm an independent contractor getting paid extremely well to do a highly specialized job. With your help, we can be out of here in two to three days tops."

"I hope you're right, because my gut says this is odd. There are too many security procedures and regulations for a simple collection evaluation."

The 1990s station wagon eased its way toward the back of the massive home that graced the property. It was a two-story Santa Fe-style hacienda surrounded by large, well-manicured cottonwood trees interspersed between ponds of grass. The trees' green buds were exploding, the mild southern New Mexico climate promising an early spring. Bloom scanned the grounds on the drive to the back of the property; two armed men were guarding what appeared to be a 10,000-square-foot house.

Bloom could see four large black Cadillac Escalades parked in the circular cobblestone driveway. One of the license plates appeared to be an official New Mexico state plate.

"Dad, did you see that blue car plate? Do you think those are state cars?"

"I don't know. I haven't seen those particular vehicles before, but maybe that's why they took your driver's license and why they needed to check you out."

"Why would an official state car visit this place, with an ex-gangbanger checking cars?"

"You don't know that man was in a gang. When you see the collection, you'll understand that the person who owns all this has money. I mean, look at this house."

"Why a black Escalade with a New Mexico state plate?" Bloom reiterated.

"Charles, does it really matter who lives here or visits this compound? Maybe the owners are going to do some kind of fundraiser for a local politician…."

"I guess it doesn't matter, but there is something incongruent about an expensive government vehicle and the men who are guarding this place," Charles said.

"Politicians often go where the money is, and this place fits the bill."

"Yes, that seems reasonable. Maybe it's a public official's car."

"Well, if it is a fundraiser I hope it's to raise money for a Democrat. We have a Democratic governor now—did you know that?"

"I did know that, but what does party affiliation matter?"

"I don't know. I guess I would feel better about doing this job for a fellow Democrat."

"Pops, I love you, but politics should never enter into business arrangements. It leads to problems. Keep politics out and an open mind; after all, they are paying you and didn't ask whether you were a Democrat or a Republican."

"Well, Son, you might be right, but at my age I want to feel good about whom I take money from."

"Ok, Dr. Ethics. By the way, it is legal to drive faster than two miles per hour. How about you pick up the pace? I want to get back for a late lunch at Josephine's."

"Nice to see you're still a young bull, Son." Dr. Bloom smiled lovingly at Charles, knowing he would never be a man to slow down.

CHAPTER 9

T.C. CANNON

A 3,000 square foot adobe building—flanked by irrigation ditches and endless rows of pecan trees filled with black-hulled nuts—was tucked discreetly behind the main house. A 6-foot chain-link fence topped with barbed wire surrounded the outside perimeter next to the grove of trees.

The construction and layout said "home," but the windows' rolling metal shutters and the heavy steel front door with two separate locks told a different story. It was unusual to see mature pecan trees that had not been harvested in March; the trees should have been picked clean by Valentine's Day.

Another large human specimen was waiting at the front entrance of the building to let the two men inside; he, too, was covered in a variety of tattoos, including a spider web on his elbow.

"There you go, Dr. Bloom. I've turned up the heat to 75; I know you like it warm inside. If you need to exit the building, please push the red button next to the door. This will let me know you are ready to leave, and I'll escort you out. Please do not lock the door from the inside. And make sure you DO NOT leave the building by yourselves; our dogs might not take kindly to you being unattended."

The man smiled, knowing the animals would rip the two men apart.

"Not a problem. I would think we'll be ready to go by noon as we didn't bring a lunch, but I'll let you know."

"I noticed your pecan trees haven't been harvested," Bloom said cheerfully. "Someone needs to give those trees a good shake; lots of tasty nuts will be going to waste soon."

"We leave them for the squirrels—they love them," the guard said, straining slightly to pull open the heavy front door. The inside of the door had two large metal sleeves and a door bolt that could be secured from the inside.

"Leave them for the squirrels?" Bloom loved pecans and knew that this time of year they were worth $3 per pound. This orchard held maybe 2,000 pounds of pecans—a lot of money left on the table. Clearly these were either very rich, secretive people or serious squirrel lovers.

Bloom and his father entered the cavernous building, which appeared to be a professionally converted art storage unit. As Bloom's eyes adjusted to the yellow fluorescent light, he could see why his father needed his help. Enormous 12-foot, black-metal framed storage cases lined the room—and all were packed with rows of ceramic forms.

"Dad, why do you think this door has such a significant locking mechanism from the inside? Why wouldn't a simple dead bolt suffice?"

"I guess for security bigger is better."

"But from the inside? Who or what are they trying to keep out?"

"Clearly they put it there so the person or persons inside would be difficult to access. I assume it would have to do with this enormous collection," Dr. Bloom said, pointing to the rows of cases filled with pre-Columbian artifacts.

Bloom considered his dad's reasoning and moved on. "I hope you haven't been climbing that ladder, Dad...."

"No, Son, that's your job. I've already cataloged everything that's shoulder high. Now the real fun begins. Hope your deltoids don't get as sore as mine."

"I feel like I'm sixteen and I've just learned that my unwanted summer job is to strip and paint our house's eaves Mom's favorite robins-egg blue—and I do still remember how sore my shoulders got that summer."

"Maybe, Charles, all those summers of painting is what led you to the art business. Let's not forget you're getting well paid this go around—and you're welcome for my help in sculpting your fine physique." Dr. Bloom smiled.

"No, Dad, it wasn't the summer house painting jobs that got me interested in art or built my shoulders. I think it was that amazing painting collection hanging in our home that kept changing that set me on my path. Remember those Santa Fe Opera posters I had to hang each month?"

"We paid good money to have those posters framed. I will point out that we also framed your high-school drawings—and, for the record, I hung our family art."

"Well, father, I WILL point out a slight mistake. I did get paid for my summer labors, 25 cents an hour as I remember, but I will give you—you did hang the FAMILY art," Bloom shot back with a childish grin that his father loved.

Charles instinctively began to walk to the front and back of each metal case, examining the pottery and stone artifacts. The art was exquisite: sienna-colored Colima dogs in various positions; Nayarit warriors ready for battle, including one large figure grasping the decapitated head of a vanquished enemy; numerous female figures with open legs and prominent breasts; and one section of white stone pieces on professional stands that appeared to be Olmec.

"This is pretty incredible. Are they all real?"

"Very much so, as far as I can discern. It's one of the best pre-Columbian collections I've ever seen, rivaling Mexico City's holdings—and some pieces here might even be rarer."

"What kind of value are we talking about?" Bloom the art dealer asked, wondering about the value the inventory represented.

"Oh, I haven't a clue, Son. That's the field of a dealer or appraiser. I have seen auction catalogs that would price many of the pieces in the $2,000 to $5,000 range, but of course I would think dozens of these intricate double figures or ferocious warriors could be double or triple that price, and God only knows on the Olmec section."

"What's back there in the dark? More ceramics?" Bloom instinctively pointed with his lips in Navajo fashion to rows of cases near the rear of the room.

“Where, Son?” Dr. Bloom asked, not picking up the subtle cue. So Bloom used his finger in a fashion a Navajo would find rude, pointing toward a large area in the dark back of the room where the sliding walls were positioned.

“I believe it’s artwork, but I haven’t really paid attention. I’ve been focused on the job at hand. They told me only to examine the ceramics and that’s exactly what I have done.”

“You think I can take a look?”

“Well, they never said we couldn’t….”

“Great, then I will.”

Bloom walked to the back of the room and pulled out his iPhone for light, peering into the rows of museum-style storage. He slid out the first wall, its brass casters making a metallic tick-tack sound as he moved it along its tracks.

The art dealer was shocked by what he saw: a vertical 72- x 48-inch T.C. Cannon hung on the wall. It was a heretofore unknown image of a Plains Indian in full regalia standing in a trading post setting with one of the Indian’s hands in what appeared to be a candy jar and the other holding a large hatchet covered with drips of red paint. It was more of a movie scene then a life setting, and Bloom concluded this was Cannon’s take on Native actors and their roles in early Western movies.

Bloom knew Cannon’s history well and had sold a few of the artist’s woodblocks and drawings in his career, though nothing as major as this piece. Cannon’s story was tragic. Of Kiowa and Caddoan descent, he trained in Santa Fe under Fritz Scholder, then joined the Army as a paratrooper, earning two Bronze Stars during the Tet Offensive.

Cannon had a breakout two-man show with Scholder at the National Collection of Fine Arts at the Smithsonian during which a Madison Avenue art gallery bought almost all his pieces and began an exclusive representation. The painter died in a car accident southeast of Santa Fe in 1978 when he was only thirty-one years old.

Bloom had never known Cannon—it was before his time—but the artist's story was eerily like that of Rachael's late brother Willard Yellowhorse, Willard's being even more tragic as he was murdered by a deranged art dealer in New York City.

Neither T.C. Cannon nor Willard Yellowhorse lived long enough to produce a significant body of work, so seeing a major painting that had never been published was astonishing. Bloom examined the work closely. Was it a fake? It appeared genuine.

Bloom's hearing was not great, but he had heard the man with the tattooed fingers when he said "no photos except for the ceramics." But he had to share this find with Rachael, who was an even bigger Cannon fan than he. He switched his phone to vibrate and snapped a couple of quick photos. The flash was off so they weren't great images, but they were good enough to show Rachael. Maybe she would recognize the piece.

The painting was hanging on a metal rack that could be best described as museum chicken wire. The back of the painting was visible through the screening, and there was writing on the reverse. "A wedding gift to my husband, whom I love more than art or life" was signed "Mrs. Roy Bryant," with a heart drawn next to the inscription. No title or date was visible, so Bloom photographed the writing too.

Lining the art wall were additional examples of early Indian paintings, but Bloom couldn't identify the artists. The caster wheels were clicking along the rails as he pushed the case back in place when he heard the large front door swing open. Bloom wished he had used the inner dead bolt to lock himself in, but this was also a no-no. He stepped away from the wall and tried to look innocent as Raoul, the large man from the entry gatehouse appeared in the doorway.

"Hi, Dr. Bloom, Mr. Bloom. I wanted to emphasize to your son, in case he didn't understand, that your activity is limited to the ceramics. All other storage vaults are off limits."

"Sure, no problem," Bloom said, as he hurried back to his father's side. Either the place was under video surveillance, which was possible, or the noisy wheels had alerted the guard to what he was doing. Either way, he was semi-busted.

For the rest of morning, Bloom worried that someone would come and ask to see his phone. He hadn't gotten his dad in trouble since he was a kid in middle school and he tried to focus on the task at hand, methodically pulling out each ceramic and stone artifact and laying them on a makeshift table for his father to examine and make notes. Bloom measured and attached identifications on a nonstick tag that corresponded with a log number on the bottom of each object. Once this task was complete, a front and back photo of the object was taken by Dr. Bloom and also given an identification number before Charles returned the object to where it had come from in the case. All the log numbers were sequential to make identification easier for later researchers.

Observing his father's meticulous identification, his magnifying-glass headset perched awkwardly on his forehead, transported Bloom back to his childhood, when he watched in amazement as the professor worked in his lab. Seeing his father's own inner world of observation and discovery made him realize that father and son weren't that different: Bloom's own curiosity about the looming darkness at the rear of the building had drawn his attention. What other masterpieces were in the storage units, and did they have anything to do with the government vehicles parked out front?

The answers lay inside the units—answers that could rewrite American art history if ever uncovered.

CHAPTER 10

HI YO SILVER

Rachael slept undisturbed for three hours, until she instinctively guided her foot toward Bloom's side of the bed to nuzzle, realized her husband was 400 miles away, and awoke. The last day had seen some improvements. She had made progress on the weaving, and her mind only wandered once to her miscarriage. She had quickly regained her composure and focused on the task at hand: her Toadlena/Two Grey Hills rug. The hormonal surge had leveled off and she was feeling better, but missing her husband.

The bottom selvage placement and first ¼-inch of weaving had been effortless; a design was mapped out in her mind; no drawings were ever needed in the Yellowhorse world. A negative background composition spoke to her current feelings. Rachael's weaving would employ twelve different shades of dark wool, reminiscent of Bear Clan rugs done in the 1930s to '40s. Her mother, a great weaver, was a fan of the deep chocolate palette her sheep provided; this rug would be a tribute to both her mother and lost child.

Rachael was invested in this new weaving from a spiritual perspective too. A lone gray strand discovered that morning while brushing her hair was plucked for the occasion. Holding the thick silver thread, she rolled the fiber in her fingers looking for an answer. "What did the gray hair mean, and why did it appear now?" She decided the sign of aging was an insight into the fleeting nature of motherhood.

The single silver strand of DNA would be firmly enclosed in the first row of the new rug's wefts, homage to the life of the rug and to her recovery from the deep sadness in her heart. Only she would recognize that this gift for Spider Woman left between the rug's wefts stood for a mother and an unfilled life, her unnamed but loved third child. The hair represented her ability to rid herself of aging, fighting back so she could be reborn and have White Shell Mother bless her with a new child. She would not share this moment of clarity with Bloom, at least not yet.

The drumbeat of the weaving comb earlier in the day had helped ease the tensions in her tight shoulders and neck, but now it was night, and there was no rug to fill her soul. A new twinge—not of pain, but of longing—was surging through her heart. She had pushed her husband away from her to his father's side. Now his gentle touch and sweet lips filled her thoughts. Why had she wanted solitude? Was it an act of selflessness on her part to encourage Bloom to be with his aging father or something deeper, a need to reflect undisturbed?

Rachael understood her strengths and weakness better than most and rarely questioned her decisions. But in that lonely cold bed this was one of those uncertain moments. In the dark room, Rachael fumbled for the phone, pulled it to her breast, and speed-dialed Bloom.

"Rachael—everything OK? It's almost 1 a.m."

"I'm sorry to call so late, but I needed to hear your voice. How did it go with your father?"

"I should have called you, I got to talking with my dad and time got away from me. I figured you were asleep, and I didn't want to wake you."

"I can't sleep well until I say goodnight," Rachael purred.

"I'm happy you still like hearing my voice," Bloom said in a lower timber, which he knew drove his wife wild.

"Stop that, Charles James Bloom! That's not playing fair when you're so far away."

"I'm sorry. I miss you, too."

"It's important you spend time with your dad. Time passes quickly and then we're alone. My mom's been gone for over a decade," Rachael said in a melancholy tone that Charles recognized.

"You and the kids could come down to Las Cruces, Rach. It's nearly 60 degrees and Dad has plenty of room."

"No, the kids are in school, and I need to focus on getting the rug well underway."

"How was your progress today?"

"Better than expected. I know the basic colors I'm going to work with, and it's going to have a three-diamond center."

"Like your mom made?"

"Very good, Charles Bloom. You are earning big bonus points. It's exactly like my mom's, a kind of a shout-out to her and my Bear Clan side."

"Sounds wonderful. Send me a couple of pictures. I like to watch the progression, and you know our buyers love to see how a rug was made."

Rachael didn't care for this salesman side of Bloom, but understood that this was who he was; she would never try to change that part of his personality.

"So how is your father doing? Is the project interesting?" Rachael interjected. Instead of promising him photos of the rug under progress, which she hated to take, she sarcastically considered showing a close-up of the hair and its meaning.

"Dad is fine, his house looks clean and neat, and he seems unchanged. He's probably going to live to be one hundred, working the whole way. He told me he's been investing in technology stocks—can you believe that!"

"All you Blooms surprise me at times. Maybe you should ask his advice if he's doing well," Rachael teased, knowing that Bloom senior, unlike his son, had an underdeveloped business sense. Bloom let the crack slide and filled Rachael in on the house, its contents, and the T.C. Cannon painting.

"Send me the pictures of that Cannon painting. I don't need to remind you I'm a proud graduate of IAIA, just like T.C. I can send the photos to one of my old professors who knew Cannon well. Maybe he will recognize the piece."

"That's why I took the photos; I know you're a fan. I'll tell you what—I'll send you images of the Cannon if you send me one of your rug," Bloom halfway joked, knowing his wife had skirted his earlier request.

"OK. OK. Herr Bloom. I'll get you some photos, but you send yours first. You know T.C.'s work is the only person's next to my brother's that I really covet."

"I'm texting you now, but please make sure your old professor doesn't share these photos with anyone. I took them on the QT, and I don't want to cause any trouble for my father. These guys didn't seem like they would brook with any misbehaving on my part, and taking the photos was a definite no-no."

"Of course I don't want you or your father to get in trouble. It's Professor Benally I'm thinking of; he's part Navajo so he will understand I want to be discreet.

"Care to send me any other pics?" Rachael giggled.

Bloom loved hearing her laugh and shot back. "I will, but you definitely can't share them with anyone else."

"Don't worry Charles, those are for me!"

Then Bloom the art dealer stepped back into the conversation. "I must admit, Rachael, that I'm curious about the Cannon's origin—especially that odd inscription on the back. I didn't see a date, but if I had to guess I would say it was a later painting, done toward the end of his career. Maybe it got sold to a friend or was a quick sale so it was never dated or titled."

As Bloom finished typing, his text message popped up on Rachael's screen.

"These are horrible photos, Bloom. Why are they so dark and blurry? That's not like you when it comes to art. The inscription on the back is clearer than the actual painting...."

"This place is a fortress and our overseers wouldn't be happy knowing I had taken photos, so these were done rather quickly in poor light. The inscription came out better because of the white canvas."

"Playing detective I see. It sounds like it's more than wanting to share the Cannon with me—you also have an itch you're trying to scratch."

"Yeah, I'm afraid you know me. There is something strange about the whole set-up. I'm sure I'm overthinking the situation, but so much art in a highly fortified home—let's just say I'm curious. Who knows? If this is truly a big-time collector, maybe I can get on the gravy train. A Cannon for a wedding gift is pretty strong sign of both wealth and excellent taste."

"That make sense, but be careful, Bloom. You should delete those photos and our texts just to be on the safe side. I have a copy now. If your bosses decide to check your photos, you would have a hard time explaining the unauthorized images you've taken of the art."

"You're the real detective, Rachael, not me."

"We Navajo are suspicious by nature. I can hear the apprehension in your voice, so I'm following your cues. With your record for finding trouble, Charles Bloom, I'm heading you off at the pass." Rachael smiled on the other end of the phone, reflecting on her shoot 'em-up cowboy and Indian vernacular.

"OK. I get it, there's a new sheriff in town. I promise not to cause no trouble."

"Good night, Bloom. I love you. Be careful; I've got plans for you when you get home, some real Wild West adventures if you catch my drift!"

"Hi Yo Silver, AWAY! Love you, too, Rachael... night."

The next two days were routine for Bloom and his father. Show up at the gate, go through a vehicle perimeter sniff with the dogs, watch their IDs being checked, and have the car ushered toward the rear of the property to do their work. No more government cars were seen and the guards seemed more relaxed.

The pre-Columbian collection was voluminous, but with a push they could finish the job in short order and Bloom could get back home to his wife. There was no word on the T.C. Cannon. Bloom took another stroll around the painting racks and no one checked on him, so either the guards didn't watch the video cameras closely or there was no interior monitoring taking place.

On the last day, Bloom noticed a room he hadn't seen before at the far back of the building; the door was ajar and a faint cobalt color light emanated from the space. Bloom took the opportunity to go past the painting racks and peek in. It appeared to be a surgical suite, not the additional storage he expected. In the room's center was a gurney with large blue straps. A complex light with multiple handles was directly overhead and in the center of the room was a gray hose with a power nozzle. A floor drain was positioned under the gurney.

The blue light originated from side counters, where a line of instruments was charging. The tools were unfamiliar to Bloom, but he assumed they were medical in nature. He decided this must be an in-house veterinary area. The straps looked too large for a human; maybe they were for the dogs, whose presence seemed to be omnipresent.

The walls were lined with counters and large panels of multidimensional wooden blocks. Their organic nature resembled art, but they appeared more functional in their design. Bloom was at a loss as to what these blocks could be—so he couldn't help himself, pulled out his phone, and took a photo. He would ask his wife about them.

Bloom decided this was his last chance to take another look at the painting racks and left the surgical suite. That room's mysterious story might never be deciphered, but the paintings hanging in the dark were his forte.

The day was nippy but the room was warm. Lights illuminated one half of the building; the rest was dark except for the cobalt light. Bloom turned on his phone light but did not pull out the walls this time, figuring the sound of the brass caster wheels moving could have been the reason he nearly got caught on the first go-around. There were no surveillance video cameras that he could see.

The iPhone camera light was powerful enough to see a third of the wall, and what he recognized was remarkable: the second wall held a Georgia O'Keeffe flower; an early O'Keeffe New Mexico landscape; a cowboy hat and gloves by Marsden Hartley; and three other modernist paintings that he couldn't see well enough to make an attribution. The third wall contained a large Depression-era image of a truck with somber men hanging out the back that looked like Maynard Dixon's work; a Frederic Remington night scene of multiple riders in the snow; a Charles Russell of Indians engaged in a battle; and two more canvases, one of which looked like either a Thomas Moran or an Albert Bierstadt. On the fourth wall was an E.L. Blumenschein painting of Angel Fire Lake with small fishermen; Victor Higgins' take on the Taos mountains with shadowy figures of despair; and a large, multicolored Pueblo Indian portrait by Nicolai Fechin next to another that was probably by Leon Gaspard and a possible Joseph Henry Sharp.

Bloom was familiar with most of these artists from the Taos and Santa Fe areas; all were very valuable. The Cannon he had seen earlier was actually the least expensive of the lot. He heeded Rachael's words and didn't take any photos of the paintings. He sent the image of the blocks to his gallery email and deleted that photo from his phone. Bloom figured he was pushing his luck and returned to his dad's side to finish up the ceramic project.

Only the Fechin was a painting he recognized as being on the market before; the rest were unknown. Bloom, as a matter of habit, methodically checked all pertinent auction records once a week to stay on top of current market prices. The Fechin work had sold at auction for well over a million dollars three years ago; it was a top painting by anyone's standards.

The magnitude of what he witnessed on the four exhibit walls was staggering—there was maybe as much as $25 million worth of art here, possibly more, depending on the valuation of the O'Keeffes. O'Keeffe prices had taken a huge leap after the Crystal Bridges Museum of American Art, funded by Alice Walton of the Wal-Mart family, purchased the piece at auction. Titled JIMSON WEED, the single white flower executed in 1932 sold for $44 million, throwing the O'Keeffe market into chaos; now everyone assumed their painting was worth millions. But the reality was that two of the wealthiest people in the world had fought for a masterpiece and didn't know when to stop. Money literally wasn't the issue.

As the immensity of the art collection in the building sunk in, Bloom wanted to know who the collector was and how the work had been accumulated without him hearing a little gossip. Paintings of this quality were rare.

"Dad, what do you know about this collection? How do people come by so much pre-Columbian art without being involved in smuggling? Is this much material available on the everyday market?"

"I'm not sure how to answer that, Son. We don't know how long this family has been collecting, but it is an amazing grouping of ceramics and stone works. Even in today's depressed artifact market, this material is worth a small to medium fortune. I would think that large gold spear alone has to equal the cost of a Mercedes."

"Can you put this kind of collection together legally?" Bloom asked, knowing the answer.

"I honestly don't know, and it's not my place to ask those questions. I'm only here to catalog and give the owner an idea of the culture, date, authenticity, and condition of each piece."

"Have you seen any fakes in this collection?"

"Not that I can tell—and most are in very good condition, too."

"That's unusual isn't it?"

"Yes, that is a bit out of the ordinary."

"What's the client's name again?"

"Veracruz Trust was what the paperwork said."

"How does this tie into a government car visiting the Veracruz Trust?"

"I haven't the foggiest, Son."

Bloom suddenly realized these questions should be asked later, as he didn't know if they were being monitored. After all, the guard had come in the first day when the caster wheels squeaked, and nothing had happened on this go-around. He had said too much.

"OK, Dad. I was just curious. It's none of our business anyway. I'm just putting off the work we have in front of us, but you know if we can finish by three we can catch happy hour at Josephine's," Bloom said, backpedalling in case they were being monitored.

"I quit drinking years ago, Son."

"I know, but I didn't and this job has me thirsty. An early weekend is coming in a few hours, so let's finish up the last few rows by 2 p.m. and call it done."

Luckily for Charles Bloom he had heard Rachael's voice in his head, become cautious of his words, and changed subjects. The room was indeed monitored for sound and Jorge had taken notice of the conversation. The younger Bloom was nosy; he had noticed the government cars the first day he was on the property and now was fishing around for answers to questions he should never ask. The guard wouldn't report what he heard to his boss, Mr. Gutierrez—at least not yet. He would check Bloom's phone as part of the normal procedure on the way out to look at the last three days of photos. If it was clean, the two men were good. But if there were any hiccups, he would confiscate the phones and pass along the devices and information to his boss to decide the next step of action.

Charles Bloom seemed a bit too curious for his own good. If he wasn't careful, he might just find himself in deep trouble with bad hombres who planted the men who crossed them in the unmarked graves that dotted the southern New Mexico borderlands.

CHAPTER 11

SILVER BEADS, PLEASE

When the burly guard requested both men's phones as they were leaving the compound, Charles wanted to tell him to buzz off. But he realized he would probably appear guilty if he did—not to mention that the man could have torn the phone out of his grip, probably with his hand still attached.

There was nothing of interest on either phone. Dr. Bloom used a hand-me-down iPhone that his son had bequeathed him. Since he only used it as a camera and flashlight, he had never bothered to activate the phone service.

"Who needs a pocket phone?" he mused. "I have a home phone that anyone rarely uses unless they are trying to sell me insurance or a cemetery plot."

Charles assumed the security guards must have heard or seen him snooping around the off-limits back wall and the surgical suite, and decided that further investigation was required. The gallerist was not normally paranoid, but under these circumstances he would watch his back for the next few days and even splurge on a new phone. Extra caution seemed appropriate considering his phone might have been hacked when it was taken out of his sight to be examined by the goons. A phone upgrade was warranted under any circumstances. His current phone was three years old and his poor-quality photos of the Cannon painting made the extravagant expenditure an appropriate use of family funds. Add the potentially dangerous pre-Columbian collection to that and it was clearly time for an asset upgrade.

Driving into the outskirts of El Paso was sobering. Bloom's time living on the rez had given him a unique perspective on population density, and this place had exploded. Like many cities in America, it too had been ravaged by a mass shooting. There was heavy traffic, smog, and high-rise buildings lining the horizon. A border fence loomed large against the trickle of the Río Grande.

The only Apple Store within 200 miles was in El Paso. Las Cruces, New Mexico's second largest city, lacked what many would consider a basic necessity, as did the Land of Enchantment's capital, Santa Fe. Bloom was used to traveling for important purchases and car repairs—usually to Albuquerque. Part of being a New Mexican was driving long distances for goods and services.

The Apple Store was packed and the staff less than helpful, which was surprising as Apple was one of Bloom's favorite companies. But, as a businessman, Charles realized that employees were only as good as the person hiring them. So he took the poor service in stride and spent a thousand dollars to purchase the latest and greatest iPhone with extra RAM. His father, who had tagged along on the shopping trip, was shocked at the price tag, and Bloom realized that he could never explain to his dad how a cell phone was a direct lifeline to the heart of his business. A smartphone provided him with flexibility, easy access to emails, the ability to update a website, make social media posts, listen to relevant podcasts, and take high-quality photos of art. It even picked up the occasional phone call.

As was their tradition, Bloom gifted the old phone to his father, wiping the memory before passing it along. One could never be too careful. Even though Bloom's phone was three years old, it had a better camera and flashlight function than his dad's out-of-date model. Professor Bloom was thrilled. "A thousand dollar phone! My god, I'm increasing my exposure to Apple—more stock is in order!" he only halfway joked. Charles had never been prouder of his dad.

Bloom figured Rachael might be in his father's sticker-shock corner. He would let the credit card bill do the dirty work, which was much easier than dealing with the fallout at this moment. The delay would give Rachael additional time to heal—and forestall the possibility that she might want a new phone too. Bloom's family was moving to Santa Fe in short order. Since he would need a new smartphone anyway, it might as well be the best. One art sale from a good phone photo and the expenditure would pay for itself.

Bloom backed up his phone's data and, after an hour-long struggle, was admiring his shiny new white phone— more a work of art than a working tool. He had decided against a buying a protective case at the Apple Store; he could pick up a cheaper one on eBay. He called Rachael on the drive home to check her mood and see how the kids were faring in his absence. His father had drifted off, the long day wearing him out. He would not be putting in any more twelve-hour workdays the way he did when Bloom was a kid. His father was moving on to another stage in life, and this was possibly his last big project.

Bloom needed to hear the timbre of his wife's voice to soothe his mind. "What did you find out from your old professor," he asked, before even saying, "Hi."

"Nice to hear your voice, too."

"Sorry! How are you, my love, and the kids?"

"Yes, we're fine." Rachael smiled on the other end of the line, understanding her husband's solidly type-A personality. "Professor Benally did recognize the Cannon. It's quite an interesting story in fact...."

Rachael paused, knowing the dead air would drive Bloom crazy.

"Give it up, or I won't tell you what happened to me today and it's pretty crazy too." Bloom said.

"All right, Mr. Ants-in-your-Pants. The professor said he remembers seeing a finished painting on the easel in Cannon's studio two days before the artist's death, and he thought the painting in the photograph might be the same one. He had come by for morning tea and conversation, which wasn't uncommon as they were long-time friends. T.C. seemed to have a lot on his mind as he had a major show coming up in New York City and was struggling to finish paintings for the event. The reason Benally remembers that piece is because T.C. told him he thought he might be able to finish one more painting for his show. I asked Benally if he knew the title, and he said that as he remembered it had not been titled yet, so he and Cannon batted a few ideas around.

"What were the titles?"

"I asked the same thing. Benally said he couldn't exactly remember, but they were something like LUNCH BREAK, SWEET TOOTH, or

AND ACTION! Apparently T.C. hadn't settled on one, but was leaning toward SWEET TOOTH.

"Two days after the car accident, Professor Benally went to T.C.'s studio to check on things, and found the door locked with what he assumed was a police padlock. He peered in the window and noticed the painting wasn't on the easel. He didn't think anything of it at the time; the family might have come for the piece, or that it could have been sold before the accident. The work was finished and T.C. always could use money, upcoming gallery show or not.

"I asked Professor Benally if it could have been stolen right after T.C.'s death, and he said he doubted that—but he did remember a rash of burglaries around Santa Fe at that time, when the economy wasn't great, interest rates were high, and cocaine was the drug of choice. There was lots of product available, so it was possible. His guess was that the estate simply retrieved the painting, or that the New York City gallery sold it in the days directly before or after T.C. died.

"He asked me who had the painting and I told him it was in a private collection in Las Cruces. I figured you wouldn't want him to know your source. I also sent a photo of the back inscription, which didn't mean anything to him.

OK, Mr. Bloom. Is that enough information? Now it's time to move on to our quid pro quo."

"You'll find this interesting, Rachael, and I would love to get your thoughts about it. The men who guard the front gate of this compound made Dad and me unlock our phones—and they took them away, out of our sight, for a few minutes. You were right to be suspicious."

"They actually confiscated your phone and disappeared inside the home—then came back and said nothing but have a nice day?"

"Pretty much. I don't know what all can be gleaned from a phone that quickly, but I'm sure they looked at my photos and text messages. It's a good thing I got rid of those photos of my nude body that I almost sent you last night," Bloom ribbed.

"Too bad; I could use those about now," Rachael shot back, her sexuality on the mend.

"You should upgrade that old phone, Bloom. Maybe they did some weird thing and can now follow you or listen in on your calls—ditto for your dad's phone."

"There is nothing among Dad's photos except the pre-Columbian art, which was authorized. I took care of getting a new phone today."

"Good boy."

"I had that Yellowhorse voice playing loudly in my head, so I knew you would approve," Bloom said, avoiding adding that he had spent nearly one thousand dollars, then quickly changing subjects.

"Rachael, did you get my email with photos of those wooden-block sculpture-looking things?"

"I haven't opened my emails today; give me a second and I'll take a look. OK, I have it open. What's your question?"

"I took that photo today. It was in some kind of surgical suite in the back of the art storage area. I couldn't recognize them, but I figured an ex-sculptor like you might know what they are."

"For your information, I'm still a sculptor—but now I prefer to use wool instead of metal, and yes, I do recognize what is on that back wall. But that's not art: those are sound-dampening blocks."

"What does that mean?" Bloom asked.

"In sound studios, they put up these large multi-tiered blocks to help deaden the room and keep noise from bouncing around. Why would they put them in a surgical suite?"

"Rachael, I didn't know they were not sculptures, and I sure don't know why they are in a surgical suite. The better question to the marvelous Ms. Yellowhorse is why do they have a surgical suite in an art storage area in the first place. It makes no sense unless it keeps the noise down when they're working on animals...."

"It's possible, I guess. I'm assuming you cleaned this block photo off your phone too?"

"Your voice is always in my head, as is the image of your face. Yes, it's been deleted."

"My voice should be ringing in your head, Charles Bloom. How much longer will you stay down in Cruces?"

"Well, I hate to report the temperature today reached 62 degrees. What is it at the house?"

"Thirty-five degrees for a high, with clear blue skies and a 20 miles-per-hour wind."

"I'll probably stay here for another week," Bloom teased.

"That's my boy, and he has a new phone. By the way, how much did the phone run?"

"I don't remember for sure; they sure have gotten expensive."

"Don't remember, huh? Bloom, I love how you try to lessen the blow, waiting for the credit card bill to come in—or maybe you're afraid I might want a new phone, too." Rachael knew her husband well.

"Both!"

Bloom switched gears to avoid answering any more questions. "Rach, you have to tell me when you want me home. I'll come running if you're having problems or the kids need me. You are my number-one priority. Dad can finish up the report on his own."

"Nice segue, Mr. Bloom. And to answer your question, the kids and I are doing fine. Marvin is going to come over for dinner tonight and we're going to spend some Navajo time together. I think he misses you as much as I do."

"How's Sal Lito's latest employee working out?"

"Marvin says it's all good, but the post in winter is dead. Marvin's bored and eating his wages in ice cream bars each day. This is the first time I can see a little fat around his sides. Sal told him he could take off a week if he wanted."

"Maybe Marvin can help fix the roof shingles; it's not my favorite task and he's like a billy goat when it comes to heights."

"For free food Marvin will cut next year's supply of wood. Tell your dad 'Hi' for me and let's plan on seeing you next week. How about I do a Mardi Gras thing? I'll make something Creole and, if you're lucky, you can throw me some beads." Rachael felt a rush of adrenaline.

"I've got a bunch of those cheap plastic beads leftover from college, so we can make this work," Bloom countered.

"I'm Navajo," Rachael quipped. "We expect silver beads, not those fake trade beads you bilágaanas think we will fall for."

"Rachael, I love you and I'll see you soon."

"Love you too—and I want a new phone for my birthday!"

CHAPTER 12

PASS THE BISCUITS

The Cannon painting filled Bloom's dreams that night, a shower of hard candy forming a river of sweets that was sweeping Bloom away from his family. Sweat trickled down his face as he awoke with a lurch and reached for a nonexistent light switch; he was not at home. Instead he found his new iPhone, the light softer than on his previous model.

The time—3:33 a.m.—was blinking. Was it an omen? The painting was churning around in his subconscious: there was something not quite right there—but what?

"How did a major painting by a famous artist avoid getting published or exhibited?" he wondered. Cannon had a small body of work and died at 31. The great graffiti artist Jean-Michel Basquiat died a bit younger at 27, yet all his works—even scraps of paper—were accounted for.

Bloom tried to consider the possibilities in his father's guestroom until the blue hue vanished from his phone. He tapped the flashlight icon and walked to the bathroom, a nightly trip more often than not. He recognized he was pushing fifty years old and could rarely sleep the night without urinating, a sure sign of disabilities to come. Time was running out for another child; he and Rachael would need to try again quickly if he didn't want to be on Medicare by the time his last child went off to college.

The splash of urine provided background music to Bloom's fading dream state.

"Stolen, that's the only thing that makes sense," he realized, as his subconscious and conscious states merged into one. "If it were lifted off the easel before being accounted for by the estate, no one would know. It probably didn't take T.C. more than a couple of days to complete the painting—especially if he were under pressure to produce work for an upcoming major exhibit. It could have been stolen by a person with access, or maybe it was just a simple robbery by someone smart enough to know that a dead artist meant opportunity. After all, it was Santa Fe and everyone there understands art equates with money. Even if you don't truly understand all the nuances, someone smarter than you will."

Bloom was wide awake now. He had visited the big Cannon retrospective at the Heard Museum in Phoenix and at the Denver Art Museum, and neither had mentioned this piece in their catalogs, so maybe it had been stolen right after Cannon's death. The art dealer would need to do some digging in the Santa Fe newspaper archives and at IAIA—maybe talk to Benally himself to be sure the painting hadn't simply gone to the estate. Charles wanted to be sure he was not overthinking a dream state and an apparently disappearing painting.

Bloom's mind ratcheted back to Rachael's brother, Willard Yellowhorse, who had been taking advantage of and murdered by an unscrupulous dealer, and how hard they had to fight to clear Willard's name and reclaim a painting that belonged to the family.

The Cannon painting had now taken on new meaning for Bloom, and provided a distraction from his thoughts about his lost child. Here was an undiscovered painting hidden in an art vault whose provenance seemed dubious. He would focus his mind and energy on this question. Little could Bloom imagine the painting's true history—and the dire consequences that lay ahead for his family if he pushed too hard.

Was the 3:33 a.m. time glowing on his new phone a warning sign? Bloom placed the phone face down on the bedside table and tried to return to sleep.

No matter how much time had passed between visits, morning coffee was a tradition at the Bloom house. Dr. Bloom rose with the sun as usual and the aroma of the fresh brew awoke Charles, who robotically shuffled to the breakfast nook. The fading flower prints that decorated the walls bothered Bloom's sense of aesthetics, and he made a mental note to send a nice small Toadlena/Two Grey Hills weaving for his dad's eighty-first birthday. It was never too late, he thought, to influence someone's sense of beauty.

"Morning, Son. Hope you slept well and that you're ready for a busy day cataloging the hundreds of items we've been measuring."

"Sure, sounds fun—nothing like a day spent listing meaningless data on material I don't own, can't sell, or understand," Bloom said, avoiding elaborating on his insomnia.

"Come on, it's not that bad. We can sit out on the patio and take in some sun, something you wouldn't get back in Toadlena."

Bloom smiled at his father's characteristically cheerful disposition.

"Sad what might happen to this information. Don't you think it seems odd to have it all cataloged by an expensive archaeologist, but not use an appraiser?"

"I have no idea. Maybe it's for a museum catalog, or just good recordkeeping where value is inconsequential. You do realize that an object's worth is not all in monetary terms...."

"True, but from my experience this is unusual to say the least. I would have an appraiser working with the authority. You give them the green light that the piece is authentic, and they give it the once over themselves to say they have seen the piece, along with a cursory condition report and a value."

"Why would an appraiser need to be there? Once I give the owner the information, the rest is superfluous, don't you think?"

Charles took a large drag of coffee and let the xanthines work their magic on his deadened neurons before answering.

"Well, if that's true, why have anyone but scientists look at art?" Bloom said sarcastically.

"I agree! Now we're on the same page, Son."

"Dad, I'm kidding. Appraisers need to look at the objects too; they might not be archaeologists, but they could see things you might miss."

"What could they observe that I wouldn't?" Dr. Bloom asked, taking his first sip of coffee.

"How about restoration, or worse, the addition of a small detail like a vintage spear that you would assume was original to the piece, but was a marriage from remnants of another pre-Columbian figurine to make it more valuable. You know we didn't backlight one of those pieces. You looked at the works for authenticity, not condition for selling."

Dr. Bloom savored his coffee, reflecting on what his son said. "I get it; one academic, one financial, different observational skill sets. So what's your point, Son?"

"It's odd, that's all. Did they give you a specific form that they wanted filled out?"

"In fact they did. We are about to work on it. Give me a second and I'll go get the form. Meanwhile, have a hot biscuit. They are out of a can, but they're nearly as good as your mom's."

"Have you ever thought that Mom might have used the can herself and didn't tell you?"

"She did?" Dr. Bloom said incredulously.

"My entire childhood was spent watching you drink coffee, eat a biscuit, and grab a piece of fruit before running to your lab. Yes, they were out of the can and we never told you. In fact, it was Mom's and my running joke."

Bloom watched for his father's reaction, not knowing exactly what to expect. Then his dad broke into a deep, hardy laugh. "I loved that woman, and she's still surprising me nearly ten years after her passing."

Dr. Bloom went to his study, where the sound of rustling papers could be heard.

"This is the form they want the information transcribed onto; they asked for the report to be in hard copy and on this form."

Charles Bloom examined the paper. "You see the last column, Dad? It says Replacement Value."

"Yes, I saw that, but they said not to worry about filling out that column because it didn't apply to this collection."

"Oh, it applies all right. Don't you see that this changes everything, Dad?"

"No, I don't see anything!"

"You signature and reputation both go into this report. See, it has your name and title already typed in below for you to sign. And look here: they want it notarized too. Yet they leave a column for replacement value that doesn't apply to this report on the form. Why would they do that?"

"I don't know. What do you think?"

"The Trust clearly prepared this form specifically for you—but they don't take out the replacement value section? Seems to me they're planning on filling in the numbers and using you as their patsy, putting you on the hook for the pricing."

"That's outrageous. I can't believe that can be right."

"Dad, how were the fresh biscuits?"

"I know I can be gullible. I don't have my son's killer suspicious instinct. But let's say they did that, filled it in with some inflated numbers, and then I get a call from the IRS questioning the form and valuations. I would just say, 'Not my numbers, not my handwriting.'"

"That's well and good, Dad—but they could type the numbers rather than write them in—and what if you're not around to verify information that's already been notarized?"

“What do you mean ‘not around?’”

“You’re nearly eighty-one and things happen to older people.”

“Please don’t call me an old person; I prefer the word ‘mature,’” Dr. Bloom said, trying to lighten the conversation.

“Dad, I’m not kidding. You can’t fill this out. It makes me very concerned. And to answer your question, the only person who could verify the information besides you is me, and if these are truly unethical people then I’m next in line....”

“You make this sound very dark and dangerous, Son. I think your imagination is getting the best of you.”

“Maybe, but maybe not. Ask them for a new form without the valuation column and see what they say. Or simply cross out the lines that say replacement value and initial them. That would take care of my concerns.”

“Fine, we will cross out each the column so there is no doubt that I’m only doing the forensic evaluation, not any commercial valuation.”

“Thank you! Now how about you pass me another one of Mom’s homemade biscuits?” Both Blooms chuckled, their two laughs harmonizing into one.

CHAPTER 13

PLEASE COME WITH ME

Charles and his father spent a good portion of the day cataloging the information they had gathered onto a single form, filled out as per the instructions of the Velazquez Trust. Dr. Bloom put a long ink line through the replacement cost section, initialized each page at the bottom, dated it, and wrote "not applicable."

After reviewing the document, Dr. Bloom and his son were satisfied.

"That's pretty good work if I may say—not bad for an old guy."

"Two old guys. I'm not getting any younger either, I'm afraid."

"Oh, Son, you have no idea of what being a senior means. Just wait until you hit eighty and the parts quit working. Luckily, the old noggin still functions."

"Let's go down to the bank where we can get a free notary and head over to Josephine's for a nice breakfast of huevos Christmas-style before we turn your masterpiece over to the Trust."

"That an outstanding plan, but I'm sure the bank will charge a fee. They don't work for free."

"Dad, I run a lot of money through that bank. They will be happy to notarize the document for free—although, from what you tell me about your stock portfolio, you're the bigger VIP."

"Oh, I don't know about that. But I like how it sounds."

The Bloom men took care of business; the bank didn't charge them for the notarization and even made them a free copy of the document. After a delightful meal, they went to the compound to deliver the package.

"Hi, Dr. Bloom. How can I help you? You're done looking at the stuff, right?"

"Believe me, I'm finished. Glad my boy was here to help. I'm just dropping off the completed form for your boss." Dr. Bloom handed the manila envelope to the giant of a man.

"See you around." Dr. Bloom waved goodbye to the guard at the gate.

"If you would, sir, let me run this in to my boss to make sure we have everything we need. If you would please pull up past the dog station, it will just take a second."

"Sure, not a problem," Dr. Bloom said and pulled over to the side inspection area, where two men with dogs walked around the car—part of the general routine.

As father and son sat listening to Dr. Bloom's favorite singer, Sammy Davis Jr., sing "The Candy Man" while they waited for the thumbs-up to leave, a long sedan with heavily tinted windows pulled close by and was waved through. Bloom peered closely at the fancy car as it drove in, but it was hard to make out the occupant(s) other than the driver.

"Dad, that must be the compound's owner."

"Hmm, looks like it. Wonder why they decided to live in Mesilla?"

The two watched as the sedan stopped at the front door of the main house. A man hurried out and opened the passenger door as the car rolled to a stop. A single female exited, and the man closed the door and stood to attention as if he were in the military. The tall, thin woman walked with an air of entitlement. It was impossible to tell anything about her other than she was female and well dressed.

"You think she's in the government? Doesn't look like it to me," Dr. Bloom said.

"The brute opening the door sure thought she was important, but I haven't a clue if she's in the government. I'm not a fan of politics, and quite frankly, I wouldn't recognize the governor much less some lower-ranking legislative representative."

"Charles, I'm sure you know who the governor is."

"Not really. I know he's an old white guy with New Mexican roots, but I don't know anything else."

"See, you do know who the governor is after all. Our last one was a woman, fairly young and Republican. All I care about, regardless of party affiliation, is that they don't touch my pension or Medicare, and that they are Democrats."

"Regardless of political affiliation, huh? I know you're a party-line guy Dad, although I've honestly never understood that position. What happens if you get a Democrat who is not a good person running? Would you still vote for that individual, even when you know it could all end badly?"

"I know a Democrat, even a bad one, beats a Republican any day—and will protect my pension and health care."

Bloom wasn't up for a no-win discussion. He was happy to be an independent. And, even if he was a poorly informed about his own state's politics, he never missed voting come election day.

A tap on the glass and the men remembered where they were. Dr. Bloom rolled down his squeaky window while Sammy Davis Jr. was still singing of world harmony.

"Dr. Bloom, I'm afraid my boss says the form has been compromised. Apparently, you crossed out the line where it says replacement value. He gave me a new form for you to fill out."

Dr. Bloom looked over at his son in the passenger seat, his eyes asking for advice. Charles took the cue.

"My father crossed that line out because it wouldn't be appropriate to leave it empty. Someone could simply fill in the valuations with his name and the notary's already filled in on the bottom."

The guard said nothing, looking at Dr. Bloom for his answer.

"Yes, that is correct. I'm an archaeologist, not an appraiser. I'm sure your boss will understand."

"I'm afraid not, Dr. Bloom. If you would please come with me you can talk directly with Mr. Gutierrez."

James Bloom again looked at his son, who said, "Fine. We are happy to talk with him."

"Dr. Bloom, would you follow me now?"

Charles started to exit the passenger side when a guard who had come around the car blocked his exit.

"Only your father, I'm afraid."

Bloom didn't know what to say or do, protesting, "I need to accompany my father; he's eighty and I need to be by his side."

"Mr. Bloom, this is a restricted area. I'm afraid you are not authorized to be here, but your father is. Don't worry. We'll take care of him."

The guard blocking the side door was not budging; it was clear Charles would not be allowed to accompany his father.

Dr. Bloom piped up: "Charles, it's fine. I've been inside before. Sit tight. I'll be right back."

"OK, Dad. I'll be right here waiting for you."

The guard on the passenger side stayed in place, his dog in a ready position, as Dr. Bloom was escorted inside.

"Dr. Bloom, so nice to see you again. I'm Carlos Gutierrez. We met a few weeks back. I understand we have a slight problem today."

"I don't think so. It's just that I can't leave an empty line for appraisals on the same form that I filled out and signed. Someone could fill in that column, which would leave me open for IRS issues in the future."

"First and foremost, don't worry. This form never leaves our sight, and all the paperwork goes into a vault on the premises. No one can touch it; it's perfectly straightforward.

"Remember that you signed a contract when you began this project that specified you must use our form for your report, and fill it out with no alterations and no exceptions. Do you remember that contract?"

Dr. Bloom was trying to figure out his next step, and wishing his son were available for counsel, realizing at that moment that he was indeed aging. He had forgotten about the contract he had received last month. He had brought his laptop to the meeting as requested.

They sent the document to his email, then printed off a copy in the office for him to sign.

"Yes, now I do. Honestly, I didn't read it closely. I figured it was just legal jargon."

"Remember that I helped you with that?"

"I remember now."

"You might want to refer back to this document. It clearly lays out your obligations to complete the task and to use only our forms, no modifications allowed—or you're not paid and YOU are in legal jeopardy for breaking the contract."

"Sorry about that. Give me another copy of your form. I'll have my son read the contract and I can get back with you. He's an art dealer and knows more about these things. I'm sure everything will be fine with your reassurances."

"Art dealer, huh? That's a wonderful profession. Where is his gallery?"

"On Canyon Road in Santa Fe. It's called Bloom's—maybe you've heard of it?"

"No, I'm not the art person, but I'm sure my superior has heard of your son's gallery. If you could get me the completed and unaltered form by tomorrow, that would be quite helpful."

Gutierrez smiled and returned to his paperwork. He was finished with Dr. Bloom and it was time for the archaeologist to exit. The large guard escorted Dr. Bloom back to his car, carrying another envelope. Once he got into the car, Dr. Bloom tossed the envelope into the back seat and made a U-turn out of the lot.

"What happened, Dad?" Bloom asked.

"They said there was nothing to worry about; they keep the papers under lock and key and no one has access to the documents but them."

"Dad, that IS the problem: THEY HAVE ACCESS."

"What's your point, Son? You make it sound like they would falsify the document."

"Correct, they could do just that. You can't fill that out."

"I won't get paid if I don't finish my work, and I've already signed a contract saying I would follow their protocol. I think you're blowing this out of proportion."

"Dad, you and I need to have a long talk when we get home, starting with this so-called contract."

The two men sat quietly on the drive home, no longer feeling the love Sammy Davis Jr. had been singing about. The world didn't feel good. Bloom felt fifteen years old, but knew he needed to be the parent in this situation. His mind raced back to his wife's recent miscarriage: being a father was difficult.

CHAPTER 14

I'LL BRING THE LUNCH

Five days had passed since Bloom's melodic voice graced Rachael's ears; only the kids' laughter now filled their small home. The solitude had helped energize Rachael so she could break through the negative thinking that revolved through her mind.

The fleeting memories of her lost baby and what that child represented to their future family dynamics had become a more solid reality. Bloom's pain was palpable, and his absence reduced her guilt to a more tolerable level. The baby names they had selected were now tainted, and she wondered if those carefully vetted identities would ever be appropriate to use again.

The pregnancy had lasted for three months, the amount of time it would take for Rachael's hair to grow only one and a half inches—yet the pain of the loss was visceral. The family was moving to Santa Fe in part because they would have needed the extra room for a baby. Was the now-reduced family size making this a moot point? Bloom had signed a lease on the La Cienega property, so it seemed—at least for now—that the family's move would occur as scheduled.

The methodical pulsation of the weaving comb was hypnotic, and the act of producing a textile cathartic. Each finished weft row pushed Rachael's sense of doom a little further away; over the course of the day her sadness, like her weaving, showed a discernable progress.

Marvin Manycoats—Uncle Marvin to the kids—arrived thirty minutes before dinner. He helped set the table, cleaned and stoked the kitchen stove, and split fresh wood while engaging in meaningful conversation. After a hearty meal, stories were told and Marvin helped put the kids down for the night.

Marvin's remarkable memory was an amazing source of stories about his life as a traditional Navajo boy. As part of one such tale, Marvin told of the lost boy he had known when he went to boarding school in 1961—the very same year Yuri Gagarin flew into space. He explained that the small, wiry boy, not much older than Willy was now, refused to go to the bilagáana's school and escaped to the high summer sheep country. And he shared how he wished that he, too, could have escaped the wicked headmaster of the school.

The children hooted and hollered about not having to go to school; they wanted to be like the brave little boy—at least until Marvin told the rest of the story.

"When I returned home for Christmas," he said, "the only break I got from school, I looked for my friend. We had no cell phones back then. That's when I heard the terrible news that he was lost and that his father, who was very upset, had died looking for him. His father is buried not far from this house."

"Did the little boy ever get found?" Samantha asked.

"No, he did not get found. No one knows what happened to him. But he's always alive in my heart and head. Every time I hear the wind blow hard or the rain bang against my hogan door, I think of my eleven-year-old friend and know he is part of Mother Earth and protecting me from bad *chindi*."

"Will he protect us too?" Willy wondered.

"Yes—you most of all, because he is the protector of children. Ricky is what made Indian boarding school better when I returned there after Christmas. I listened for his voice in the tree branches at night, and felt his touch when the snow fell hard against my cheeks, and heard him saying, 'You are safe, do not worry.'

"Now, children, it is time for sleep because, unlike the wind's song, you do have school in the morning."

"Ahhhh...," Willy and Sam protested in unison as Marvin clicked off the light and gently closed the door, leaving a slight crack of light.

"What was the little boy's name?" Willy asked as Marvin left the room.

"His name is Ricky Begay, and he is the kind of friend you never forget."

Rachael, who had pulled up a chair outside the kids' door, had also listened intently to the story.

"Marvin, you sounded so sad. Is that a true story about Ricky Begay? Did he really disappear and his father die looking for him?"

"Yes, I'm afraid it's true. There is no close clan left so their memories only live through a few people like myself who are still kicking."

The thought of the tragic deaths of Marvin's friend and the boy's father struck a nerve with Rachael and she began to weep.

"Rachael, I'm sorry. I shouldn't have told that story. Forgive me. The recent loss of your child has affected me in ways I never would have imagined. A long-buried ghost has been released and I feel responsible for my friend's death. For so long the pain was like a small ant, something you can brush off. But with your sorrow added to the burden, the ants have grown into a single velvet ant—a lone wanderer on the desert floor waiting to ambush its prey, with a sting so powerful it can bring a grown man to his knees."

"How could you be responsible for this tragedy that is still causing such pain so many years later?"

"Your baby's passing triggered my memory. I thought I had buried this part of my childhood forever, but I now realize I must deal with my loss somehow."

"What happened, Marvin?"

"I was a child, but even children can make a difference in life and death. Not acting to help a friend is my curse. The ghosts began haunting me again with last night's full moon. I have not told anyone this story in fifty years.

"My friend and I had played the day before we were to leave for boarding school. Our families had given us time away from our chores so we could be kids. I guess they knew what was coming. Anyway, I remember my friend being happy, and I asked him why he was so happy on such a sad day. He told me he was running away to his summer sheep camp on Chuska Mountain in the morning. His father had given him permission to not get on the white man's yellow-squash bus—and he asked me to join him on his run to freedom.

"I wanted to go, but my father was not like Ricky's father. My family would be dishonored and I was afraid my father might get in trouble if I ran away—though I still wanted to go. I told Ricky he could count on me, and that I would try my best to meet him in the morning. The night before I was supposed to leave for Indian school, I packed a set of clothes and two days worth of venison and hardtack in my knapsack. I planned to leave when everyone was asleep and meet my friend at the spot we had selected in the morning. But that night a full moon awakened the old juniper outside my folks' hogan. In my mind, it had turned into a witching tree that would not allow me to pass and I backed out.

"I always felt that if I had joined him, I would have been able to help Ricky somehow, and he wouldn't have been lost in the backcountry. I assume he died out there."

"Marvin, you were following the law and your family wanted you to get an education, even if it was a seriously flawed system. Your father, as I understand it, was a man who played by the rules; he wouldn't have taken your running away and being truant from school lightly."

"Oh, I know. It makes no sense, but trauma is never a rational thing, at least that's what a shrink told me in Vietnam."

"They never found any trace of your friend?"

"Nothing, and they looked for many months after the tragic death of his father. But after a while there was no one to really care about Ricky other than me, and I was imprisoned at boarding school. The locals simply stopped looking and chalked his disappearance up to shape-shifters."

"What do you think happened to him?" Rachael asked, wiping the last of her tears away.

"My guess is that he slipped and fell in some deep crevice or put up in some cave for the night and a lion found a small dinner. Huge mountain lions roam the backcountry, especially back in 1961. Those are the most likely possibilities, I guess. What else could have happened?"

"Those scenarios do seem logical. Have you ever tried to find his remains?"

"No, although I thought about it a hundred times when I was younger. I wanted to bring closure to his disappearance and give my friend a decent burial. But life presses on, rugs get made, boys turn into men, move on with their lives, and put away childish thoughts."

"Marvin, you're retired and have more time now—plus you love to hike. Do you have any idea what path your friend would have taken to get to Chuska Mountain?"

"I have some ideas of the route he would have traveled. We went to his house after our play day and planned the details of the escape as best as young kids could. I remember sharing those plans with the tribal cops over Christmas break, but they said there was nothing they could do, and that Ricky's father was on the same route when he died. He had not found anything and neither had they."

"Well, Marvin, like you I'm dealing with my own demons over the loss of this child. Maybe you and I should take a couple of days and see what we might discover. We know this area like our own faces. We both raised sheep as kids and understand the backcountry. The worse thing that can happen is that we'll burn some extra calories."

"You sure you want to do this, Rachael? It's unlikely we will find anything and, if we do, it will be human bones."

"I understand. I don't like human remains any more than you—but chances are slim we will find anything and it could help you close a chapter of your life that has remained open way too long. I felt the pain in your voice when you told that story. You clearly have remaining issues, and frankly, so do I. This will help me as much as you, Marvin."

“Well, if helps you, Rachael, I’m all in. We can go out tomorrow. I think if we start at my friend’s old home some details might come back to me so I can draw up a good map. What time do you want to meet?”

“How about leaving after I drop the kids off at school?”

“You mean like you always do, then have a cup of coffee and a donut?”

“Yeah, something like that—except this time I’ll bring food for our lunches. I hope tomorrow will be a good day for both of us. I need to put the full moon behind me too.”

They smiled, each knowing the other needed closure. Tomorrow the healing process would start in earnest.

CHAPTER 15

THE BLUE CHAIR

With moonbeams illuminating his hogan, Marvin's sleep produced a torrent of dreams. Ricky Begay filled his subconscious. Why hadn't he run away from Indian school too? His friend's snaggle-toothed smile kept saying, "Come on, Marvin. There's plenty of rock candy in my father's summer sheep hogan."

The boys had planned to make their way up to the mesa northeast of Toadlena, then cut due north to Chuska Mountain. Ricky was alone in the world, his dad his only relative and friend—not counting his best buddy Marvin, of course. They had been helping each other herd sheep and learn silversmith skills from Marvin's dad, whose jewelry-making was legendary.

At 3 a.m. Marvin awoke, yelling, "Don't go! Don't go!" Realizing that his mind was floating close to another world, he decided he needed a cookie and some warm milk. A rusty cast-iron pan clanked on the stove's metallic surface as Marvin poured a large cup of milk into it. One day he would get a microwave—he had electricity—but somehow the act of stoking the fire and cooking on the stovetop kept him connected to his long-gone family; he too was alone in this world.

The aroma of simmering milk wafted through the tiny room as Marvin poured the contents into a coffee-stained cup that read, "Best Dad"—ironic considering he had never had kids or a wife. But the words made him hopeful. He owned five mugs—each inscribed with words or a funny logo—but this was his favorite. None had cost more than a quarter and all were from a second-hand store.

Small chunks of the cookie disintegrated as he dipped the sweet's edge deep inside the cup. Why was his subconscious working overtime? Was it the moon? He had a rudimentary idea of where he wanted to start the search, but something was missing. What? Then, like a clap of lighting, it hit him: he knew where Ricky's father had been found dead and he understood the basic direction Ricky had headed in. Maybe the answer lay somewhere between the two points.

Marvin smiled a half-awake grin. A concrete plan was what his mind was hoping to discover. Not aimlessly wandering the backcountry, but a real plan. Maybe redemption was nearby....

Ricky escaped from Indian school alone. Why hadn't Marvin been with him? After all, he was the boy's best friend. Marvin hated the fact that he had spent decades wading through the negativity of this subject, but until Ricky Begay was physically accounted for in the Fourth World, this part of Marvin's soul would never heal. Tomorrow was a new beginning; maybe some answers would push through the darkness in his mind.

* * * *

Sam was particularly ornery in the morning, refusing to eat her eggs and tossing the plate Frisbee-style across the kitchen floor. Rachael couldn't help wondering if her daughter's mood was a reflection of her own semi-despondent state of mind. She had sent Bloom away so she could recover. Now Sam was missing her dad and Marvin was revisiting old ghosts at least in part because of her pain, so this had to be a day of healing—not by weaving but by helping a friend.

Marvin opened the hogan door to find Rachael on her knees, trying to rein in the last of the egg globs hiding under the refrigerator.

"You need a broom; it would be a lot easier," he said. "And if it's food you're looking for, you know the mice need to eat too."

"You're not helping, Marvin Manycoats—and I don't have mice. How about you check the coffee? It's about ready."

Marvin smiled; the delightful aroma permeated the room. He retrieved two colorful matched cups from her well-organized cabinet and filled them half full of the deep chocolate brew. Rachael liked her coffee with plenty of milk, Marvin the same, although he added two teaspoons of sugar to his for an extra kick.

"Here you go, Rachael, just like you like it," Marvin said as he handed her the steaming cup. "I've made a small change to our schedule today. Instead of a long, aimless hike without a real goal, I figured that after we visit Ricky's abandoned family hogan we could go drive down to Gallup and see if we can dig up any files on his father's death, where the police found his body and such. It seems like a more organized place to start, and I know you like organized."

"That makes sense, and you're right—I always seek clarity of action. Do you think the police would still have records from 1961?"

"Yes, October of '61. It was a warm month as I remember."

"Of course you do. What don't you remember?"

"I don't remember what your leftover chocolate cream pie tastes like, especially with an extra-hot cup of coffee."

"Marvin, when is the last time you went to the dentist?"

"Oh, I go about every two years. They say the water out here has got so much fluoride I'll never have to worry about cavities—but when it comes to crooked teeth, all us Navajo have a similar smile."

Marvin grinned to prove his point, and Rachael grinned back, her perfect teeth belying his stereotyping.

"Well, Rachael, everything about you is perfect in my eyes."

Rachael blushed at Marvin's assessment; if he only knew how broken she felt.

"OK, Marvin, enough of that. I'm not perfect, but I'm a good detective. So when do we leave?"

"As soon as you bring out that missing pie."

March weather in western New Mexico is fickle; a sunny 60 degrees or a blizzard were both possibilities. Thankfully, today there were clear blue skies and a gentle wind; only a light jacket would be required. The gear in Rachael's truck included two down jackets, wool hats, gloves, and a gallon of water for unexpected adventures. Knowing Marvin's stomach never filled up, Rachael also packed an extra sack lunch of peanut butter and grape jelly on homemade bread.

"Marvin, I looked at the website and you're supposed to apply online to get access to police records. Are you sure it's worth the trip to Gallup?"

"I'm old school, like most us Navajo. We prefer to go in person and I know a lady that works at city hall."

"You do? How?"

"Well, I never told you but about a year ago I got a parking ticket for a space that wasn't even zoned. Either the gods were angry with me that day or the city needed money. Either way, I went to the city hall to find out what I could do and this nice Navajo lady helped me. We've talked a few times since, and I even ate a burger with her last month. I think she's sweet on me." Marvin blushed.

"Well, you are quite the catch."

"Because I'm Navajo, not married, in good health, and have all my teeth?"

"Precisely, that and your great smile!"

Marvin flashed his teeth and they both broke into a hearty laugh that filled Rachael's home.

Ricky Begay's ancestral land was almost ten miles from where Marvin grew up, but his father and Ricky's had shared an interest in horses, which drew the boys together. At least once a week, Marvin would ride his mare to his friend's home, where they would roam the base of the steep cliffs that encompassed the property and help each other with the sheep. The earth's bright white transformed into a deep, blistering red in the morning and evening—the wonder never failing to amaze Marvin.

A supposed Begay third cousin had taken over the land and built a new structure not far from the old hogan. Marvin had met the owners on a few occasions; they didn't seem to know anything about the Begay family and cared less. The thought of Ricky's and his father's lives having little importance to anyone but him was disheartening. The reddish cliffs and the remains of the home jarred Marvin; it had been years since he was there. Marvin guided Rachael's truck to a parking spot next to the Begay family home; the new owners were nowhere in sight.

"Marvin, what's wrong?" Rachael asked, noticing the change in her friend's demeanor.

"Sorry, it was a rough night, and well—see that faded blue chair?"

"Yes, by the abandoned hogan...."

"I vividly remember that chair. It's made out of heavy cast iron. Ricky and I would rock back and forth in the chair. The goal was to not tip it over, which of course, one day we finally did—and in a big way. Feel right here," Marvin said, pointing to the left side of his temple.

"You feel that?"

"You mean that lump?"

"That lump was the result of us taking that chair over the top. We fell onto each other and our heads cracked together like the clackers we use to play with. You remember that toy?"

"Before my time."

"They were glass balls you knocked together to make a loud noise. Our heads sounded like that, the sound of the collision of our skulls ricocheting off those cliffs. We must have damaged our heads. We were both knocked silly and got these knots that never went away. I had a headache for a week, and we never took that chair over the top again."

"You had a concussion," Rachael said, smiling at the picture Marvin had painted with his words.

"Probably, but we were kids, and in the remote rez no one took you to see a doctor unless you cut something off. That blue chair has brought back memories I hadn't thought about in years; there's a flood of thoughts sweeping through me," Marvin said.

Having waited the courtesy time required in Rachael's truck, they opened the doors simultaneously, their inner clocks in harmony, and stepped out.

"Marvin, no one died in these buildings, right? They were simply abandoned?"

“They’re fine; it’s just my own childhood *chindi* gone wrong.”

Marvin plopped into the fading turquoise chair, his hands gripping the rusting arms for support. He gently rocked the metal chair back and forth as he sang a chant that matched the rhythm of the beat of the chair.

Rachael watched; her friend was clearly dealing with some serious childhood demons, thanks to Indian boarding school.

“Rachael, I remember everything. We talked about our great escape plan right here. We would meet along the long flat mesa just east of the post where the Nasazi spring bubbles—you know, the one where the graffiti rocks are?”

“Yes, I know that place. It’s just over the rise on the south side of the road.”

“That’s the one. We would fill our canteens, then head north toward Chuska Mountain, following the washes until we hit the juniper stands, camp for the night, then go to his summer hogan. If trouble came, we would leave a note for his father and head toward Canyon de Chelly, where we could disappear into our ancestors’ hideouts. Rather silly to think about that now.”

“You were kids, dreaming of adventure and escaping the *bilágaanas*’ grip. And you had each other.”

“Yes, each other....” Marvin said, again lost in thought.

“Marvin, why was the mesa the meeting place?” Rachael asked, trying to bring her friend back to the present.

“Well, you could see a long way from the top of the mesa, plus there was a water source there. We figured if anyone was coming for us, like my dad, we could spot them and hide out near the spring in one of those slot canyons.

"I wonder how long my dear friend waited for me?"

Marvin's voice trailed off again before he resumed the story, this time in a lower octave. "I told him if I wasn't there by the time his stomach started growling to go without me. I was supposed to bring the food. I hope he brought something to eat...."

Marvin's voice faded away as he thought of his friend. Then he began speaking again.

"Ricky understood that my father was a strict man who followed the *bilagáana* laws, even the bad ones. He was a man of unbending principles. My friend must have been devastated when I didn't show up. I'm sure he waited until lunch before he pressed on; that kid was hungrier than me. I was going to bring my pinto pony along, and that could have made a difference. Walking may be what had gotten him killed."

"First of all, Marvin, you don't know for sure that he's dead—and your not being there didn't cause his disappearance."

"I try to convince myself that this is true. I was only eleven and that witching tree guarding my house warning me not to leave. My father had given me his special necklace as a gift.* I simply could not disobey my father, no matter how much I wanted to go with Ricky. We all make choices, and I made mine that night. We had no phone to call...."

Rachael saw tears welling up in Marvin's eyes, something she had never witnessed before. This was a battle-tested Marine, a war hero who was on the verge of tears. His connection to Ricky Begay ran deeper than guns or battles.

"Marvin, let's look around. Maybe we can find a clue," Rachael said, hoping to break the melancholy mood engulfing Marvin. "Let's start with the family hogan. Maybe something is there." Rachael pointed with her lips.

*See *Indian School Days,* the sixth book in the Charles Bloom Murder Mystery Series for the full story. for the full story.

Marvin cautiously opened the off-kilter door and used his phone's flashlight to peer into the darkness. The hogan had been abandoned a long time ago. There was a large pack rat's nest, a group of flattened beer cans, and a few pieces of broken furniture. Marvin entered with Rachael close behind, her phone light illuminating every step.

"Wow, I hope my place doesn't look like this when I pass onto the next world. Rachael, I want you to know that I put in my will that you would get my land and house when I die."

"You did?" Rachael said, surprised.

"Yes, I thought maybe one of your kids might need a nice home in the future. It's close to the trading post, not far from your place, and has good running water. I don't want my hogan to ever look like this," Marvin said, his lips flashing in all directions to point out the overwhelming dilapidation.

Under a crinkled metal bed frame whose mattress long ago disappeared, Rachael found a half-dissolved "Big Hunk" candy wrapper. She carefully fished it out with her shoe, watching for any unexpected creatures.

"This looks old, maybe from the 1960s?"

Marvin came closer and put the wrapper close to his face, smelling the fragile paper before sticking it in his pocket. "That was Ricky's favorite candy. We would split a Big Hunk and occasionally, if we could afford it, some of those giant jawbreakers. We use to get two jawbreakers. He preferred purple and I got yellow, then we made ourselves look like chipmunks with overstuffed pouches, sticking our tongues out like blue-tongued skinks smelling the air for a roadrunner—and we would laugh and laugh. My old friend was even funnier than me."

"That's hard to believe," Rachael said as she stuck her tongue out at Marvin in jest.

The two looked around for another ten minutes, not finding anything more than the candy wrapper. All the crushed Pabst Blue Ribbon beer cans were recent. There were no maps, or clues, or notes—just human detritus and serious decay.

They stepped out of the musty enclosure into the bright sun. Marvin took a deep breath of cold air and gave one last glance to the old blue chair before getting back into Rachael's truck.

The two started down the dirt road, with no words spoken for many minutes. The drive to Gallup was less than upbeat for Marvin, but Rachael was determined to help him through his deep emotional barriers. For the first time in a week, Rachael's mind didn't return to her recent miscarriage and her own fears that somehow, because she had been weaving during her pregnancy, she had been the cause of her devastating loss.

Like Marvin not showing up at the meeting place, Rachael feared that her prayers had not been strong enough, and that she was to blame for her unborn baby's death. But today Rachael focused on Marvin's needs and his childhood friend's disappearance. The old home provided a significant reminder of the past. There were no significant clues there, but the visit had unintentionally dredged up deeply buried feelings of remorse. These were emotions that could break a man if he was not careful: the road could be treacherous from here on out.

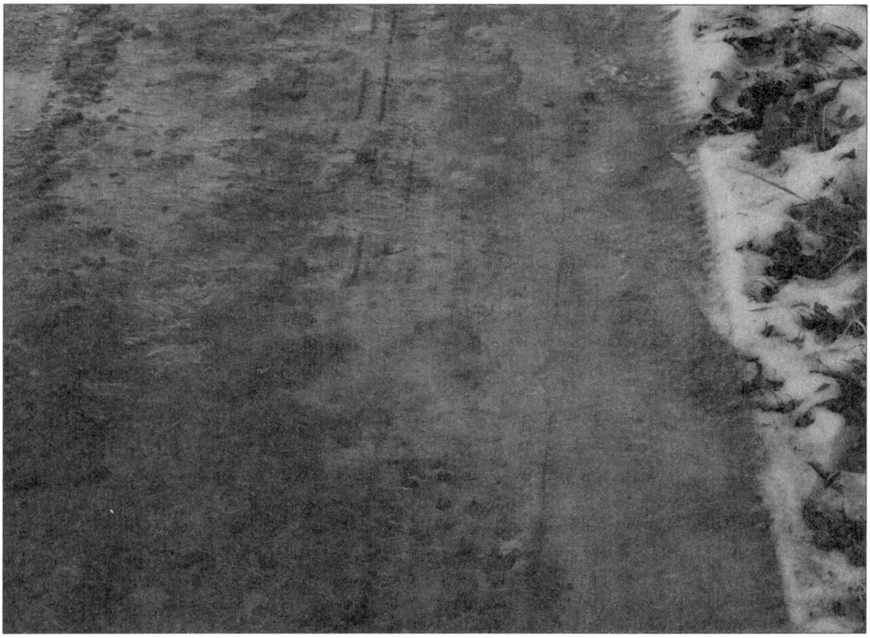

CHAPTER 16

LILLY NEZ

City hall's parking lot was near capacity; Rachael circled twice before finding a remote place covered with a black slick. Her truck's weight cracked the ice as she slowly maneuvered into the narrow spot, the sound signaling possible danger.

"Careful, Marvin, that's black ice," Rachael said as she pulled in.

"Could you get my walker for me, my granddaughter?" Marvin teased, his sense of humor resurfacing. He understood all too well why this parking space was open; black ice was a way of life on the rez. Marvin was getting older, but refused to focus on the frailties that came with aging, his sense of humor his best defense mechanism.

Bypassing a small clump of people huddling under vibrating fluorescent lights in an austere waiting room, Rachael and Marvin snaked their way through a side door to the courthouse, where an aseptic odor filled the air. Marvin used his instincts to trace a path to an unmarked door that popped them out next to Mrs. Nez's office.

Marvin had called ahead; the courthouse official was awaiting their arrival with a single steaming Gallup District Court coffee mug on an empty, red-stained table. Apparently, Nez was aware of Marvin's taste in coffee beans.

A short, stooped woman in her mid-fifties, Nez's smile waned when she saw Rachael, who noticed the subtle cue. This pleasant-looking woman clearly liked Marvin.

"Hi, Marvin… this pretty girl your daughter?"

"Nah, she's my third wife, Rachael!" Marvin's quick wit broke through Nez's tension.

"You're a devil, Marvin Manycoats."

"No, not a demon—just a man who loves to joke. This is my good friend Rachael Yellowhorse from Toadlena. She's come along to help an old man in need."

"I thought that was my job," Nez shot back, not missing a beat.

Rachael noticed Marvin's face flush; this so-called casual friendship might be more serious than Marvin had let on.

"So, Mrs. Nez…."

"It's Mrs. Nez now, is it Mr. Manycoats?" Nez interrupted.

"Sorry, just trying to be professional. So, Lilly, do you have that case file I was hoping to see?"

"Sort of. I have every file for the year 1961, and I'm afraid there is no order to them. You're lucky we have any files at all. They are overdue to be destroyed—we aren't required by law to hang on to anything longer than fifty years. I guess the powers that be figure anyone who would be interested in something that happened fifty years ago would either be dead or so far gone they wouldn't care."

Nez noticed Marvin blushing again. "Of course, Marvin, you're barely old enough for Social Security."

"It's OK, Lilly. It's true I'm a senior, but I was old enough to remember when my friend disappeared, and I'm with it enough to still care—so I'm thankful old guys like me can score a win."

Nez smiled affectionately at Marvin, and Rachael smiled too, seeing the connection this woman had with Marvin, even if it looked like a one-way road.

"Well, Marvin, even though these are technically 'dead files,' they have to remain in this building and nothing in them can be removed or copied. You can, however, request copies or simply write down the information you want. I'm not telling you this, but I doubt anyone would know or care if someone were to take a photo or two.

"You're not supposed to have liquids in the reading room, but I don't see why you can't bring your coffee." Lilly smiled, letting Marvin know he was special.

The clerk guided Marvin and Rachael to a cluttered side office that reeked of moldy paper. Boxes were stacked haphazardly to the ten-foot ceiling, and the only source of illumination was a hanging, humming fixture producing a glowing, yellow light.

There was a six-foot plastic fold-up table and a single metal chair in the center of the room. The small space heater in the corner buzzing one octave higher than the ceiling lights was undoubtedly a code violation. All were courtesy of Mrs. Nez.

"Nice digs," Rachael blurted out as she took a step into the stale air, immediately wishing she could retract her comment. She realized that Nez had put some effort in making the room semi-livable.

Nez ignored Rachael's comment and pointed to one wall: "That half of the wall is 1961; apparently, it was a busy year. You might find some internal organization by date once you start. I did a quick look for October 1961, but didn't have any luck.

"We close at five, Marvin, and I get off at noon for lunch. Rachael, I'll get you a chair," Nez said, recognizing that Rachael, the third wheel, was in the way of her plans to have lunch with Manycoats.

"Great, Lilly. We can get a lot done in that time. We'll probably work through lunch. Rachael made us some PB and Js and I've got a couple of Dr. Peppers in my pockets."

Marvin pointed to his bulging coat, then noticed Nez's face falling.

"Lilly, you're welcome to join us at noon and share one of my sandwiches and DPs," he added.

Nez's faced perked up. "OK, Marvin. I'll be back for lunch and give you an extra hand sorting—plus I have some of my homemade biscuits to add to the mix."

Nez quickly brought in another chair, then made a brusque, military-style exit, clicking the door shut behind her.

"Marvin Manycoats, you have been hiding Lilly Nez from me. Why?"

"I like your dinners better and Willy and Sam are like my grandkids. I figured if you knew I had other friends you would stop inviting me over."

"Marvin, you're one of the smartest people I've ever met, but when it comes to understanding women you need a remedial course. You are and ALWAYS will be part of our family—and that woman really likes you."

"Thank you, Rachael. I really appreciate you helping me look for this file. I know the whole idea is kind of a wild goose chase, but I need closure and this might help me find that even if we don't discover anything of use."

"Marvin, we both need some healing; this is for me as much as you—and I loved chasing geese as a kid. How about you start on the far right end, I'll start on the left, and we will meet in the middle?"

"Rachael, I've never been on the far right before, but if I find what I'm looking for I'm open for a change."

They both smiled, knowing their politics lay more on the left side of the spectrum.

The answers they sought were indeed hidden in those files; if they were uncovered, powerful forces would push back hard to make certain lost clues never came to light.

CHAPTER 17

FINDING RICKY

Reviewing Gallup's crime records reminded Marvin and Rachael that the city was a dangerous place for Navajos even in 1961. Multiple accounts of robberies, rapes, and the occasional homicide were interspersed with otherwise boring police reports. The common thread among the defendants and those injured were their Navajo surnames.

After two-and-a-half hours of searching, Marvin found a thin file with "Orville Begay" typed in bold letters on the front.

"Here it is!" Marvin yelled to Rachael, loudly enough that he instinctively covered his mouth with the file. "Sorry!"

"I take it we have found our Atlantis?" Rachael asked.

"No—it's Gallup, New Mexico, 1961!"

Marvin flashed a smile as he plopped into one of the chairs, its metal legs screeching under his weight. He opened the yellowing file and there was Ricky Begay, smiling back at him. A small black-and-white photo of Ricky was paper-clipped to the first page—possibly the only photo ever taken of his friend. The young boy had a big smile, with most of his teeth showing. Marvin was taken aback by the image, and it showed. He shifted in the chair as he focused on the file he was holding, his formerly happy expression shifting to one of concern.

"You OK, Marvin?" Rachael asked in a low voice.

"Yes. It's just that I have not seen my friend's face since I was eleven years old, and now here he is, staring back at me. I'm that kid again, transported back to September 15, 1961—the last time we talked before he disappeared."

"Marvin, we can take a break. Let's go get some fresh coffee."

"No Rachael. I'm here to help my friend, and that is exactly what I'm going to do."

Marvin took half the pages in the file and handed the rest to Rachael. A rudimentary map was attached to the folder with rusting paperclips. Points of interest on the sketch were noted by the letters A to G:

A: Cellophane wrapper near large rocks, close to trail B

B: Road assumed to be the path where Orville Begay's horse fell

C: Large rock outcropping where cellophane wrapper found

D: Displaced rocks following a slide area to bottom of the mesa

E: Single dead horse with two packs and Orville Begay's body found here

Pack contents: one peanut-butter sandwich on a single piece of folded-over bread; a single broken bottle of Coke, cap intact; one unopened Big Hunk candy bar; a small military-sized folding shovel

F: One 1940s Colt Commando revolver with dull finish and 2-inch barrel, holstered, weapon safety on, the chamber loaded; one brown leather wallet containing five one dollar bills neatly folded; and one worn black-and-white photograph identified as Ricky Begay, the missing child assumed deceased

G: A secondary map sketch revealing Orville Begay's body's position and the gun holstered to his side (the paper had turned a honey yellow and the graphite was fading badly); and a 2-inch symmetrical round white object awaiting analysis, possibly a piece of candy

Rachael's half of the file contained the forensic findings:

—Analysis of the composition of the found objects: plastic: cellophane; round object: sucrose (hard candy); the words "probable incidental findings" written in bold letters at the bottom in red wax pencil

—A three-page typed autopsy report on Orville Begay's body. The summary statement page read: "Death secondary to exsanguinations of systematic organ contusion/failure and right complex femur fracture. Severe trauma includes cerebral trauma, basal skull fracture, large cerebral hematoma; lacerated caudate lobe of the liver; contused renal system-bilateral; ruptured spleen; ecchymotic lungs-bilaterally; complex open fracture, right femur spiral fracture; displaced fracture, 4-5 metatarsals."

Rachael's usually strong voice quivered slightly as she read the coroner's report. Marvin's face was frozen as he stared up at the buzzing light; he had seen men in combat with similar injuries.

Final conclusions by officer-in-charge Ned Tsinnigine: accidental death secondary to horse fall, probably caused by inclement weather (see attached weather report). No sign of foul play, no further action required.

"What do you think?" Marvin asked Rachael, his gaze moving from the ceiling light to her deep brown eyes.

"I don't know, Marvin. It appears that nothing was taken from his horse's packs and there was poor weather that day. We both know how slick that white rock can be if it's wet. Maybe something spooked his horse and he took a bad fall down the hill."

"The timing seems odd, though—that it happened just after his son goes AWOL? And he's carrying a revolver?" Marvin asked.

"Odd, yes, but if he was that distraught, he simply might have not taken care of himself or his animal. Being sleep deprived can make you careless too... I know," Rachael said, reflecting on her own poor sleeping habits.

"But why carry a pistol? Most Navajos I know didn't carry a gun, even back then, unless they were hunting...."

"Well, if he thought a lion killed his son, he might have been hunting," Rachael said, picking up on Marvin's train of thought.

"But what about the hard candy?"

"Well, Marvin, he liked sweets—something you can relate to. There was an unopened Big Hunk in his pack. Maybe when the horse took a tumble the hard candy popped out of his mouth."

"I agree it's possible—a distraught father dies in a tragic accident while looking for his lost son, and that's that." Marvin's voice trailed off.

"I think that is the most likely story," Rachael agreed.

"But Rachael, we now have a map. I can find those boulders and we can explore where Ricky's father passed to the next world. If we search the area maybe some clue the police missed could turn up." Marvin words sounded pathetic even to him.

"Marvin, I'll take a few photos of these reports with my phone and place this file on top of the stack in case we need to come back. Take your sandwich and go have lunch with Lilly somewhere in the sun. She clearly wants to see you alone. I'm going to call Bloom. I miss my husband."

Marvin retrieved the cell phone stuffed in his back pants pocket and fiddled with the buttons. There was only one piece of evidence he wanted to capture—the image of his friend's smiling face. Marvin also missed someone greatly, but could not talk to him until they had both reached the next world.

The return trip to Toadlena was somber. Marvin's eleven-year-old mind had resurfaced, trying to recapture and understand his father's decision to follow orders to attend Indian boarding school and a friend's defiance of the *bilágaanas'* laws. Marvin couldn't help but wonder how this traumatic incident set up the rest of his life's journey. He was a decorated war hero in Vietnam, but without a family; he had friends and was respected in his community—but could there have been much more to his life?

Could finding Ricky answer questions he had been too afraid to ask? The rusty old blue chair was once again in his life, this time holding a mountain of buried emotion.

Rachael broke the deafening silence: "Marvin, this is the quietest I've seen you since I served you steamed broccoli...."

"Sorry, Rachael. It's hard to believe, but at nearly 70, I'm traveling back to my childhood, searching old maps and moldy papers for a thread of hope that probably doesn't exist."

"Marvin, Indian boarding school was traumatic for you, and quite frankly, for many others who were forced to go."

"The adult man in me understands that, but I was just right back in that spot, looking at the moon-drenched witching tree in front of my dad's place and trying to make myself go with Ricky. But I was stuck. I couldn't disobey my father's command and lose his trust, and then my friend disappeared...." Marvin's voice trailed off.

"True, but that was a choice Ricky and his father made. You're not responsible for that. You were a good son and did what your family wanted."

"Yes, a good son, but maybe not such a good friend. I should have talked Ricky into coming to school with me instead of running away, to face the adversity head on."

"Marvin, you're right. We now have a starting point, a roadmap to follow. We may not find out what happened to that little boy lost to Mother Earth's embrace, but we can possibly put a close to this unfortunate chapter in your life."

"I'm sorry I've dragged you into this Rachael. You have a family and other more important things in your life than an old man's wish for redemption."

"That's where you are wrong, Marvin Manycoats. I need closure too. I can't explain this in any rational way, but helping you helps me."

Rachael's eyes shone with unshed tears as Marvin gently placed his hand on her arm.

"Well, we are a fine pair, aren't we? I'm feeling hungry—any chance we could stop at the Speedway station? I'm in need of an ice cream bar."

"Make that two."

CHAPTER 18

FOLLOW THE MAP

The harsh night wind that had blown into the Toadlena basin was showing no signs of letting up. Yesterday's blue skies had turned ominously dark. Marvin dropped Samantha and Willy off at school. Rachael's neighbor, Mrs. Bennally, agreed to pick Sam up at noon; if the two investigators had not returned by 3 p.m. she would also get Willy—assuming Marvin and Rachael didn't get blown off the mesa by Mother Nature.

"Rachael, the kids got off nicely, even Sam. They're happy that Mrs. Bennally is picking them up instead of you or me. Kids are nice, huh?"

"Feel lucky, Marvin. You only have to deal with your emotions; kids can tear your heart out without even trying."

"You sure you want to start our search today? It's pretty miserable, and we might even get some sleet."

"I've got my Gore-Tex rain jacket," Rachael said, "and my rabbit fur hat. Unlike kids today, I did herd sheep—and not with a cell phone in my hand. This is as good a day as any to follow a map."

A large smile spread over Marvin's face. Rachael was the kind of woman he hoped to find for himself. Maybe Lilly Nez was a senior version of the feisty weaver?

"All right. Here's a rough copy of the map Officer Tsinnigine drew in 1961." Marvin laid the single page of paper he had copied from Rachael's photos on the dining room table.

"See this mesa? This was where Ricky and I were supposed to meet. When I didn't show up, I think he would have headed in this direction, toward the Chuskas. It would have been a two day hike, depending on how fast he was traveling. I remember the weather was good that week."

"Marvin, what is it with that memory of yours?" Rachael asked the question she had thought about a thousand times.

"I know it's an odd sort of gift. I used to think of it as a curse, remembering all the dates and encounters of my life in such vivid detail like they happened yesterday, not fifty years ago. But I've accepted it's what the Holy Ones wanted for me. I've learned to take what comes and avoid sharing too much."

"But how does it work?"

"It's like a film that runs in a loop. I think about a day and a time and a place, and images pop up like snapshots so I can see the exact moment I'm thinking about. I think my mind is a camera that never runs out of film."

"I'm on digital," Rachael teased. "Film is old school."

"Not in my mind," Marvin shot back.

"I have a problem remembering what I did last night, and my camera's battery is always low," Rachael riffed.

Marvin smiled, letting Rachael know he understood and that he, too, was human.

"So do we start where you were to meet Marvin or use the officer's map?" Rachael asked, her curiosity about Marvin's memory quenched for the moment.

"I've been thinking about that. The only real hard evidence we have is what was written in the police report. I figure this place on the map is where we begin, see if we can find any clues, and then head over to the place my friend would have started from without me. Maybe the Holy Ones will point us in the right direction."

Marvin and Rachael thought they knew how to find the rock formation and trail marked on the map. They went as far as they could go with Rachael's four-wheel drive. They both knew it was risky to go in too deep with the truck; the road was rough, and if the weather changed to sleet—or worse, ice—they might get stuck for the night.

Using his hunting binoculars, Marvin scanned the horizon through the passenger window, the truck's heat on full blast to help cut the cold wind. After about ten minutes, he pointed his lips toward a far mesa.

"Those have to be the rocks and the slide."

He handed the spotting glasses to Rachael, who nodded her head in agreement. She drove the truck over to the general location and parked on a high knoll. If anything happened to them, their truck would be easy to spot.

Coats buttoned, gloves on, and caps pulled low, the two exited the truck to face the harsh wind. Rachael hid her keys in her usual place under the right front tire wheel. Losing keys in the backcountry could be a deadly error.

The two walked slowly toward a distant boulder field, both scanning the ground as they walked. No talk was necessary. The methodical search took nearly an hour before they reached the spot where Orville Begay and his horse had died. Fragments of a horse's skull marked the tragic spot.

Marvin stopped and scanned the area, then looked to the heavens. "My best friend's father died in this very place." He pulled out his corn pollen pouch, put a small amount in his mouth, a pinch over his head, and tossed a little more in the air as he said a prayer. Rachael said her own prayer; this was sacred ground.

After a few minutes passed, Rachael broke the silence. "You know, Marvin, he may have died on the fall down the hill. We don't know exactly when or where he expired."

"You're right. We don't know the whole story. Keeping an open mind is important, but this feels like sacred ground."

"Marvin, let's explore this area. We can take photos for backup in case our eyes miss something. There is the boulder outcropping up above us. How about I look there and you work this area?"

"Afraid a man of my age can't make it up that steep grade?"

"No, Marvin. I need the exercise and I figure you get enough with the ten miles you walk each day."

"OK, you're forgiven. When you get up in those large rocks see if there are any signs, like a cave a lion could use to attack and spook a horse."

The amateur detectives spent the next two hours carefully walking the area until Rachael signaled Marvin to join her. The wind was biting at her red, chapped cheeks, and she hunkered down, using the rocks as a windbreak while she was waiting for Marvin.

"You find something?"

"Yeah—our lunch and this nice warm spot."

"Unfortunately, I didn't see much either. I found a few pieces of bone from the horse's leg. See that line of smaller rocks? That's where they fell from the top of these boulders. I can understand how a fall like that could kill a man and a horse."

"Here, take a bite of this. It will make everything better." Rachael's maternal mode was in full tilt as she handed Marvin a sandwich.

"You want to keep going? The weather's holding even though the wind has picked up...." Marvin lisped, the peanut butter sticking to the roof of his mouth.

"I'm game if you are, Marvin."

"Yes I am. I walked this area a couple of times when I was a teenager. There is a long ridge of cliffs with undercuts where the Nasazi used to live running along that edge."

Marvin used his hand to give Rachael a better idea of the length of the search area.

"Once we hike to the top of the mesa, we can search all the caves and undercuts. If Ricky was hurt, I'm sure he would have sought shelter there. It was lion country then, even though they are now rare in our lands."

"There was a big cat killed last winter behind the post, so they're still around," Rachael countered.

"True enough. We need to keep our eyes open and our ears to the wind."

"How about we split up, Marvin? I can take one side of the ridgeline, you the other. We can meet up where they merge. Looks like a two-mile walk; if we find nothing we can call it a day and get back to Toadlena before dark and that sleet blows in."

"Sounds like a solid reconnaissance plan; my Marine platoon leader would approve. I'll take the north side, that's where the Nasazi houses were located to catch the winter sun. You're young, Rachael, and don't need to be witched. I would feel better if you let this old man explore that area."

"That's fine. I'm not a fan of our ancient enemies. Bloom thinks I'm crazy, but I know better. Once I reach the mesa's end I'll text you if I can get service. If you don't get a text, go to that last little ridge with the clump of junipers, find a nice protected but visible spot, and I'll look for that orange cap of yours."

"How about you start a smoke signal? That's more likely than me getting and answering any of those small texts," Marvin laughed, spewing small fragments of Rachael's homemade wheat bread in the air: technology was not his strong suit.

The two bundled figures traversed the white caliche mesa, stopping at a high point for a final check. Rachael moved the message icon on Marvin's phone to the most prominent location on his homepage and increased the phone's font size so he could easily find her text—although one-bar service didn't bode well for digital communications.

"Drink up, Rachael. It may not be hot, but it's still easy to get dehydrated. That's another thing I learned from my captain in Vietnam. There's nothing worse than a Marine going down because of dehydration; you have to stay on top of your fluid intake."

"Aye-aye, sir," Rachael responded playfully.

"I was not an officer. I was an enlisted man and worked for a living." Marvin joked back.

They both took sips of water from their canteens, then started hiking toward their respective goals. If nothing was discovered in two hours, and they couldn't reach each other by phone, then they would meet back at the high point.

The mesa was composed of bleached outcroppings of finger-shaped rock structures leading to a single, large slot canyon; the entire mesa top ran about two miles, with the highest point elevated by 150 feet. The topography was dotted with ancient junipers, many killed by the harsh cyclic climate while trying to eke out a life on a seabed of fossils deposited in better times.

The runoff water from the slot canyon funneled down a ravine, supporting a lone massive cottonwood whose stark limbs spoke of the cold enveloping the land. This refuge in the desert was an ideal resting spot for game and a few prehistoric men or early Navajo settlers. Marvin wondered how many cottonwoods had come and gone in this canyon over the last 10,000 years.

He walked carefully along the bottom edge of the mesa, where dozens of flattened Nasazi rock homes had been built into the edge of the south-facing wall. Pottery sherds blanketed the area; he could hear the brittle clay cracking under his feet.

An ancient Navajo stone sheep pen built into a two-foot-tall rock wall cut into a natural rock bridge. Nearby were two disintegrating Navajo rock hogans, neither more than five-by-five-feet wide, probably dating from 1600 to 1700. The chimney in one of the homes was intact; the remaining hogan walls were a foot-and-half tall, with two sun-bleached juniper roof beams still standing.

Marvin had never closely examined one of his ancestors' homes, and was amazed at how similar they were to some of his neighbors' modern hogans. But instead of pottery sherds, his neighbors' yards were decorated with smashed Pabst Blue Ribbon beer and Vienna sausage cans.

The small cramped room was close enough to the sheep pen to protect the precious animals from wolves or the plundering Spanish. Parts of a wood- and dung-burning rock hearth with a roof no taller than four feet remained in the space. The major change from that ancient day to this one, Marvin thought, was a regular protein-rich diet, which had made the modern Navajo people taller and stronger, but no wealthier. It was no longer the Spanish or Navajo who raided their neighbors: the casinos had taken on the job of keeping the people poor.

Generations of Navajo had been raised in this small outpost of humanity—and he wondered about the stories that hearth must have witnessed. These people were rich in animals, food, fuel, shelter, and undoubtedly love—though the wolf's jaws were a constant threat to men and sheep. Maybe Kit Carson's men had been responsible for the demise of this family when they moved them to the Bosque Redondo in 1864. Marvin considered the history of his people and his place among them as he searched for a Navajo child lost a half century ago.

Marvin fished a crushed, rusted can out of the hearth. "Modern-day people have been here," he thought—and at that moment the possibility that a human had been the cause of his friend's disappearance washed over Marvin. He searched meticulously through the remains of the hogan, but found no other clues. "Keep on task, this is not the place," Marvin's inner voice said, so he continued west along the mesa ridge, exploring each undercut and gully.

A massive cut through the heart of the cliff made a large slit worth exploring carefully. It was too dark in there to see the back wall of the cave. Marvin turned on his phone light; there were no service bars and no messages. Then he bent to one knee, supporting his weight with both hands, and began easing his way into the darkness.

"When did I get so old that crawling took a concerted effort?" Marvin wondered to himself.

In the extreme far corner of the underbank, he could see a yellow squash-shaped pot, an ancient Hopi vessel that had probably been made before the Navajos arrived. Marvin smiled thinking of his friend Bloom, who would say the galleries in Santa Fe would kill for a pot like this, old and intact—the only downside being it was illegal to take a relic off Indian or federal land.

Marvin knew Bloom would leave the pot, but many other *bilágaanas* wouldn't care about rules or laws; the dollar signs flashing in front of their eyes would win out. For Marvin, though, the artifacts were simply part of the structure of the land. He trained his phone light up and down the walls, found nothing else of note, and moved on.

He stretched his legs and brushed off the white coat of dirt covering his jeans. One bar, no messages from Rachael; she was still searching. Marvin was nearing the end of the mesa, and his sprit was starting to flag: he had found no signs of his long, lost friend. Then he noticed a subtle rift in the side of the canyon.

The cut in the wall was straight, small, and easy to miss. Once again Marvin forced himself to his knees and slowly crawled into the abyss. Once he was inside the cut, the cavernous area seemed to open up, the space jet black and smelling of musk. He turned on his phone light again to orient himself, and saw what he had been fearing: men had been here. Rocks had been stacked in a neat line from the floor to the cave's ceiling,

"A tomb, maybe more ancient Hopis?" Marvin whispered to himself, the hair on his arms standing to attention. There were *chindi* here.

He backed up reflexively and considered his options; this could easily be an ancient Indian burial site, maybe 200 years or older, the remains probably intact. The structure was definitely manmade and untouched. Should he be disturbing ancient *chindi*? But what if it were something else? Marvin was on a mission, and this was his path, good or bad. He could get a healing sing if it turned out to be a human burial site. He reached into his pocket and once again pulled out his pouch of corn pollen. He put a small pinch in his hand, his mouth, and on his head, then sprinkled some in front of himself before moving more deeply into the cave, chanting loudly as he went.

Marvin inched his way toward the back of the space, scanning the area for hibernating rattlesnakes. The wall was intact except for what appeared to be a small window, the opening large enough for a fat packrat or an unfed snake. The fenestration was tight. It was impossible to peer in without good light, and the phone was too large to fit through the opening. Marvin gathered his strength, slid his hand into the small window, and removed three large, flat rocks. He carefully positioned his camera light inside the hole and peered in, expecting the worst. And his fears were realized: death stared back at him.

A small human skeleton curled into a fetal position was visible at the far edge of the cavern. The body looked as if it had been deliberately placed in that position. There was no clothing visible, and only a few isolated patches of dried skin around the pelvis. The skeleton appeared to be that of a Navajo, but Marvin was no archaeologist. It must be old, he thought, but was it ancient? He knew that an early Diné grave would include the deceased's favorite clothes, blanket, and jewelry, but this skeleton was stripped bare. Maybe it was Nasazi?

Marvin noticed that the light on his phone was wavering. He was not a man to scare easily, so he assumed his nerves must have been frayed by the cold dampness. But the smell of human remains, even ancient ones, had him spooked. *Chindi* enveloped him; he could taste their presence.

The question was what to do now. Was it possible this could be Ricky, and if so, where were his clothes? Could rats have eaten all the fabric in fifty-plus years? It seemed unlikely, but the skin also was gone. Marvin realized that no matter how much he hated to approach the dead, he must inch closer to the body to understand the truth. He owned his friend this much courage.

As Marvin meticulously removed a large section of the rock barrier, a flat insect with pinchers scurried away from its winter hideaway. He eased himself over the remaining rock wall on his hands and knees. The inner cavern was dark and claustrophobic; he pushed forward until he could advance no further. When his knees and back were simultaneously touching the wall, he brought up his phone to illuminate the space. It suddenly went dark, and he felt a surge of panic as he fumbled to find the flashlight button. The light popped back on, and Marvin was face to face with death.

He jumped, banging the woolen cap that protected his head hard against the roof wall, and his phone tumbled free, its precious light buried in the fine brown sand coating the burial grounds, a single strand of filtered light from passageway door bouncing off the stark white skeleton. Marvin regained his composure and began searching for his phone the way a blind person would hunt for a misplaced cane. When a round object touched his left hand, he gripped it, knowing it was manmade and thus important—then continued searching for his phone with his right hand. When he found it, he was amazed the light was still on.

He brought the round hard object he had found earlier closer to his face. It was covered in a cellophane wrapping—a hard candy, a faded purple jawbreaker. Marvin's hand started to tremble again, the fear not induced by the cold but emanating from a deep well of emotion. His usually practical mind was spinning like a bike wheel without a chain as his internal brakes fought for control. Marvin felt his heart pounding, his mind racing back to a dark night in the Nam jungle, bullets screaming past his head. What had he discovered?

Marvin mustered his inner strength, slowed his breathing, and focused his light on the nearby skeleton. The mouth was wide open in a permanent scream. A row of chalk-white teeth was visible, and they were crooked! Marvin's unflagging memory recognized Ricky Begay's jagged teeth frozen in time and horror. The parietal portion of the gleaming white skull had a small protuberance that was not an artifact of evolution, but a scar of brotherhood—the bumping of heads thanks to one blue chair.

Was there a connection between the cellophane-wrapped candy he had found and a fifty-year-old police report noting a cellophane wrapper discovered near Orville Begay's body? The possibilities seemed ominous. Was his lost friend calling for justice from beyond the grave?

CHAPTER 19

A DROP IN THE MARKET

Bloom spent the afternoon trying to decipher his father's contract. Most of the verbiage seemed like boilerplate, but one paragraph was particularly pointed and disturbing: "Failure to complete the project and inventory form in full and without any alterations within thirty days of the project start date, which is considered the date of execution of this contract, will be considered in breach of said contract and liable for all damages associated with loss of income or any associated devaluation of the collection as determined by mediation. Such mediation will be confined to the village of Mesilla court system."

"This is not good, Dad. You are liable if you don't complete this form as dictated by your contract. I'm not sure what to tell you. The contract was signed February 15th; when did you actually start work?"

"I first checked in to examine the artifacts two days later. I did briefly view the collection before I started the project. I called you not long after that when I realized I had bitten off a bit more than I could chew—not to mention that the pieces on the top shelf looked daunting."

"I'm glad you called me, Dad, but we're about out of time. Don't sign the form yet. I'll see if I can get a lawyer friend to take a look at it. I guess the worst case scenario is that you fill out form and hope they don't monkey with it—although I don't know how you would ever know."

"Charles, the reality is that I'm 80—and what if they do mess with the form? Chances are it won't affect anything, except maybe soil my reputation for whatever that's worth—and who cares if I'm dead?"

Bloom was shocked to hear his father make such a negative, matter-of-fact assessment of the situation. James Bloom was a man of integrity, or at least that was what Charles had always thought.

"Dad, you don't really mean that, do you?"

"I don't know. Does it really matter, Son? I'm happy enough and don't need the conflict in my life. I signed the damned contract; that was my mistake, and I have to take responsibility for it."

Bloom saw where his father was coming from: it was the integrity involved in having already signed the form that he was concerned about, not the form itself.

"Well, Dad, I can't tell you what to do. This is your call, but at least let me have a lawyer look this over and find out if we have any options."

"I'll tell Mr. Gutierrez it will be a few days before I can finish up project, but it will still be done within my thirty-day deadline. How's that sound?"

"Perfect, Dad. Now how about that early lunch? I can't get enough of those fresh Hatch green chiles."

The two men headed to their favorite Mexican restaurant. Bloom understood that his role in the family had flipped, and that he was no longer the kid but the person in charge. Maybe the gods had more control of his life than he had previously realized.

Bloom called a longtime art collector and lawyer in Santa Fe and emailed a copy of the contract for his review. It didn't take long to get a response.

"Charles, I wouldn't mess with these guys. That clause should never have been allowed, and the arbitration has to take place in their own backyard. You and I both know that in New Mexico this means trouble if you're not a local with long family roots in the community—which your father is not."

"I understand. I was afraid of this. Any recommendations?"

"Well, considering what you have told me, I suggest you have him sign the paper, make copies of what he turned in, and write down everything that has transpired in case you get pulled into court."

"Where should I start the log?"

"As far back as your dad can remember—then document when the notes were written, and that they were created on advice of counsel."

"Thanks! I'll call you first the next time I get a great Scholder painting."

"Charles, I'm still looking for a 1970s piece, so hurry up. I notice his auction prices have nearly doubled in the last year."

"Tell me about it—$288,000 is a new auction record. The good news is that when you get a record sale, lots of fresh paintings hit the market. They might not be a bargain, but finding material is the name of the game."

The two men hung up and Bloom made a note on his phone to let his lawyer/client have the first shot at the next Scholder. He'd also make a few inquiries to see what might be available. It would be months before Santa Fe's selling season kicked in.

Bloom broke the news to his father that night and the professor seemed to take the lawyer's advice in stride. It was clear Dr. Bloom had made up his mind to complete the project as contracted, and this advice eased his worries. He would finish the form tonight, have it notarized tomorrow, and drop it off by noon. Then he would collect his final paycheck and invest it in the market. Maybe this was the high note he was looking for to make a good exit.

Unknown to the Dr. Bloom, though, his portfolio was the least of his worries. If he didn't answer some tough questions correctly, his investing days would be over—forever.

CHAPTER 20

ONE WHO STANDS IN THE SUN

Dr. Benny Benally never slept more than five hours a night, and the discovery of the stolen T.C. Cannon painting made things even worse. His mind had been racing since he got the phone call from Rachael Yellowhorse.

Tonight the elevated head of his mattress was unforgiving, and he struggled to find a cool soft spot, flipping from side to side and slowly curling up into a shriveled mass. His body felt like a piece of bacon on a griddle. Poor health was now his reality, and this new, unwelcome stress might tip him even further over the edge. His mind was reeling, images of the Cannon painting playing out like a microfiche scroll as he struggled to breathe.

Santa Fe's elevation was too high for him these days; he needed to live below 7,000 feet, but where? Too many years of smoking and inhaling paint fumes had led to a diagnosis of early COPD. The doctors called his condition terminal, and warned that he could die sooner rather than later if he did not relocate to lower ground. Benally could hear his physician's voice playing over an image of the Cannon painting, the two making it even more impossible to sleep.

Why had he acknowledged the piece's existence? He had never discussed MAN WITH SWEET TOOTH before, even though there had been ample chances to do so for a man who was an often-quoted source in the Cannon literature.

"What an old fool I am," Benally said to himself, his lips pursed as he tried to ease himself into a better breathing rhythm.

Rachael Yellowhorse had been one of his favorite students in his forty years of teaching; she was smart, driven, and talented. An intuitive woman, he knew she would be able detect a lie, so Benally told her the truth as he perceived it—or maybe his conscience was just in need of a healing.

The weaver knew of the deep bond he had with T.C. Great friends, they were more like brothers than fellow students. Benally, who was three years older, performed the role of big brother, protecting T.C. at every corner, recognizing the man's talent, and after he returned from Vietnam, his vulnerability.

Did Rachael realize he was lying about not knowing the painting's title, and what if she checked with police records that showed him at the scene the day of Cannon's death? Benally did indeed know the title—MAN WITH SWEET TOOTH—it had been his suggestion, a mate to Cannon's 1974 painting MAN IN WICKER CHAIR, which had quickly achieved critical success. Benally knew the importance of strong wording. The original title for MAN IN WICKER CHAIR had been COLLECTOR #5—which did not have enough pizzazz to interest a viewer. A simple title tweak, like a catchy song, was all it needed to get more attention.

MAN WITH SWEET TOOTH was one of fifty paintings scheduled for an upcoming exhibit at Aberbach Fine Art in New York City. It was sure to be an international success, but T.C. had told his dear friend the piece would not be sold. Once the show ended, MAN WITH SWEET TOOTH was to be his!

"My painting—that's what he said, for all the good deeds I had done over the years. It was marked NFS (not for sale), and once the piece had received the important New York City buzz and the masses had viewed it, T.C. would present the painting to Dr. Benally in front of the IAIA staff and students with a message for each group: "Treat your fellow students as brothers and sisters," and "And to the staff, students should be considered your precious children. Do that and you will be rewarded with love and creativity."

The Vietnam conflict had damaged T.C. He was a war hero, but didn't feel like one; too many of his brothers had been killed, and for what purpose? T.C. had a premonition that his life would be short; he talked about it often and lived in the moment. But his sudden, tragic death didn't seem preordained; he was too talented to leave this earth at just thirty-one.

Benally remembered that horrible day in vivid detail. It was May 8, 1978, finals week during his tenth year as a professor at IAIA. He was preparing to pass out the last test of the semester on color composition. Sitting in an oak chair with metal rollers, he was neatly stacking the multipage test papers when a Kiowa artist burst into the room, tears streaming down her face: "T.C.'s dead, he's dead!" she screamed, before dashing out to spread the word to the next classroom.

He remembered the chair biting into his back and the squeaky wheels screaming as he reflexively pushed away from his desk and smashed into the chalkboard. Pandemonium broke out in the class. Was it a rumor, or some kind of sick performance-art prank? Then the overhead intercom crackled to life, the school's president breaking the news with a trembling voice. The unthinkable was no rumor—it was true.

T.C. Cannon, one the brightest stars that had ever streaked across the IAIA campus, had flared out. The circumstances were sketchy—it was some kind of accidental car wreck—but what did it matter? He was dead. There would be no more paintings, no more impromptu visits, no more conversations, no more laughs, and no more "One Who Stands in the Sun," T.C.'s Kiowa name. The man's soul had moved into the next world, leaving only his paintings to remind us of his vision and talent.

Benally sat silently in his chair with his eyes downcast for a solid minute before he announced in a low monotone: "Grades are superfluous on a day like today. Everyone in this class receives an A on the final test."

A young Navajo student who was struggling to pass the course spontaneously shouted, "Cool!" Benally lifted his tear-strewn checks and peered into the classroom. "An 'A' can just as easily turn into an 'F,' so get the hell out of here and go create something. Think of T.C. and pray for his passage to a better place. This is a dark day for all Native people."

The memories brought back the anguish of that fateful day, and Benally's eyes spontaneously filled with tears. Why had his friend died so young when he himself had lived so long? The pain continued to haunt him, the shame of his actions that day too much to bear.

* * * *

Benally's eyes fluttered open: it was nearly 9 a.m. He had finally fallen asleep, but his subconscious had continued to churn, his mind replaying that awful day as if it were yesterday.

May 8th had been a beautiful, warm spring day, the skies crystal blue and the fruit trees in full bloom, their sweet aroma saturating the air. Benally bolted from the classroom and drove directly to Cannon's studio, to which he had a key—the only one in existence besides Cannon's. All he could think of was HIS painting, the piece T.C. had wanted HIM to have. If he didn't retrieve the piece now, it would be lost to the estate or taxes. There was no paper trail backing up his claim, only his word about what Cannon had told him—and the word of a Navajo teacher and friend would never carry the day when it came to a valuable painting.

The studio appeared empty. T.C.'s truck was gone, wrecked on a deserted highway. He peered in the dark window; his painting was still propped up on the easel, as it had been earlier in the week. Time slowed as Benally unlocked the studio. The plank door swiveled open as a wave of turpentine attacked his lungs and music filled his ears. KANW, T.C.'s favorite Native music channel, was playing loudly. The painter must have run out for a quick errand, one from which he never returned.

The lights were bright and the music blaring, but there was no T.C. The studio was now just a memorial to a departed friend. The drumbeat of the Native music faded and a Bob Dylan song took its place. Benally gulped and tears filled his eyes. T.C. had loved Dylan—was this song coming on now a sign? He wiped his face and thought of turning off the radio, then realized he would have to act quickly. Removing the large painting from the easel, he ran through the open door, balancing the unframed canvas on his foot as he relocked the plank and used the sleeve of his sweater to grab the door handle, leaving no fingerprints behind.

Guilt washed over him. He was acting like a criminal. If caught, he would be a thief rather than someone claiming a gift that was rightfully his. He wasn't stealing this painting for money or prestige; he would never sell it, which was what T.C. had wanted. The painter might not be able to present the piece to him in person, or exhibit it as he had hoped, but the work was going to its rightful home.

Benally's mint-green station wagon, parked with its hatch open, accepted the painting with inches to spare. He had just placed the image upside down in the vehicle when he heard a police car rounding the bend. He threw a Pendleton blanket over the painting, shut the hatch, and jumped back into the front seat, opening the driver's door as the police pulled in to make it look as if he too had just arrived.

The officers' voices and words were etched into Benally's mind, even though both men must be long dead by now.

"Officers, I'm glad you're here," the professor said. "I was told at school that T.C. Cannon died last night, and I had to come and see for myself. He's a dear friend."

"I'm sad to say it's true," one of the men replied. "He died in a one-car rollover just south of Santa Fe. I'm sorry for your loss."

"That's tragic—he was so young," Benally said, the heartfelt tears again rolling down his face as he shook his head in disbelief.

"May I ask your name?"

"I'm Dr. Benny Benally. I'm a professor at IAIA. T.C. and I were close friends. We went to school together."

"Do you have a key to Mr. Cannon's place? We would like to look around."

"Yes, I do. As I said, we were very close. We used to have coffee at least three times a week. T.C. was getting ready for a big show in New York City—his career was just taking off."

"Anyone else have a key to Mr. Cannon's studio?"

"Maybe the family. I'm not sure. Why?"

"Well, as I said, this appears to be an unfortunate accident, but our job is to completely check out all sudden deaths. I'm sure you understand."

"Of course, officer." Benally started to open the studio door when the policeman interceded. "If you wouldn't mind, let me do this. We might want to dust for finger prints."

Benally handed him his key ring. The officer opened the door with a gloved hand, then handed the keys back. The professor, now accompanied by the two policemen, walked into the studio.

A multitude of paintings in a variety of sizes were stacked against every wall.

The smell of an artist's workspace surprised one of the officers. "The fumes in here are quite strong. Does Mr. Cannon's studio always smell like this?"

"I'm afraid so. It's important to have ventilation, but T.C. said that it wasn't near as bad as napalm and laughed it off. He always thought he would die young and lived for the moment, not worrying about cigarettes or fumes. I guess he was right."

"Why is this music on?" the other officer asked.

"T.C. loved music. It was always playing. He was a good musician as well as a painter."

Satisfied with the answer, the cops asked, "How come there are so many paintings here. This guy must have been awful fast—or maybe he didn't sell much?"

"No, just the opposite. T.C. was getting ready for a show and these paintings represent about six months of work."

"Are his paintings valuable?"

"Yes, quite. Go down to Elaine Horwitch's gallery off Palace Avenue; she has a couple for sale. I wouldn't be surprised if she's doubled the price by now," Benally said sarcastically, knowing how dealers work.

"Then it's extremely important, Mr. Benally, that we make sure no one comes into this building. We need to complete our investigation even though it all seems straight forward—and the paintings need to be accounted for."

"It's Doctor Benally: I'm a Ph.D."

"Dr. Benally, we need to make sure this studio is secure so it would be best if you give us that studio key. It will protect you from any possible future problems. When money is involved, especially in Santa Fe, you can expect relatives and friends to come out of the woodwork saying, 'this painting is mine,' or 'he said he was giving it to me.' I'm sure you can imagine the possibilities."

Benally understood it all too well—and felt a sharp pain of guilt when he realized he was one of those people.

"Not a problem. I don't want to be dragged into anything. I'll let his New York City gallery know what's going on. I'm sure the owner will want to contact whoever does have legal claim to these paintings. Unfortunately, when painters as talented as T.C. Cannon die young, their work immediately becomes in great demand, so there will undoubtedly be a traveling retrospective."

"I understand, Dr. Benally. One further question...."

"Sure," Benally replied.

"Mr. Cannon was obviously working in his studio. We have paintings everywhere, the lights are on, and there's music playing. How come there isn't a painting on the easel? Don't artists usually have a piece in the works?"

The officer looked directly into Benally's eyes.

"True, they do. But T.C. had finished everything for the show and was taking a break before starting again. He was at the point where he was organizing his paintings and getting them ready to ship to the gallery," Benally said, looking at the ground.

"Yeah, it's a real shame," the policeman agreed.

Benally sat down in a worn blue studio chair and watched as the officers took photos and inventoried the paintings. The cosmic die had been cast and was rolling toward its ultimate, destructive destiny.

CHAPTER 21

RIGHT ON SCHEDULE

With the discovery of the jawbreaker and small human skeleton, the day went from being cold and uncomfortable to utterly dismal. Marvin was visibly shaken. Rachael had never before seen this strong man reduced to such a catatonic state, and took charge of the situation. She sat Marvin in a sheltered windbreak and gave him her leftover peanut butter sandwich, assuring him that she was there for him.

Rachael also feared the *chindi* that surrounded the dead, and girded herself before she entered the tomb to look for any pieces of the puzzle that Marvin might have missed. She was less convinced than he that the skeleton was that of Ricky Begay—it appeared to her to be an old Nasazi grave—but if Marvin's remarkable memory said these were his friend's teeth, she would be in his corner.

The child's skeleton was exactly as Marvin described it—an anthropologist's dream find if were ancient, or a grieving Navajo mother's worst nightmare if it were more recent. Rachael put her phone in her mouth and used her hands to gently sift around the bed of the floor. She was looking for other candies, or artifacts that might point toward a Nasazi skeleton instead of that of Ricky Begay, but found neither. It plainly appeared to be a burial site, but it would be up to a specialist to determine the age of the deceased; she had seen enough.

There were only a few hours of daylight left, and the kids would want dinner soon. Rachael hated to leave them at Mrs. Bennally's for too long; they needed her and she needed them. She convinced Marvin to let everything be for the moment, and put the rocks back in place to prevent any animal from coming in and destroying the grave: there was always the possibility this was a crime scene, though it seemed unlikely to her. They could simply leave the past buried if the gravesite was in accordance with ancient Navajo ways. But then again, Ricky's father's grave was waiting for his son's return—assuming the burial wasn't his doing. She would talk with Bloom and get his take on it.

Much depended on Marvin's feelings; these were his ghosts, not hers. Rachael invited Marvin to stay the night at her house, and was surprised when he accepted: he clearly needed human contact. The two made their way back to the truck without speaking. Marvin—the man who walked 10 miles a day—needed help getting into the truck. The day had clearly taken its toll.

Rachael's house was warm with kids running in circles and peppering Rachael with questions. Marvin sat on a stool, staring into the boiling pot of day-old mutton stew. Rachael tried to control the moment by having the kids talk about their day before she tucked them in for the night. The next part of the evening would involve serious conversation. She knew Charles would be calling precisely at 9 p.m.—he was a man who stuck to his routines.

"Marvin, I know today's discovery is disturbing and weighing heavily on your heart. The question I have for you is what do you want to do about the grave."

"I've been thinking about this for hours, and I'm torn. My heart says to let it lie. Ricky is dead, and his father has passed. He is probably the one who buried his son there and the grave is as he wished. Maybe now I can put the mystery of my friend's death behind me...." Marvin's voice trailed off.

"That's reasonable. You know, Marvin, if we dig much deeper those intense emotions you felt today are only going to get more intense."

"That does concern me, but part of me wants to know how my friend ended up nude and pushed into the back of that tomb. And what about the cellophane wrapper and the candies? Could those help answer that question, or is my mind working too hard to solve this riddle?"

"Marvin, I see the thread," Rachael responded thoughtfully. "The candy and the wrapper seem to be connected to the tomb, but in what ways?"

"I keep thinking that my friend's father found his son dead from some sort of trauma. You saw his skull; there was large crack on the front part that must have been what killed him. Maybe his dad discovered his body and buried him in a traditional fashion. Maybe he was so upset that he decided to die on his way home, purposefully lost control of his horse, and fell to his death. Traditional Navajos would often have their favorite horses killed near their graves."

"Maybe so. I guess it's plausible."

"But, then, why the two candies? You don't say. 'Oh, I'll suck on a candy on the trip home after burying my son, and then commit suicide.' No matter how much you might like sweets, your mind would be on the afterlife. Was the jawbreaker at the burial site a gift left for his son?" Marvin was trying to work out the riddle.

"Maybe his father didn't eat the other jawbreaker; maybe he tossed it out along the way to his own death so he wouldn't have any reminders of his son's passing?"

"That makes more sense. He could have been so distraught that he was searching for anything that bound him to his son. And maybe that caused the horse to spook and they took their death tumble. Suicide or accident—both are possible."

"Why didn't you put the jawbreaker back where you found it?"

Marvin paused for an uncomfortable second, like a comedian waiting a beat for an awkward punch line, then reached into his pocket and pulled out the candy. He laid it on the table, the old cellophane making a crinkling noise, its elasticity long played out.

"I guess I wanted something more than a photograph to remind me of my childhood friend. Maybe I'm like his father. I wasn't thinking straight."

"I understand, but we don't know what the implications of the candy might be—don't you agree?"

"You're right," Marvin responded. "But if we don't do anything about the grave then it doesn't really matter, does it?"

It was Rachael's turn to be silent. "Let me talk to Bloom and get his take on all this."

"I like that. He will see things from a different angle than we can—but I think this is ultimately my decision."

"Agreed."

The two sat drinking hot cocoa, waiting for Bloom to call. They both jumped when Rachael's cell phone rang out with her favorite Beyoncé song.

Bloom could sense from Rachael's voice that there was a problem, so he let her talk first, before launching into his father's problems. She quickly explained the day's events, giving Bloom all the details so he could understand the situation.

"Rachael, are you positive Marvin recognizes the skeleton as that of Ricky Begay?" Bloom used the deceased's name in a not-so-Navajo fashion.

"Yes, he says he's sure."

"Well, you know Marvin's memory, so it must be Ricky. Is he staying at our house tonight?"

"I asked him to—he was shaken up pretty badly," Rachael replied in a low voice.

"Wow! Marvin's so calm under fire; this must really run deep. How about you? Are you holding up?"

"I'm not so good. Seeing that child in an unmarked grave in an isolated canyon, with no family to grieve him, hit a raw nerve."

"I can come home tomorrow if I need to, I'm getting close to finishing up with my dad."

"I'm fine. I have Marvin and together we seem to be working out issues we have in common. I promise I'll tell you when I need you. Spend time with your dad while you can; it won't last forever," Rachael said; both her parents had died young.

"Only if you promise you will tell me to come home when you need me. I really miss the kids."

"They miss you too, but we're getting by OK, and my rug is making progress, at least until the last couple of days. Marvin needs to clear his demons, and I'm sure finding his friend's grave will help with that."

"I don't know what to tell you, but I believe Marvin needs to go to the authorities. His childhood friend deserves that much—and maybe it's all more sinister than we think," Bloom cautioned.

"That's what I figured you would say, and I believe Marvin is leaning in that direction. I will tell him your thoughts; he really respects your opinion.

"How's your dad?"

"We have a few little legal issues to work out but nothing big yet. I'll let you know if things change. He's definitely getting old; it won't be long before he will need to live closer to us."

"I love your dad, so I'm fine with that. When we move up to Santa Fe in June, you can let him know he's welcome anytime."

"I love you, Rachael Yellowhorse."

"And I love you, too, Charles James Bloom. And don't worry: we are not through having babies. I'm ready to start working on that again when you get home."

Rachael and Bloom talked for nearly an hour before retiring to their separate beds. Tomorrow would be a long day for them both—longer than they could ever expect.

CHAPTER 22

NEWS TRAVELS FAST

Rachael relayed Bloom's impressions of the situation and his recommendations to Marvin, who decided to see how he felt in the morning before he made any decisions. He recognized that Bloom's advice was well thought-out, but still came from the heart.

Rachael's unfamiliar couch kept the older man on the edge of sleep and compounded his disturbing dreams. Ricky's skeleton was running in circles, his mouth fixed in a permanent scream. Marvin's mind bounced from desert crypts to the deep jungles of Vietnam, where he was taking heavy fire while rescuing his badly injured captain from certain death.

He draped the injured officer over his shoulders as he tried in vain to reach the safety of an awaiting Jolly Green Giant helicopter. In the dream, Marvin didn't make it to the bird: it took off without them, with Marvin screaming, "Don't leave us, don't leave us." Disoriented, he fell off the couch, scrambling for cover.

"Where is my horse poster? Where am I?"

Resurfacing from the dream, he recognized Rachael's kitchen and realized that his mind was advising him about the action he should take: he must let the authorities know about his deceased friend's whereabouts, no matter how many bad memories were dredged up. His redemption depended on it. It was the only way he could forgive himself and be released of the haunting dreams of childhood; a father's grave was waiting for a son's return.

Marvin arose early and said his morning prayer as the sun breached the front door. He could see the light streaming under the door, just as it had on the day he had left for Indian boarding school, and Ricky had made his dash for freedom. On that day, he was 11 years old, about to turn 12. Today would be a rebirth; it would start with a strong cup of coffee and a call to the Navajo Nation Police in Shiprock. Marvin wasn't exactly sure how to handle an inquiry into a possible half-century-old homicide without sounding like a kook, so he decided to make the forty-five minute drive to the station, figuring he would be more believable in person.

Rachael wanted to accompany her friend, so as soon as the kids were at school they headed north on U.S. Route 491, a second steaming cup of coffee shoring up their courage. They would tell the authorities an abbreviated story of how they found the body, and why they had been searching—leaving out only one detail: Marvin insisted he didn't want them to know about the jawbreaker quite yet. That piece of candy was a thread connecting him to his deceased friend, and he refused to let the charm out of his possession. He wanted to see what conclusions the cops reached before giving them a key piece of evidence.

Rachael thought that was a bad idea. If by some chance Ricky had been murdered, that candy was important piece of evidence and Marvin was potentially altering a crime investigation. But he would not relent, and she didn't feel it was her place to force the issue. This was Marvin's journey; he had found the candy for a reason, and until the Holy Ones showed him why, this artifact of his past life would remain in his deerskin pouch, bathed in life-giving corn pollen.

Shiprock's monolithic outcropping was nearly obscured by a low-hanging cloudbank as they approached the town—an omen, Marvin thought. The Shiprock police building was located near the Bethel Christian Reformed Church, along with a dozen low-slung block homes and a few trailers. Wells Fargo had strategically placed a branch across the street—more for security than convenience, Marvin reasoned. A *bilagáana* bank vice president back East would probably be concerned about the abject poverty of Shiprock, and want to keep the institution's precious assets safe. Marvin laughed at the notion. Did the reformed church feel the same way, wanting to keep the traditional Navajos at bay?

The police desk attendant was a young officer in a sharp khaki-brown uniform with a yellow and green patch that promised "to protect and serve since 1868." Marvin recognized the date; it was the year his people were released from the *bilagáana's* prison at Bosque Redondo, near present-day Fort Sumner, New Mexico. He hoped the motto was true.

The officer's nametag read Kenneth Katoney. He looked about eighteen years old, and Marvin immediately asked for his superior.

Katoney frowned, but relented out of respect for Marvin's age. An older officer emerged, not looking too happy to be interrupted during his morning donut-and-coffee time, his expanded belt line exposing a weakness Marvin could understand.

"I'm Lieutenant Brown. How can I help you, Mr....?"

"I'm Marvin Manycoats, and this is my friend Rachael Yellowhorse."

"The weaver Rachael Yellowhorse?" The officer's demeanor changed dramatically when he recognized her name.

"Yes, I'm a weaver, like my mom. Are you familiar with our clan?"

"Yes, ma'am, I'm a fan. My daughter is a weaver too. I'm pretty sure you taught her for one semester at Newcomb High School. Her name is Elva Brown."

"I remember Elva," Rachael smiled. "She was a great student, very creative. I'm happy to know she has found Spider Woman's gift."

"She will be excited to hear I got to talk to you today. I hope we aren't meeting under bad circumstances...."

Marvin re-entered the conversation: "Well, lieutenant, I'm afraid they are. Rachael and I have found the skeleton of a childhood friend of mine who died fifty-plus years ago, and we need to report the finding. I'm hoping you can put one of your best officers on it."

"Fifty years! You don't hear a story like that every day. Where are these human remains? Is it a complete skeleton? And how do you know it's your childhood friend and not Nasazi?"

Lieutenant Brown fired questions at Marvin. Finding Nasazi and early Navajo skeletons on the reservation wasn't out of the ordinary; clearly the officer was looking to clarify such a specific charge.

Marvin retold their story of what had happened and how they discovered the remains, with Rachael filling in gaps. The lieutenant seemed engaged and promised to send his best detective to the location right away. He asked if they would be willing to show his team the grave, and they agreed.

A crew of three accompanied Marvin and Rachael to the tomb. A detective, a young officer, and the acting coroner followed Rachael's truck until the road became impassable. The remaining two-mile hike felt refreshing to Marvin and Rachael; the two officers in their heavy boots, military-style hats, and Glock 22s were less enthusiastic.

Once Rachael and Marvin pointed out the crime scene, the men went into professional mode, the detective barking orders in Navajo. The area was coordinated off into a large square with yellow police tape. The incongruity of the fluttering yellow words, "Police Line Do Not Cross," in the barren New Mexico desert was not lost on Rachael, whose keen artistic mind sought out such oddities: "Performance art Navajo style," she thought.

Multiple photos, measurements, and notes were recorded before the team proceeded to the skeleton's hiding place, where the same process was repeated. After what seemed like hours, a black body bag was finally removed from the crypt.

Marvin and Rachael watched intensely from behind the yellow tape. Marvin pulled a small pinch of corn pollen from his pouch; inside the deerskin bag, the cellophane-wrapped candy was staring back at him. He placed the pollen in his mouth and on his head, chanting as the two men unceremoniously dragged the remains in its plastic-wheeled black sarcophagus across the red dirt, leaving an odd track no hunter would be able to identify. When they reached the police van, they placed the bag on a small cart.

Marvin was clearly bothered and Rachael instinctively put her arm around his stout neck.

The detective took Rachael's and Marvin's affidavits as his partner struggled with the bulky stretcher in the unforgiving sand. Marvin's opportunity to share the jawbreaker with the authorities had passed; Rachael also remained mute.

Once the police officer was satisfied his forms were complete, he asked Rachael and Marvin to return home and advised them not to mention the day's activities to anyone. The police wanted to see what they could find out before the information became public. It was clear that the story would leak, as they would need to exhume Orville Begay's body to look for a DNA match to the skeleton. No match would mean no Ricky. They promised to give the pair more information as soon as they could.

The drive back to Toadlena was quiet; the usually talkative Marvin went radio silent, so Rachael opened the conversation: "They seemed interested and very professional. I think the police will take this seriously, don't you?"

"I know they were impressed that you're a famous weaver; that probably made all the difference."

"You sound skeptical Marvin...."

"I guess I am."

"Why, Marvin? These are professionals; they will do their job."

"Except this is a cold case, with no family in the picture, no one but an old man and a weaver interested in the outcome. I'm afraid they will want to put this to bed quickly and with as little investigation as possible. 'To protect and serve' may only go so far with a fifty-year-old case."

"Well, I hope not. Maybe seeing our deep concern for this child, they will be afraid to be too cavalier with their findings."

"What's 'cavalier?'" Marvin asked

"It means the police would be indifferent or casual about the case."

"That's a new one for me, Rachael. I guess you're never too old to improve yourself—or should I say, I wouldn't want to be too cavalier about learning a fancy new word." Marvin smiled faintly for the first time that morning.

News travels fast on the reservation. By the next morning, a reporter for the *Navajo Times* was on Marvin's front porch asking for comments regarding the body he had found. Marvin was taken back by her questions and was not sure what to say, but he decided to invite the young woman into his hogan—even if she hadn't waited the proper amount of time in her car before knocking on his door. Her inquiries were direct and to the point: how long had he been looking for Ricky Begay? Why did he think the boy had been lost for so long? Did he think there was foul play involved?"

Marvin was surprised by the cub reporter's use of the deceased's name, but she was young and clearly wasn't traditional. He listened intently, then slowly answered the questions to the best of his ability. He said he didn't know if there was any foul play, but was sure the tribal police would get to the bottom of the story; he had full faith in their abilities. In truth, Marvin was less than sure of the cops' commitment to the case, but hoped that seeing his words in print might motivate them to put more effort into the case.

The reporter soon found her way to Rachael's home. The weaver was less accommodating than Marvin. She had seen both her own and her husband's names in the papers before, and nothing good had ever come from the exposure. Reporters were looking to sell papers, or, in today's world, clicks. Rachael referred the woman to the Navajo Police Department for comment. The reporter frowned, then continued to pepper Rachael with questions, hoping to badger her into talking.

Rachael's temper flared: "If you spent more time at your grandmother's knee and less time on your phone," she said to the reporter, "you might learn to respect your elders."

Rachael was shocked by her own outburst. When did she become such an adult, she wondered, much less an elder? Maybe being a mom made her feel old enough to talk that way to the young woman.

When Marvin called Rachael and told her he had spoken with the *Times* reporter, she warned him that the press was not always on your side, and to be careful.

"I'm at that stage in life where I don't care what people say or know of me," Marvin replied. "I just want to know the truth of what happened to my friend. If I have to get into the mud with the pigs, that's not a problem. I can afford a bar of soap."

Rachael respected this man of honor and courage. He was a rare find, she thought, and she was surprised he had never found a soulmate. Maybe the childhood trauma or his Vietnam experience had damaged Marvin in ways she could never understand.

Within two hours a reporter for KTNN AM 660 had called Rachael. The story was out, and there was no putting it back into the bottle. Again, Rachael deferred to the tribal police office in Shiprock. This time the reporter was polite and thanked Rachael for her time, so she decided to give her a bit of the backstory on Marvin Manycoats, his history at Indian boarding school, his Marine service, and his two Purple Hearts. He was simply trying to put to bed what happened to his childhood friend, Rachael said. She couldn't help but smile as she hung up the phone, thinking of the rude *Times* reporter hearing this story. Maybe next time she would show a little courtesy, whether she was talking to an elder or not.

Rachael should have paid more attention to her reluctance to interact with the press. This last bit of information about Marvin's history would cause his world to unravel. The tightly wrapped threads of his life were about to unspool, and there was no way to stop the evil born on a hot fall day a half-century earlier.

CHAPTER 23

HONOR AMONG THIEVES

Benny Benally was fully awake as he considered the implications of his vivid dream. Removing the T.C. Cannon painting from its easel in 1978 had been a personal low point. He loved the connection to T.C., but like life itself, possession of the painting had been brief. It was no longer his to admire, the bond with T.C. broken forever. The painting that brought him such joy left a deep void in his soul when it was gone. Why couldn't he have had the will power to quit drinking on his own so he could keep the painting instead of having to pay for rehab?

Taking the painting had damaged Benally's sense of right and wrong, but he could live with that. It was a gift of sorts and he never wanted the work for the money it represented. The minute he monetized the art, his self-esteem became the bigger casualty. He had managed to stop drinking with professional help, but the emotional costs of quitting were deep and long lasting.

What should he do about Rachael? Benally had been considering his options for four tortuous days, and concluded that the Cannon painting's owners would need to be notified of her inquiry. Rachael had said the painting was in a private collection in Las Cruces. Perhaps the Cannon had changed hands again; the person he had sold it to lived in Santa Fe. The inscription on the back also was new to him. Benally didn't recognize the dedication.

Rachael Yellowhorse was memorable—a woman with a persistent drive for success who would doggedly complete any project she was given. She was now interested in obtaining information about the Cannon painting, but why? And how worried should he be?

Alcohol had taken a heavy toll on Benally's work and health. The habit had become so severe that his tenure at IAIA was in jeopardy. Intense medical intervention helped kick the addiction; unfortunately, his inadequate health insurance paid for only a small portion of a stay at a rehabilitation center. Two months of intense inpatient therapy and counseling had been needed to increase the odds of permanently kicking such a long-standing dependence.

In retrospect, Benally wished he had sold his home instead of the painting, but a real estate transaction takes time, and he didn't have time. With his marginal credit, a home loan wasn't a possibility either. He had only one liquid asset—the T.C. Cannon painting—but would he be able to sell the piece? Collectors don't like big gaps in provenance, and his was as large as a Mack truck.

A Jean-Michel Basquiat that had never been seen or exhibited, with a scanty provenance as a gift to the musician Matt Dike, had recently sold for $10 million—but that sale happened after Dike's death. No one cares about the fine details, all parties are dead: that should have been him and his Cannon painting. He wanted to leave the Cannon to IAIA in his will so he would be remembered, if only by his name, but he needed fast money and he had only one resource, so he picked up the phone and called a wealthy private dealer with a reputation for paying top dollar for good pieces and keeping ownership questions to a minimum: Angel Veracruz. He had met her at a senior student's final art project. That year's class included two promising students, and many of the Santa Fe art sharks were sizing up the fresh bait.

Angel slipped Benally a business card and talked about her great love of Cannon's work. She had done her homework and was aware of the relationship between Benny and Cannon. She was self-confident enough to ask right away if the professor might have anything to sell, or know of any Cannon paintings for sale. He had been noncommittal, but his twitching body told her Benally knew more than he let on. So she ended the conversation by saying, "I'm always interested in buying Cannon's work; just let me know if you hear of anything." She had followed up a few times over the years, reminding him of her interest in Cannon—almost as if she knew he had a painting hidden away. So when he decided he must sell the Cannon, his first choice of buyer was Angel Veracruz.

The phone call had gone better than he expected. Angel was definitely interested in the work and came to his house that same day. Benally had never sold a painting, so he took his cues from the art world. The painting had been hanging in his bedroom, where he could look at it every morning and night, but the light was poor and space cramped for such a large painting. He moved the Cannon to a wall behind the living room couch, which had ample natural light. The large, empty space accented the importance of the painting; it had never looked better. When Angel walked through his front door, it was apparent she recognized the importance of the painting. She wasted no time on small talk, taking no chance on losing such an important and rare find.

"The painting looks fantastic. You have hung it beautifully, but with the proceeds from this sale, you can put two paintings in that place and have money left over. So, Dr. Benally, are you ready to hear my offer?"

A half bottle of tequila had fueled his courage, yet even in that altered state his mind was clear. "Sure. How much for my precious Cannon?" he asked, slurring his words slightly.

"How about $60,000? You must agree that's a strong offer, Dr. Benally."

Benally had no idea of the Cannon's value on the secondary market and was shocked. The sale would easily cover two months of rehab—but the liquor gave him the courage he needed and he pushed for more.

"I don't know what I want. I need a lot of money to cover some medical issues. That's the only reason I am considering selling this painting, so I need to get the most I possibly can."

"Well, give me a number that works for both of us," Angel countered.

"I would sell it for $70,000," Benally blurted out, his slurred speech more noticeable this time. "I could live with that. I love this painting and hate to sell my friend's gift."

Angel, a seasoned dealer, waited a few seconds before responding, not wanting to be too quick on the trigger, then calmly said, "Done!" and thrust her hand out to consummate the deal.

Benally was shocked. He had made an additional $10,000 dollars just like that. It would take him three months to make that much money at his regular job. He stuck out a limp hand, which Angel gripped tightly, a smile flitting across her face. He would never forget that smile—it was not one of joy, but more of a smirk. She had bested him.

His dignity in shambles, Benally continued to press: "Can you do some cash?"

The professor understood that the entire sale would be taxable unless he received some of the money in untraceable funds. At his age, he also was concerned about the IRS's cut. He could be dead before the government caught up with him, and with no family, there was little to lose. Once upon a time he might have been more cautious, but his beloved wife had died at thirty-six, and he was now an old man with no children. The rehab facility might even give him a discount for paying cash.

"I can do better than 'some,' Dr. Benally. How about I give you all of the funds in cash. Does that work?"

"Even better!"

"What can you tell me about the provenance of this painting?"

"Well, like I said, it was a gift. T.C. wanted me to have it because we were close friends. It was painted in 1978."

"The year he died?"

"Yes, that's correct."

"So it's one of Cannon's last paintings?"

"Yes, that's fair to say," Benally said uneasily, the tequila's grip beginning to wear off.

"Tell me if I'm wrong, but to my recollection I have never seen this painting in any of the catalogs, or for that matter, any images of this painting. I'm surprised that you of all people didn't want your painting documented." Angel watched Benally's face closely as she quizzed him.

"Well, I never wanted to share it with the world. It was a special gift, and I didn't want people bugging me to sell it. I'm sure you can understand—but I do guarantee authenticity."

"I do understand," Angel replied. "I, too, am a very private person, and I have no doubt the painting is authentic. Do you have any paperwork from Mr. Cannon stating he gave you the painting?"

"No. T.C. handed it to me one day saying 'this is for you.' It seemed wrong to ask for a bill of sale, as if I only cared about the painting's value and not the piece itself."

"Not a problem, but I will need you to sign an affidavit detailing the painting's history as you remember it. I'm sure you understand that I need a provenance paper trail, even though I plan to keep this piece for my own collection—so there is no need to worry about the painting coming back on the market, if you know what I mean."

Benally did know what she was indirectly telling him. She didn't care how he got the piece from T.C. and she would not expose the sale, but she did need to cover her butt in case there were any future issues with provenance.

"That's not a problem, Ms. Veracruz. I can give you a bill of sale with the history." In an instant, Benally had succumbed to the power of money, and the painting was gone forever.

Fifteen years had passed since that day, and he had never seen or spoken about the painting since. He bumped into Angel Veracruz at a few social art gatherings in Santa Fe, and ran into her once in Whole Foods Market, but no words were spoken—only a collegial nod of the head gave a clue of their shared secret.

The sale of the painting had unburdened Benally of the alcohol addiction and saved his teaching job, though an unfortunate side effect of rehab was that he had started smoking again, which in turn led to his current health issues. Karma was a bitch.

Benny understood that he needed to talk to Angel, and that she would want answers that he didn't have. Rachael had gotten images of the front and back of the painting, apparently in a storage facility. But where was it? She was being very cloak-and-dagger about it all, avoiding telling him how she had come by the photos. Rachael trusted her old professor, and now he was going to betray that shared bond—and for what? His so-called reputation? His fear of a possible lawsuit from the Cannon estate? Or, even worse, Angel Veracruz coming after him?

The professor's wealth was not counted in dollars, but in his tireless work as a teacher and his well-known friendship with the great artist T.C. Cannon. His savings were in the form of a Southside adobe home and a school pension. He could never face the shame of being exposed for stealing from his friend's studio the day after the painter died. It was easier to let the gods decide the outcome.

Angel Veracruz was a powerful figure, and from what he had more recently come to learn, not someone to be crossed. His decision was made: he was firmly in Angel's corner—and Rachael was on her own.

CHAPTER 24

IN THE CROSS HAIRS

Benally slipped his hand into the back drawer of a worn desk for Angel's creased business card. The glossy 2- by 3-inch card had aged better than he had. He stared, unblinking, at the small piece of paper with its bold red type: the letters began to vibrate as tears rolled down his sunken checks. This card had been his undoing, providing the outlet to sell his beloved Cannon. He numbly dialed the phone number and was amazed that Angel's landline was still connected after fifteen years.

The call went directly to voice mail, the dealer's seductive voice unchanged: "This is Angel. You know what to do...."

Benally left a cryptic message: "Hi, Ms. Veracruz, this is Dr. Benny Benally. I need to discuss something regarding the painting I sold you. Please give me a call at 505-820-7451. I look forward to hearing from you."

Two hours later, Angel returned his call. Benally had never moved from his desk, the card on the table in front of him no longer pristine. Tears now splotched its surface.

"Dr. Benally, it's been too long. I hope all is well with you."

"I'm fine thanks, and I appreciate you returning my call. I wanted to let you know I received an inquiry from a former student asking me questions about the Cannon painting I sold you."

"Hmm... that's interesting."

"Yes, I thought you might think so. This person asked if I knew anything 'bout the painting. I told them I remembered seeing it in Cannon's studio a few days before his death."

"And what else did you say?"

"Well, I told them that I didn't know where it was and suggested it might have gone back to the estate, or been sold off to some private collection."

"You didn't tell them it was a gift from the artist to you?"

"No, I didn't."

"Why not?"

"I don't know—I just didn't. I never had any proof that T.C. gave me the painting. I was taken off guard, and frankly I panicked."

"You don't have anything to worry about, Benny. It was a gift, and I'm assuming this gift took place around the day the artist died?" Angel asked, already knowing the answer.

There was silence on the other end of the phone as Benally considered the question before he laid his cards on the table. "Yes, that's correct. T.C. had given me the painting a week earlier, because I had helped him and was such a good friend. When he died, I went to retrieve my painting the next morning. It was mine."

"I see; you took it off the easel."

"Yes, but I swear he had given it to me."

"I understand. You don't have to explain any more. I'm not upset. It was your painting, but you're afraid of the repercussions if this part of the painting's history gets into the ethnosphere."

"Yes, Angel. I am very concerned."

"Who is this student?"

"I really don't want to say; I like this person a lot and I think it's better if I keep their name out of it for now."

"Then what do you want, Benny? You called me...."

"I'm not sure, but I figured that if one person is sniffing around there might be others. I can tell you this much: the person who contacted me didn't know your name or anything about the painting's backstory."

"I have a question, Benny. How can you sure be sure it was my painting they were talking about? It's not been published, and there is no title."

"They emailed me a photo."

"A photo? Was it a professional photo?"

"No. I believe it was a cell-phone photo. It looked like it might have been taken in an art storage unit—maybe yours?"

"Why do you say it was an art storage facility?"

"Because the wire mesh the painting was hung on is the type found in a professional unit—something I'm assuming you would use."

"Right. Can you forward me that photo? I'll give you a cell number. If you would text it to me, I would appreciate it."

"Ok, I can do that. I've learned how to forward photos, but I'm not the greatest so you will have to let me know if you receive the photo."

"I will, Benny. I appreciate the heads-up and don't worry: you're fine. T.C. gave the painting to you, and it was yours to sell. My concern is how and why a photo of my painting was taken from my storage room."

"Honestly, Angel, I don't know."

"Well, I would appreciate it if you can find out anything else, Benny. I'm going through a transition in my life right now and prefer not to have any unnecessary media exposure. If you could stay on top of this matter, I will owe you one."

"I promise I will do what I can."

"Thanks, Benny, and just to be clear: I'll make sure it's well worth your while if you keep me in the loop." Then the phone went dead.

Benny Benally had drawn a line in the sand. He was in Angel Veracruz's camp; she knew the whole backstory and didn't care. He would find out what he could and report back to Angel. Maybe there was a large finder's fee in his future. He could use the money; all those medications to ease his breathing were expensive. But he had left out one critical piece of information by not mentioning the inscription on the back of the painting: this part of the story could be future leverage. Before he brought it up, he would see if he could decipher its meaning.

Angel waited anxiously for the text, which arrived on her burner phone thirty minutes after they talked. She responded to Benally with a white thumbs-up emoji. Benally flashed a black thumbs-up emoji back to her; he might be old, but he was not dead yet.

The photo was blurry but it was definitely a picture of her painting that appeared to have been taken in her art storage unit. Her questions were twofold: who took the photo—and why? Blackmail seemed possible. A stolen painting by a famous Native artist could make for bad press, especially at this time in her life. She couldn't afford any issues right now. Benally had said the person making the inquiry was "an old student," so they were most likely Native.

Angel was in the process of de-accessioning her family's pre-Columbian collection; a museum in Mexico had accepted all the works, sight unseen—as long as the pieces were authentic and had been properly valued. Pre-Columbian art had come under scrutiny of late, and she didn't need any pesky reporters asking how the pieces had been acquired. Mexico didn't ask pointed questions when it came to getting its heritage returned, and the hefty charitable deduction from the donation was equally important. This was going to be a good year.

She needed to make a reconnaissance trip to her Mesilla compound, and pronto. A talk with Gutierrez might help her figure out who took the photo and why. An inside job by one of her family's men seemed unlikely—it was too highbrow for that bunch of Shreks—plus they were loyal. Men who break bones for a living wouldn't understand this kind of treachery. She would find out who was involved, and when she did, she would dispose of the problem.

No one blackmailed Angel Veracruz—and anyone who tried would pay dearly.

CHAPTER 25

TIME TO MAKE THE CUT

Leaving the cold air of Santa Fe for the warmer clime of Mesilla was a break Angel would normally have appreciated, but today she was preoccupied. She traveled solo, not wanting any additional scrutiny as the press was starting to keep track of her whereabouts. Angel needed to look Gutierrez directly in the eyes when she showed him the photo of her Cannon painting. Her father had taught Angel well; she would know if her second-in-command was lying about any involvement. The man was a furiously loyal lieutenant, and betrayal seemed unlikely.

Two men snapped to attention when Angel's red Mercedes G550 slipped into the front lot of her family's compound: they recognized the vehicle.

"Ms. Veracruz, you were not on today's schedule. Is that correct?" The huge man asked apologetically as he pulled hard on the leash of a barking dog.

"I know you didn't have me listed; that was the idea. Park my car close by and not under those damned fruit trees, unless you prefer a job as car-wash attendant. I doubt I'll be here long."

Angel left the car running, flipped the keys onto the seat, and walked into the house, settling her slender frame in a blue-trimmed chair prominently placed in front of Gutierrez, who immediately stood to attention.

"Ms. Veracruz, so nice to see you. Were we expecting you today?"

"No, you were not."

"I hope nothing is wrong. May I offer you an espresso?" Gutierrez asked, glancing over to his third in command, silently asking him to fetch the drink.

"No espresso. I'm not going to be here long and for YOUR sake, I hope nothing is wrong. Please tell your man to leave the room."

Gutierrez gulped and pointed to the exit. Once the bruiser left, Angel, who had been leaning back in the chair, leaned forward, both hands on the desk, while making eye contact with her lieutenant.

"Mr. Gutierrez, you have been running our family's operation for fifteen years now, correct?"

"Almost sixteen years, so yes, a long time," Gutierrez said nervously, his eyes locked with those of his boss.

"Do you know if someone is trying to screw me?"

"What do you mean?" he asked, in a shocked tone.

"Well, someone has taken a photo of one of my precious paintings in the art storage area and is sharing it with who-knows-who. I would like to know how something like that could happen under your command."

"I have no idea. What painting? When?"

"As if you would know one painting from another. It's my T.C. Cannon."

Gutierrez's blank face confirmed what she suspected.

"The one with the Indian eating candy...."

"Yes, I know that painting. It should be in the storage area. I can go check right now."

"It had better be there—but that's not my question. I have a photo showing my Cannon on the metal grid. Look here...."

Gutierrez leaned over for a look at Angel's phone.

"Do you have any idea who could have taken that photo?"

Gutierrez looked at his desk for a moment while he was thinking, then looked up. "Yes, I think I know who took that photo."

"Well, who?"

"The retired professor we hired to do the appraisal for the pre-Columbian material. His son came along to help him, and we heard the metal wheels of the art walls squeak the first day he was here. I sent Jorge to check it out, and he told them the painting racks and all other parts of the storage unit were off-limits. They could only look at the pre-Columbian material, and take no photos. I didn't think much of it at the time, but I did check both the men's phones before they left and there were no photos of any paintings on either one."

"So you were concerned enough to check their phones but not alert me?!"

"Sorry, I didn't think it warranted a call. He's an old man and his son was only there for a couple of days."

"I remember hiring one ancient professor from NMSU—not two men! What are their names?"

"Dr. James Bloom is the man you hired; his son Charles Bloom helped him for two days."

"Charles Bloom, the gallery owner from Santa Fe?"

"Yes, I think so. I take it you know of him, boss?"

"I can't believe you let a gallery owner from Santa Fe into my god-damned art storage vault. Who knows what photos he's taken? I'm sure he snooped—it's in every good art dealer's blood. Bloom used to handle Willard Yellowhorse—he loves contemporary art! Jesus!"

"I didn't know this was important. He was the old man's son, so I figured the professor needed help to reach those pieces on the top of the shelves."

"Yes, Mr. Gutierrez, it was VERY IMPORTANT. You let a hungry fox into my henhouse. Is Bloom's father qualified to do the appraisal or was this whole thing a set-up to get in to see my art holdings?"

"No, the father is one the best archaeologists in New Mexico. Remember that we checked him out. Here's his finished report; it looks very legit to me. We are going to get our guy to put the values in next to Dr. Bloom's identification of the artifacts. That's what you asked for...." Gutierrez pushed the multipage document across the desk for Angel to inspect.

"I remember my wishes. What I don't remember is authorizing another art dealer to come into my most sacred storage area—and let in by my own men?"

Gutierrez didn't like where the conversation was headed, but knew he needed to fill his boss in on all the details.

"There was one hitch. It took Dr. Bloom two tries to fill out the paperwork, but the second time it was done correctly."

"What does that mean—two tries?" Angel asked, her anger growing as a new wrinkle appeared.

"Well, when he originally turned in the papers he had crossed out the value line, and I reminded him that his contract said he couldn't change anything, or he would be liable and not paid. He came to his senses and brought back an unaltered notarized sheet that had been filled out properly, the value section left empty."

Angel considered this, looking at the form. "Did Dr. Bloom say why he had initially crossed out that area?"

"Yes, he was afraid someone might fill in the valuation numbers for the objects since that information was on the same page. He had signed each page and was concerned that someone might assume he had also done the valuation of the pieces."

"Of course, he's right about that. Did he seem upset when you made him leave this section empty?"

"No, not really, though my security man tells me his son wasn't too happy about it."

"Well, there's our motive. The old man is pissed about the form, and he's looking for leverage to screw me if I do something untoward. Or maybe Charles Bloom is trying to sell a painting he doesn't own. Either way, the Bloom boys are on my shit list—and that's not a good place to find yourself, is it?"

"No, Miss Veracruz. I wouldn't want to be them."

"Go get me the Cannon, and make a note in my painting log that I'm taking the piece to the governor's mansion. And, Mr. Gutierrez, make damn sure you have the correct painting! Blanket-wrap the Cannon and put it in my Mercedes, image facedown with a piece of cardboard over it.

"I'll let you know what I decide about the professor. He lives in Las Cruces and will be the easiest to deal with. I want Dr. Bloom's movements and house monitored. Put Louis on his scent, and bug the house if possible."

"You got it, boss."

"One more thing I want you to do...."

"Sure, what?"

"Get the surgical unit prepped and tell Doc he's on standby; we may have some business coming his way soon."

CHAPTER 26

JOHN F. KENNEDY'S BOY, 1961

The dusty two-lane road between Gallup and Shiprock was bumpier than usual for early September. The last of the summer monsoons had passed through two weeks earlier, a final gully washer leaving ridges of packed red earth on the road. When the wind blew or a vehicle went by, a line of blood-colored dust lifted off the dry packed dirt and spread across the horizon.

Earnest Smiley hated Mondays and today would be worse than most. The Indian boarding school would officially open tomorrow and herds of Navajo kids would be bused off the reservation—which translated to a lower consumption of sweets along his trading post route. Today the children and their snacks were being caravanned out on the "yellow squash," as the Navajo called the buses heading to the dreaded boarding schools. For the next four months, his candy and chips orders would be precipitously cut in half. Less money, unhappy traders, and an unhappy boss would take it out on the guy whose only job was to deliver the goodies and request payment.

Sweets and chips were big sellers at any Navajo trading post. Smiley was amazed that the customers had any teeth left with the numerous jawbreakers they consumed, but their dental health wasn't his concern—he was only responsible for making the delivery and booking the next week's order.

Today marked a low point: it was Smiley's two-year anniversary driving a delivery truck for Perry Mason's Sweets, Candy, and Potato Chips located on the north side of Gallup. His tenure with the company felt more like a decade than twenty-four months.

Smiley despised his boss's holier-than-thou attitude, which was only outmatched by the man's narcissism. Perry Mason, the company owner, might share a name with a hit television show, but unlike the TV character—Raymond Burr was smart, handsome, and witty—this Perry Mason's death would only be noticed by a few suppliers who were owed money.

Smiley's Perry Mason was more dunce than dilettante. He didn't care about his clients' concerns. They were all putzes to him, jerks to be taken advantage of, unlike the TV defense lawyer who strived to protect and serve the hapless defendants. If Mason's candy company had not had close to a monopoly in the Four Corners region, he would have never survived in business.

For the five years the TV show had been running, Smiley's eponymously named boss had been reshaping his own persona to line up with that of his namesake. Mason never missed an episode, writing down terms that his idol used in court, so he could banter them about in his own boardroom of sorts, the manufacturing plant.

"Hey, Smiley, we got a big case today... we need to fill that order at Crystal Trading Post by tomorrow; the inmates are hungry and we can't disappoint."

At the end of each month, Mason called in all the workers to review their performances for the last thirty days. All were forced to sit in a long line of seats, arranged like a jury box, as Mason paced the floor summarizing the facts in his closing arguments. No one but Mason was allowed to speak.

"Well, it's clear to me that we have some issues in the potato chip arena. We need to crack the code to get more Navajos to eat that crispy goodness. This critical information could be the difference of us surviving, or being thrown out on the streets. Did you realize if one truck breaks down for a single day we could lose as much as 5 percent of our gross income for the month? Check your vehicles diligently, so I won't be forced to prosecute you. Any truck that breaks down from willful neglect will have the heavy hand of justice applied to the guilty party or parties. I am assuming there are no objections?"

No objections were ever voiced during these tirades of legal gibberish, although snickers were inevitable, the employees knowing their boss had slipped into his TV persona.

Smiley, who was never thought of as jovial, kept his mouth shut. He needed this employment, bad as it was. He had lost a cushy job working for the GM dealership when his dad's boss had caught him sleeping off a hangover in the back of one of the new pickup trucks. His father was called in from a closing to witness his son's sloth, and he was forced to fire his own son in front of the entire staff.

The two had never reconciled, Smiley's father was unable to forgive his son's poor judgment, which had humiliated him in his most precious place, the GM sales floor. Smiley vowed never to be put in that position again: no snickers, no back talk, just work to earn enough money to go to college, so he could get the hell off the reservation and away from Gallup's small-town attitude.

The yellow bus was leaving the parking lot as Smiley pulled his large delivery truck into his second stop of the day, the Toadlena Trading Post. Dozens of families were milling around the building, many on horseback. Women were crying and at least one man was riding his horse at full tilt alongside the bus, screaming something to one of the kids. It looked like a western movie minus the cavalry.

Smiley was struck by how backward the reservation sometimes felt. Penetrating brown eyes followed him through the post's front door. Their hostility toward whites—especially bilágaanas with blond hair and blue eyes—was palpable on this day. Smiley regretted he hadn't stopped for a cigarette and listened to the new Ray Charles song, "Hit the Road Jack," before pulling into the trading post. If he had, the crowd would have dispersed before he arrived.

"Hey, Smiley, you know I'm not going to need as much candy or chips for a while, right? The kids are off to boarding school, and for what? So they can learn to plant corn? Give me a break!" Toadlena Trading Post owner Logan griped.

"Well, I understand, Mr. Logan. No one seems happy to see their kids off to school, though I got tell you a good number of them didn't seem to like me much either."

"Well, hell, kid. You can't blame these people can you? They got zero choice in the matter; the feds say give up your kids for months at a time or risk going to jail. A few parents risk jail each year by sending their children to hide out at their family's winter camps or to stay with relatives. Pretty pathetic all around if you ask me."

"I'm no judge or jury, but it seems like some of these kids might could use the schooling as a way off the rez." Smiley hated himself for using Perry Mason lingo; deep down, he knew it was him who wanted out.

"Not for most. Those schools aren't like the one you and I went to. At Indian school they cut their hair, tell 'em to stop speaking Navajo, and then punish them by washing their mouths out with yellow soap if they don't speak English. Not much good comes from that—it just makes people bitter. You'd best keep your guard up today, Earnest. It's not like these folks would want to hurt you, but on a day like today, things can spiral out of control, even for me."

"Yes, sir. That's good advice."

Then Smiley tried some salesmanship: "Mr. Logan, are you sure you want to cut your order in half? It seems like it's been pretty busy since that Kennedy has been in office. Folks seem to have more money to spend."

"If you say so, Earnest. But I'm more likely to know who our local chapter president is than who the U.S. commander-and-chief is. The local politicians are the people with real power as far as I'm concerned. They can close me down with a single phone call. Kennedy—well, he doesn't even know what Navajo means."

"Well, Mr. Logan, I'm a lifelong Democrat, not like my father. I think Kennedy's the best, and I'll bet he does know about Indians, even Navajos. I want to be just like him someday."

"Kid, politics is a dirty business. You're better off staying in the candy business. It's as sweet a job as you can find," Logan said, chuckling to himself.

After two years, Smiley had heard all the candy jokes: "At least it's not a bitter pill to swallow;" "sticky business you're in;" and his least favorite, "I'd be Smiley too with all this candy." He forced an awkward grin and headed for his truck. He had aspirations, and being someone's candy joke boy wasn't one of them.

CHAPTER 27

WATCH YOUR BACK

Smiley enjoyed the physical part of his job. Loading and unloading boxes eight to ten hours a day had helped strengthen and develop his body: at nineteen, his physique was that of a grown man. He would have considered as a long-term job in the snack industry if he had a decent boss and a few more mental challenges.

The Toadlena Trading Post owner opted for few extra boxes of Big Hunk taffy bars. He wanted to help Smiley and realized the sale would make the kid look good for his boss, who was a well-known jerk. Logan understood all too well that without the Navajo kids on the rez, he would not be able to sell the extra candy bars right away, But those white strips of sugar never went bad; in fact, the texture became stickier as they aged, and the Navajo children loved that. The bars would be ripe for eating by next summer.

Smiley kept his head down the entire time he was restocking Logan's shelves. It was good that he did, as a few Navajo men entered the post looking for a fight. They would not be able to match Smiley's physical strength, but they were mad at the white man's rules and size wasn't a factor here—numbers were. The Candy Man watched his back as he squeezed into the cab of his truck and quickly left the post. He wasn't interested in spending any more time on the reservation today than need be. He hoped Logan would be OK.

Since he was ahead of schedule, Smiley decided on an early lunch overlooking a large patch of white cliffs that were off the beaten path. He knew the back roads on this part of the reservation well, spending many days after work searching for prehistoric artifacts, which were plentiful. The Navajo didn't care if you removed an old pot or arrowheads from their lands—they looked at the stuff as bad medicine—so, when time allowed, Smiley would park his truck out of sight and search the nearby cliffs for caches of pots.

The location of his midday meal had a panoramic view with Shiprock peeking out in the distance, and the Chuska mountaintops, tipped in a splash of yellow, to the west. Only sheep, cattle, deer, and the occasional mountain lion roamed in this remote area.

Smiley stuffed his red and white transistor radio into his pocket, slung his worn knapsack over his shoulder, and hiked up to a flat ridge with a beautiful overlook. When he reached the top of the white stone outcropping, he sat down, popped open an illegal Pabst Blue Ribbon beer, and balanced it precariously on a semi-flat stone while he retrieved a soggy peanut butter and jelly sandwich and two bags of crushed chips—spoils of the job—from his pack.

Hands almost as large as a baseball gloves fished out the radio and fumbled with the two small, black-plastic knobs. When he found his favorite non-Indian radio station, he turned the music up loud. The sound of clapping hands echoed along the ridge as Chubby Checker started singing, "Come on, let's twist again...." Smiley stood up, sandwich in hand, and started twisting to the new song on the whiterock platform. He took a huge bite of his sandwich and immediately felt better about life, twisting and swallowing simultaneously. A swig of the beer helped ramp up his movements.

"Do you remember...."

Smiley tried to sing along, but the peanut butter stuck to his upper palate, making him laugh at the absurdity. But the song was infectious: "Twisting time is where... I mean here!"

Laughing and gasping for air, he took another big hit of beer, and unclogged a chunk of peanut butter and white bread that hurt as it went down. For the first time that day, Smiley quit feeling sorry for himself, with a lousy boss and dead-end job. He had big plans to become a leader in his field, if he could only get an education and get away from Gallup's thumb of mediocrity. Of course, he would have to figure out what his field might be....

A creaking noise broke through Smiley's inner happiness. His heart, already racing from his wild twisting dance, began pounding faster.

"What the hell?" he said to himself, already knowing the answer. He instinctively crouched low on the open ridge, knocking over the stone balancing his precious beer as he reached to turn off the radio.

"God damn it," he cursed as he righted the can, its precious liquid disappearing into deep cracks in the earth. Then he heard another sound, one he recognized: the creaky back door of his truck closing. Someone was in his vehicle!

Smiley didn't know what to do. He was over six-feet, three-inches tall, and two years of lifting boxes had developed his physical strength. But now there was an unknown entity in his truck, parked in the middle of nowhere. Had someone been stalking him?

"Possibly Navajos out for frontier justice," he thought.

Logan had warned him to be careful today. Smiley stuffed his radio in his pocket, swigged the last of the beer for added courage, then crushed the can with his hand so it would fit in his front pocket. Hugging the curve of the rock for cover, he made his way back to the candy truck. He had the vehicle's keys in his pocket, so it was unlikely anyone could steal the truck. If they were looking for a fight, he was going to give them one. He grabbed a large, dead juniper branch to show he was serious. Smiley might have despised his jackass boss, but those chips and candy were his responsibility; he was the Candy Man, and no one was going to screw with his load.

CHAPTER 28

YOU'RE OUT!

Smiley crept down the ridge, trying to avoid any loose stones, his heavy work boots making the task nearly impossible. He grimaced with every cracking stick and displaced rock; each sound might betray his position.

When he finally got close enough, he could see that the truck's back door was ajar; someone or something was in the back of the vehicle, his sugar-laced load in peril. Smiley was sure he had shut the door firmly when he retrieved the two bags of chips before heading to his ridge restaurant reservation for one. Maybe it was nothing more than a ground squirrel helping itself to corn nuts; he crept closer and paused to listen.

The sounds were not those of a rodent. He could hear a cardboard box being ripped open and candy bars being stuffed into some kind of scratchy material, maybe a bag or a pants pocket. Smiley gripped the branch stick firmly in his right hand and threw the door open with his left, jumping into the back of the truck bed as if he were stealing home base.

"Get the hell out of my truck," he screamed as he leaped.

The intruder jumped straight into the air, hit his head on the roof of the truck, and crumpled to the ground. A preteen boy lay there, visibly shaking, his pants pockets stuffed with Big Hunk candy bars, Cracker Jacks, and hard candies.

The boy let out a scream and tried to crawl past Smiley, but the kid didn't get far. Smiley reached out with his left arm and scooped up the boy like a net scooping up minnows. The Navajo boy fought hard, kicking his little legs and wind-milling his arms to get free. Smiley tightened his grip until it hurt and the kid melted into a puddle in his arms.

"What the hell are you doing in my truck stealing my candy?"

The boy didn't answer; he just stared at the large man, more with anger than fear. The look surprised Smiley, and he shouted louder: "You heard me, boy. Why are you stealing candy and what the hell are you doing out in the backcountry alone? You are alone, aren't you?"

Smiley realizing at that moment that he might be in real trouble and twisted around, still holding onto the boy, to face the open door of the truck. Would someone else come to the kid's rescue? There was still no answer, so he applied a little more pressure to the boy's chest with his large arm, the force causing the boy to gasp for air.

"Stop, please," the boy pleaded. "You're hurting me. I'm alone, running from the yellow squash."

"You mean the Indian school bus down at Toadlena?"

"Yes. I was suppose to leave my family today, but I would rather die than go to school. Those white men forced my dad to boarding school, I won't go."

"Kid, I can't say if that's a good or bad decision, but you and your family are going to get in big trouble if you are truant. Do you know what 'truant' means?"

"No."

"Truant means if you don't go to school they can put you in a worse place than school, the white man's jail—and you don't want that, do you?"

"Both are jails, one is no worse than the other."

Smiley considered the statement and realized that from what he had heard about the Indian school near Gallup, the kid might have a point. But he was also pretty sure that running away from the school was against the law—and stealing his candy definitely was.

"Your folks know you're gone?"

"My dad didn't know for sure when he woke up, but he does now, and he's fine with me leaving."

"Hell, kid, you're going to put your poor dad out of his mind with worry. Here's what going to happen: I'm going to take you home and you can work it out with your family. And I will forget you stole my candy."

The boy looked up as the hulking man bent down and bit Smiley's forearm with all his might.

"AHHH, you little shit! I'm going to kick your butt," Smiley screamed, as he automatically released his grip on the boy, shaking his injured arm violently. The boy broke free from Smiley as bright blood flowed from his captor's arm.

The young Navajo made a jackrabbit leap out of the truck, leaving a trail of candy in his wake as he ran toward a nearby arroyo. Smiley jumped out of the truck and saw a giant cellophane-wrapped blue jawbreaker lying in the dirt next to the vehicle—part of the kid's plunder. He reflexively picked up the apricot-sized candy and heaved it at the kid with all his might, yelling, "Kid, I'm going to kill you when we meet again!"

Amazingly, the jawbreaker found its mark, hitting the child squarely in the small of the back and knocking him off his feet, the force causing the boy to tumble down the adjacent wash.

Smiley yelled again: "All right, one for the good guys. You better get up fast, kid, cause I'm coming after you."

The Candy Man ran full tilt to where the boy had fallen. It was payback time, and he was going to scare the living bejesus out of him before he turned him over to his folks. He expected to see the kid getting up, crying, when he reached the edge of the wash—but the boy was lying face down in the dirt.

Smiley stopped, his expression shifting from one of anger to deep concern: the kid wasn't moving.

"Hey, kid, get up. Don't screw with me, and no more biting. I just want to take you to your dad." No sound or movement came from the boy.

Smiley slid down the chalk-colored embankment of the ravine and stood over the boy's body, his shadow covering the child's motionless head. The cranium told the story: the boy's head had landed on a small, triangular gray stone—the only stone visible in the sea of brown soft sand running the length of the wash. The lone rock had witnessed millennia of heavy runoff and wind, yet held its position in the deep Navajo earth, waiting silently to punish wrongdoers.

The rock was the proverbial tip of the iceberg, but this wasn't the *Titanic* sinking with fifteen hundred lost souls on board. This tragedy only involved two: Smiley and a dark-skinned boy whose beautiful shoulder-length hair was now glistening with a bright red color.

Smiley truly had not meant to hurt the boy; throwing the jawbreaker had been a reflex reaction of sorts. Yes, he had aimed for the boy's back and hit the target dead center, but not to kill—just to stop him from running, or maybe pay the kid back for his severely throbbing arm. It was not a premeditated act of murder. How could he know the jawbreaker would hit with such deadly force that it would cause the child to fall and roll down the slope to find the one submerged boulder in the ravine, a life-changing rock of doom?

In full panic mode, Smiley started shaking the boy violently, yelling, "Kid, kid, wake up. I'm sorry you hit your head. I didn't mean for you to get hurt."

As he shook the boy, blood from his own wound dripped onto the kid's shirt and hair. When Smiley rolled him over, he could see the impact of the devastating blow. The beautiful face of the child had been split open. Tumbling down the hill had been hard, and the shape of the rock acted like a wedge splitting firewood. The unmovable force had stopped the boy's momentum, killing him instantaneously.

Smiley stood up, trying to come to grips with the macabre scene and the crumpled body sprawled out in front of him. What now? His mind worked overtime trying to play out the possibilities—all of which were dire—as he realized he had dripped his own blood over the dead boy's body.

The magnitude of the situation slowly sunk in. He had killed a child, some would say murdered him, over what?—a few bars of candy? He played it all back in his head. "I'm going to kill you." He had said those words. He didn't mean them, but if it somehow came out in court, along with the fact that he was his high school's leading baseball pitcher, his specialty the fastball, he was toast. No doubt he would be found guilty—and maybe he was? His strict father and probably the rest of the Smiley family would completely disown him.

Smiley collapsed in a heap next to the child and gently turned the boy face down in the blood-soaked sand, unable to face the child's death stare. He gently stroked the back of the boy's hair with his hand and sobbed. His torrential tears were for both of them: his life and the child's family's life had been irrevocably altered by the single, stupid act of throwing a jawbreaker in anger.

Smiley needed a plan of action, but at that moment all he could muster was grief and regret. He was no longer on a good trajectory; an evil force had pushed him off his path, and his life might never return to normal again.

CHAPTER 29

FINAL RESTING PLACE

An hour passed, each minute stabbing at Smiley's heart as he mourned the tragic turn of events. Standing and raising his eyes toward the crystal-blue heavens, he said in a monotone: "God, I am sorry for this boy's death. I swear it was an accident. You must give me a chance to redeem myself. It was a horrific sin and I'm afraid my evil ways are not yet over. Please find it in your heart to pity me and let me succeed in life. I promise not to fail you."

Smiley gingerly picked up the remains of someone's loving son and tossed the small child over his shoulder as effortlessly as if the body were a bag of flour. The boy's long, bloody black hair dangled at Smiley's waist as his assailant began walking west down the soft sand wash. Droplets of fresh blood and fat globules—the cookie crumbs left behind by a departed human—dribbled off the straight, coarse hair onto the sand, leaving a distinct map of Smiley's route.

Fortunately, this part of the reservation was well known to the Candy Man and he knew exactly where he could find an eternal resting spot for his young victim. Isolated, low caves abounded on this mesa; he had once found a 16th century Sikyátki pot in one. A place that until recently had held its secrets for over 400 years would hopefully hold one more, and for as long a period as a protohistoric pot cache. Finding the Hopi vessel carefully wedged in the back of the earthen structure—as if the jar had been left just that day by its maker—was a wondrous moment for Smiley. The disc-shaped ceramic was a rich yellow color, its condition pristine; no natural elements had ever reached this far into the hidden dirt fortress.

The crevice was four miles from the nearest dirt road and deep into Navajo lands. Ironically, it was only a few miles away from Smiley's favorite place. He wondered if this would now be sacred land for him, too, as it was for the Navajo and Hopi. He would never again be able to visit this remarkable geologic structure that had once made him so happy. He remembered exactly where it was and how to get into it. The last ten feet required him to crawl in on all fours, making it an ideal place for rattlesnakes to cool from the heat of an early September day.

The dead boy was now reduced to a lump of meat, soulless and losing heat quickly, his life-giving blood reduced to a red trickle. Smiley dragged his rag-doll victim the last fifty feet along the fine silt floor of the hidden cave. Reaching his destination, he took out his cigarette lighter and illuminated the deep hole. He was glad he smoked and had the lighter available for some light. A five-foot western diamondback was contently curled up in the furthest cool corner, too far away to strike at him and of no concern for now—but he would keep a close eye on his new-found guardian of the dead.

Smiley removed all of the boy's clothing and bundled the garments. He slipped a small silver ring from the child's left index finger and stuck it in his front pants pocket next to his radio, which just an hour before had been playing his favorite new song. Now it was time to mold the child's body into a fetal position. Working his way down the tight crevice, he positioned the boy on the ground directly in front of him. He took off his heavy boots and lay down on his back. His stocking feet gave him a better feel and would not leave any marks in case the child was discovered sooner than he hoped—a Perry Mason case was playing in his head.

As he pushed the body as far into the structure as possible, a loud buzz filled the tight chamber when the body touched the back wall. Mr. Diamondback was not appreciating his newest bedmate. The snake's dissonant tones told Smiley his job was complete. The rest was up to god, nature, and hopefully not the tribal police.

In the Navajo world, the rattlesnake is both a protector and strong medicine that can be used to witch someone. Smiley had been around the Diné long enough to recognize that the presence of the snake could be a very dangerous omen, so he decided to say another prayer.

"Oh, Holy Ones of the Navajos, please protect this poor soul who died too young and let him rest in peace in the next world with his ancestors. I will not harm your friend the rattlesnake; please tell him not to harm me. Amen."

Smiley backed out of the crevice, boots in hand, his body covered in sand and sticky drops of blood. Once out in the hot sun, he put on his boots and looked at his arm: it was still oozing blood and hurt like hell.

He cradled the boy's clothes under his massive right arm, before setting the garments on a stone outside the newly minted crypt. He then started scavenging for heavy, flat stones to close up the entryway and make it a proper Navajo grave. He promised the gods that no coyotes would defile this body. He would leave a small opening so the snake could escape, but coyotes couldn't break into the boy's tomb.

If the body were discovered, he hoped the finders would assume it was an old Navajo or Anasazi grave; there were many of those throughout the Navajo reservation. If it were Navajos who discovered the place, they would avoid the grave out of fear of the evil *chindi*.

Three hours of heavy labor was required to close up the small vault. A slight smile crossed Smiley face as he looked at his masonry job; there were no gaps other than a three-inch escape route for the snake. His smile quickly turned to a frown as he realized his craftsmanship was helping to hide a capital murder, not building a retaining wall. This act of deception insured that any chance of an accidental death verdict was now impossible. Watching all those Perry Mason episodes had taught him that he was now responsible for his actions, a murderer in the eyes of the law as well as his own. The thought sent a chill down his spine. He would have to clean up around the crime scene and remove any remaining evidence around his truck. He needed a solid alibi and a story he could stick to if asked.

Smiley headed back to his truck and fashioned a cleaning device of sorts out of the child's shirt and a juniper branch, wiping away the blood trail as he retraced his footsteps. The child's clothing would be burned so there would be no chance it could be used as evidence: he would visit a favorite backwoods campfire tonight.

Even with the best planning, though, all crime scenes harbor clues. In Smiley's case, it was a small cellophane-wrapped purple jawbreaker that had slipped out of the kid's pocket when his clothes were removed. The candy fell unnoticed into the last millennium's accumulation of fine sand. This key piece of evidence could be a killer's undoing, a clue that would not stay hidden forever.

CHAPTER 30

HEAT STROKE

Smiley skipped two of the smaller posts on his route, barely making it to his last big buyer as the sun dipped below the horizon. The trading post owner had waited thirty minutes longer than usual, knowing the Candy Man would eventually show up.

The human bite throbbed unmercifully after Smiley unloaded the last two boxes of the day, using his good left arm to open the tops. He covered the wound with a semi-clean T-shirt and donned a ragged paisley long-sleeved shirt from his toolbox to hide his bad wing. It was hot for early September, and Smiley was afraid the heavy garment might catch attention, but decided it was less risky than a blood-soaked makeshift bandage.

Smiley pulled into Gallup two hours late. He knew Perry Mason would be livid, but stopped outside of town anyway to ditch the kid's clothes before rolling into the dark lot. Mason was pacing the loading dock. The Candy Man could hear his cranky boss complaining as he backed in: "Goddam it, Smiley. You sure as shit better have a good excuse for being this damned late. My dinner is as cold as a witch's titty and my wife won't be happy."

Smiley knew his boss well enough to know a cross-examination would be forthcoming, so he had prepared and practiced an alibi.

"I know. I'm sorry, boss."

"What the hell put you in this late?"

"Got a good start today and I was running ahead, so I took the time to eat an early lunch. I pulled off on a little dirt road and damn if I didn't get stuck in one of those monsoon mud holes. It was way deeper than it looked. Anyway, I didn't want to leave the truck to get help; you never know who might come by for free food or tires or something. So I used my dad's army spade and dug her out. By the time I got free I was over two hours late. But I did manage to get an extra order of Big Hunks from Toadlena."

"Big Hunks? You think that's going to take the edge off my mood or make my dinner warm again?"

"No, sir. I just thought...."

"You're not paid to think, Smiley, you're paid to get my goddamn candy and chips to the vendors on time and not take lunch breaks in the boondocks."

"I understand Mr. Mason. It won't happen again, I promise."

"I know it won't, because if it does, your ass is toast and you can take your good-for-nothing spade back to your salesman dad and start washing junkers again."

"Yes, sir. I like my job, and I don't want to do that. I'm sorry."

"You screw up my axle or oil pan when you buried her?" Mason asked, getting down on his knees in the dark to see if there were any damage to the truck.

"No, sir. I was careful. There are no problems; she's running tip-top. Do you want to take her out for spin to see?"

"No, I don't. Go punch out. You're costing me even more money jawing out here. I'm going to take two hours off your paycheck. You better be on time tomorrow. And what's with the long-sleeve shirt? Hell, it's damn near 100 degrees."

Smiley had hoped Mason wouldn't notice the shirt, but apparently the TV show had improved the old man's observational skills. But he was prepared for all possible lines of questioning.

"Well, sir, I think I might have gotten a little sun stroke out there digging in the heat. Got chills and couldn't get warm or stop shivering. Strangest thing you ever seen...."

Mason knew this was not a good sign and that his idiot deliveryman might have actually gotten himself seriously hurt, so he abruptly changed his tone. A workman's comp claim was the last thing he needed.

"OK, maybe. You better get some water and drink a lot, and for god's sake get out of the heat. Come in around noon tomorrow. I'll have you do the short route."

Smiley kept his head down, not wanting his boss to see his slight grin, the first ray of happiness he had experienced in six hours. He would go get some peroxide, salve, and a proper cotton wrap for his arm, clean his wound, then retrieve the kid's clothes and burn them. There was a lot to think about. His life had changed and nothing would ever be the same.

Flaps of flesh in odd jigsaw configurations were the result of the human bite. Ugly scars would be a constant reminder of his dastardly deed; he was a child killer on the loose. Smiley couldn't chance getting stitches; only time could close up the wounds the boy had made.

The young Navajo's teeth had never seen braces. Each tooth mark, at forty-five degree angles, told the story. Smiley used a peroxide solution to bath the laceration, the bubbles confirming its effectiveness. He repeated the process until only a small amount of solution sloshed in the bottom of the bottle.

A wave of panic rushed over Smiley as he stared at his clean arm. "What if the kid had seen a dentist and had fillings?" It was a chink in Smiley's defense; no Anasazi skeleton would have modern dental work. As the panic passed, Smiley relaxed. With dentition this poor it was unlikely the kid had ever seen the inside of a dentist office. His pulse slowed and he took a deep breath, then wrapped the arm tightly with gauze.

A bundle of the child's clothes and the tiny silver ring lay next to the medical supplies in Smiley's small trailer. The clothes would disappear tonight in a fire of redemption, but he would keep the ring, not as a trophy, but as a reminder of his deed, a cross he must bear.

His "I've got sun stroke" ploy would only work for so long, and he could see just two choices for his next steps: call his boss, quit, and simply walk away and wait for his wounds to heal—or come up with a plan to explain the bandage and hope there weren't too many questions.

Smiley prayed for a cool snap. The calendar might say fall, but the temperature still said summer. The aspens were changing at the top of the Chuskas, so cool weather must be close at hand. He had no extra money and the rent for his small metal crackerbox was due in less than two weeks, so he couldn't afford to be unemployed. There were few jobs in Gallup and none on the rez.

He considered different ways he could explain the bulky bandage, finally landing on roughhousing with his neighbor's dog, Pepper. He could say that things got out of hand and the usually good-natured dog bit him. It was no big deal, just done in play, and the dog's vaccinations were up to date.

Smiley had played Harold Hill, the lead in his high school play *The Music Man*, so he could sound convincing: "Don't blame the dog. It's my fault for riling the old boy up. I'm current on my tetanus shot, so there's no need to worry."

Finishing his wound care and having decided on a plan of action, Smiley started to feel a tinge of relief. Soon he would be back to normal and the weather would turn in his favor. He could switch to long sleeves and avoid preying eyes while the wound healed. By the time spring came, it would be a distant memory.

There was the real possibility of infection. He had once read an article that said that human teeth were dirtier than a dog's mouth—a headline to sell papers, he hoped, not one based on medical fact. If his arm did get infected, though, he would have to seek medical treatment. An Albuquerque doctor would be his best bet, far away from the Gallup gossip train. He could change the story to fit the circumstances: "A party brawl got out control and some drunk asshole bit me." He didn't want a record of the injury, but he also didn't want to lose an important limb to gangrene. It was his pitching arm, and one never knew when the big leagues might call.

Smiley's favorite radio station no longer played the latest dance music. He was now tuned to KTNM AM 660, the Voice of the Navajo Nation, looking for news about a runaway. Who was this child he had accidently killed and left for the ages?

Delivering his goods over the next few days would be perilous. Thanks to Perry Mason, he knew that most homicide cases were solved within the first week. Fear filled Smiley's mind as made his usual rounds. The Candy Man was scared, and scared men are dangerous.

CHAPTER 31

NEVER GIVE UP

Radio silence on the missing kid broke open on day three.

"Ricky Begay, an eleven-year-old runaway, has not been seen since Monday." The announcer repeated the report every thirty minutes in broken English—Amber Alert rez-style, 1961.

The story became more explosive after an interview with the child's father, Orville Begay. The story was in Navajo, so Smiley could not understand what was said, but the message was unmistakable: the distressed man was desperately looking for help finding his son. Unfortunately for Mr. Begay, only Smiley could respond to his pleas, and the Candy Man was never going to talk. But hearing the distress in the father's voice brought Smiley to tears—he was a monster.

The day the news first aired, Smiley donned a light, long sleeved-shirt, a paisley pattern that he wore over a blue T-shirt. Left unbuttoned, it looked like a work shirt, with worn cuffs and two missing buttons. In fact, it was his "going fishing" shirt.

"A sunburn," he would say if anyone asked. People would be on the lookout for anything out of the ordinary, especially from a *bilagáana*, even a harmless Candy Man. Smiley began to nibble at the edges of the rez for additional information. His first stop was the Toadlena Trading Post. Orville Begay lived five miles from the post and would use the place as his community gathering spot. Old man Logan, the owner, would know as much—if not more—about the missing boy and his father than the police.

"Hi, Mr. Logan. You need the usual?"

"Actually, I need more Fritos. The locals are upset about Orville Begay's missing son. I reckon the nervous eating is good for me, but very bad for our community."

"Yeah. I heard about that. What do you think happened?"

"I've heard about ten different stories. The one that sounds most reasonable came from Ricky's great aunt. She told me the kid was running away to his winter sheep camp to avoid going to Indian boarding school, and that Orville Begay knew this, but waited a few days before breaking the story. He figured he could find Ricky on his own, but when it became hopeless he called in the tribal police."

"What do the police think?" Smiley probed.

"No word from our local tribal authorities yet."

"Maybe the kid ran away from a bad home life. It happens out here," Smiley said, trying to plant the seeds of other possibilities.

"Not a chance. Orville Begay is a standup guy and a great father. Little Ricky was his only family; his wife died in childbirth. If anything, he probably cared too much. He hated the thought of his only child being sent off to boarding school for months at a time."

"So what do you think happened? The kid couldn't just disappear into thin air...."

"I don't know, Smiley. I hear people saying Shapeshifters steal kids as punishment for past deeds. If I had to guess, I'd think Ricky might have fallen into a crevice, or maybe a lion snagged him. Whatever happened, it can't be good."

"That's too bad. If I hear anything on my route, I'll let you know."

"Please do. Orville's going out of his mind. That man will never give up looking for his son. He'll search the damn reservation acre by acre to find an answer."

"How do you know that?" Smiley asked, trying not to sound too concerned.

"Ever since the story of his son's disappearance went public, he shows up as soon as the post opens. He buys a sandwich, a bag of peanuts, and a bottle of Coke—and here's the sad part—he gets one Big Hunk in case he finds his son. It's a way of counting days, I think. Then he rides off on his old roan."

"Gone all day?" Smiley asked, trying his best to sound concerned for the man.

"So far as I can tell he searches all day. The best I can figure is that he's methodically investigating every crevice and slot canyon, and he won't quit until he gets to the family's winter sheep camp on Chuska Mountain. Then I would guess he'll start the process all over again. He's a driven man, always has been."

Smiley gulped, hearing this news. "Anybody helping him? It seems like a big task for one man...."

"Besides the Navajo police, who aren't doing squat as far as I can tell, most folks are afraid of a Shapeshifter wanting retribution. Seems like this is something Orville must do alone."

"Hard to believe someone isn't helping him...."

"Smiley, I've been here a long time and it's not that folks aren't worried for Orville or his son—but Navajos are afraid of death. They know that's what's waiting at the end of his journey, and they don't want to be the ones to find a dead body. They figure that's a job for the police, and Orville understands this."

"Well, I'm sorry to hear about his troubles. It's amazing to see a dad who cares so much about a son." Smiley's closed facial expression belied his own dysfunctional father-son relationship.

"Yeah, it's going to be hard on everyone. Begay lives not far from the post, and with no family left in the area, I'm guessing he'll be here a lot. Tough times ahead, I'm afraid. Those damned Indian schools aren't good for nobody, no how. Why can't those big shots in Washington figure out that they hurt more than they help?"

Smiley nodded in agreement, but his head was spinning. "He never gives up?" What should he do next? His throbbing arm brought his mind back to the present. Was there an infection setting in? A ghostly human bite filled with sugar from a past life Big Hunks was returning to haunt him.

Smiley had been sleeping fitfully since the boy's death, his mind racing from images of Ricky's makeshift grave to being shackled and dragged off to prison. He could think of three possible options:

1) Run! Head to Mexico and never look back. Maybe he could come back in five years or so if it all blew over.

2) Do nothing and hope he wasn't found out. If Begay discovered that grave, he was probably sunk. The crevice he left the body in was isolated, but a driven man with local knowledge would ultimately find the crypt—and something there would tie him to the murder. There weren't many suspects to choose from, and he was the white one. He had taken the boy's clothes off, so the jury would probably think he was a child molester; it would be the electric chair. The "Perry Mason" show had taught Smiley that all criminals leave behind evidence, no matter how smart they think they are.

3) The last, and the most unthinkable, option: eliminate the problem, Orville Begay.

Smiley decided to shadow the bereaved father before deciding what to do. Time was running out.

CHAPTER 32

WICKED FASTBALL

Smiley needed a few days off to focus on the task at hand, and delivering candy was not on the agenda. He approached Mr. Mason complaining that he was still feeling weak from the sunstroke and, in fact, Smiley didn't look well. He was pale, sweating, and running a low-grade fever. The condition of his injured arm was tentative at best. The wound had festered on one end, and was oozing a yellow fluid that smelled like cowhide being tanned. The red edges of the bite had formed a large scab, an overripe plum waiting to burst. The entire forearm was tender and, even worse, a small red line was creeping up from the perimeter of the wound toward his armpit. Smiley wasn't sure how much longer he could go without medical attention.

Mr. Mason, who had once been nearly sued by a disgruntled employee, turned to his favorite television show for advice. His doppelgänger, the actor Raymond Burr, convinced him though his weekly court case that he would be in jeopardy if Smiley died from his work-related sunstroke injury—so he relented.

"Sure, Smiley. Take a few days off if you need it. In fact, take the whole week. Get lots of rest and drink a lot of water—but don't drink any alcohol. That could make you worse."

Smiley assured his boss he would take care of himself and would be better by next week and turned over the keys to the company vehicle. Mason documented the exchange in his business log; one never could be too careful.

Hiding his truck on an isolated dirt road west of the Toadlena Trading Post, Smiley climbed the back mountain trails. From his vantage point on a flat ridge overlooking the Toadlena Basin and a deep ravine, he could see the comings and goings of all the post's visitors.

Begay galloped up the dirt road from the northwest on a reddish Navajo horse and hitched the reins to the broken post railing before heading inside; it was 9 a.m. on the dot. Five minutes later, he walked out with a small brown grocery sack that he tucked into the horse's saddlebags, then remounted and headed due east. Smiley watched Begay until he was almost out of sight, focusing on his prey with his father's old army binoculars. He could see the small horse halt near Tsinnie Butte. Begay appeared to dismount and begin what Smiley assumed was the day's search.

"Why the horse?" Smiley wondered. Surely the man had a truck. Most Navajos used trucks these days. Maybe the animal grounded him to the land and slowed his pace so he didn't miss anything? Whatever the reason, riding horseback would make Begay's search slow and methodical, which could be an advantage if Smiley chose option three—which he was leaning toward.

Smiley left his Chuska Mountain vantage point and headed toward the twin towers of the Toadlena Basin just east of the post. He would take a dirt road north, then head west once he was clear of Orville Begay. The rez was sparsely populated but its communication system was very active. There was a third eye that watched everything, especially with rumors of a Shapeshifter haunting the land. The Candy Man wanted to eliminate any chances of being seen, by Begay or any other preying eyes.

A large outcropping of fading petroglyph-pecked rocks was the perfect place to set up watch, and it didn't take long to spot Begay. The man was on foot, methodically examining every rock, bit of disturbed ground, and small crevice—even the trees.

Begay called out his son's name in Navajo every ten minutes. "Ricky, Ricky. It's me, Father!" The palpable pain in his voice was haunting. Maybe, Smiley thought, he would be doing the man a favor by ending his grief. Watching him stop and dig with a small spade for forty-five minutes told the story of the man's angst and perseverance.

The pattern didn't take long to establish. Begay would plant his horse, walk east for a half-mile, go a quarter-mile north, then turn west to walk back, collect his pony and advance his position north by a quarter of a mile. Then he would repeat the process. The man was methodical, covering about three miles a day. Unfortunately for both men, he was on the right path. At this rate, Begay would discover his son's crypt in three days or less.

The sun was hot for late fall, and Smiley felt faint; he took a long swig of a sugar- and salt-water concoction, a drink he had discovered during long summer baseball games. The sugar gave him energy and the salt seemed to help replenish what was lost through sweat. Sunstroke would never get Smiley, but at that moment he wished it would. Realizing his predicament, he began to sob, a new phenomenon since Ricky's death. Smiley had never been one for emotion—he was the closer for his baseball team—but something had changed in the last week, a weakness had emerged. He lowered his head into his oversized hands and cried for five minutes. When the tears subsided, reason, and the closer's mindset, returned.

"OK, Smiley. Get a grip on yourself. You know what has to be done. You're not going to run and you're not going to just wait out the inevitable. There is only one choice, and it's number three. I have to kill Orville Begay, and it needs to look like an accident. A missing son and a missing father would be too much of a coincidence, and the feds might get involved."

But how and when would he do it? No clear plan had yet emerged. He must find the right place, one that would make the "accident" look plausible and where it would take passersby or the police a few days to discover the body. The longer it took to find Orville Begay's corpse, the better.

Smiley had a huge advantage. He understood Begay's search pattern, so all he needed to do was figure out where and how to ambush the grieving father. As he considered his options, he jammed a huge jawbreaker into his cheek. The massive candy rock took up his entire mouth, making him feel like a chipmunk packed with piñon nuts for winter. As he sucked and caressed the global lump of sugar with his tongue, trying not to choke, he had an epiphany.

The plan was wacky, but Smiley could pull it off once he found the right setting. He smiled for the first time in nearly a week. His overextended cheek hurt. He spit the huge candy treat into his hand and tossed it up and down, gauging the ball's weight. It was perfect. Smiley may not have made the pros, but his arm was as good as most in the big leagues. The scouts had watched him in action and told his high school coach, "Your boy's got a wicked fastball, but nothing more, and the big leagues need that something else. Otherwise he's just another kid with a screaming fastball."

A well-thrown object had started Smiley's cascade of troubles; another would be his way out.

"You're right, Mr. Big-Shot-Scout. I only got that fastball, but it's a hell of a good one, and amazingly accurate. You should have drafted me and seen what I could have done. I would have slain them." Smiley smiled grimly at his black humor, then dusted off his pants, wiped the last of the tears from his eyes, and headed to his truck. He would cry no more.

Later tonight he would secure the perfect kill zone, and tomorrow he would take care of business. He was once again the closer. The moon was full and he was sure the gods were with him. But what kind of gods protected the murderer of a father and child?

A long line of cliffs covered with well-preserved petroglyphs and alcoves carved into the steep stone faces were accessible by a good horseman. It was an ideal habitat for mountain lions. At this point in the search, Begay must have figured that his son had become a food source and he would be checking the high places for a lion's den. The largest mountain lion in the southwest had come off the nearby Chuska Mountains and was the size of a female African lion. Ricky Begay wouldn't have had a chance if an animal of this magnitude had run across the boy on the run. Orville Begay must have been using his spade to look for a lion's kill hidden in the dirt, a grim proposition for a father to face.

Smiley was sure Begay would check this higher area if he hadn't already. He figured that for the first three days, the man had made a wide, fast search looking at the most probable places. When he called in the tribal police, he had given up hope of finding his son alive, and was now on a detailed cadaver hunt. Begay would reach the highest cliff point in mid to late afternoon. It was the perfect place for him to end his search for the day.

The nearest decent dirt road Smiley could use to stash his truck was a little under a four-mile hike away. The kill spot he thought of as "ambush rock" was a group of large boulders that were precariously balanced on a steep cliff, with an animal path along the edge. Begay would undoubtedly guide his horse along this ridge.

Smiley brought additional supplies with him in case his plan didn't materialize as he hoped, or if he had to spend the night on the ridge: a sandwich, canteen, three oversized jaw breakers in cellophane wrappers, a fifteen-foot rope, a razor-sharp buck knife, a ratty Pendleton blanket, a fold-up army spade, and a handmade broom that would help wipe away all traces of his presence in the area. There must be no prints left behind but those of Begay and his horse. Smiley couldn't risk having the bereaved father see recent human activity in such an isolated area.

He used the blanket to bundle all the gear and slung this over his right shoulder; his father's .30-06 was over his left side. Part of him wanted to set his father up as the killer to pay him back for all the mental anguish he had caused him when he was growing up.

The late September morning brought the first dusting of frost; the chill was magnified by Smiley's low-grade fever. His arm ached, and he hoped he was up to the task. The full moon was setting as he settled in. The faint halo of clouds outlining the golden hue was a sign of an approaching storm front.

Smiley set up camp and locked his scope into the spot he would use to fire the rifle if things deteriorated. Killing the man by shooting him was a last resort, and he had no back-up plan for disposing of the body. He couldn't let his mind go there.

The Candy Man unwrapped two of the three purple jawbreakers and stuffed the flimsy cellophane into his back pocket. When he stood up to stretch, a morning breeze whisked one of the wrappers into a small, but deep, crevice. Smiley watched the silvery covering float away and considered retrieving it, but that would take energy he didn't possess. His fever was sapping his strength and he figured trash on the rez was unlikely to be of any concern, even to the cops.

The two apricot-sized jawbreakers, minus their cellophane wrappings, were lined up on the ledge ready for action. Smiley picked up the nearest jawbreaker and nervously tossed it up and down, gauging the weight as he waited for Begay's horse to come into view. The dense candy felt like a hard ball, and with each toss of the candy he felt his confidence grow. When he placed the jawbreaker back on the ledge, he looked at his hand: it was a plummy red. The sweat from his hands had melted a bit of the sweet treat's covering, the white sugar inner core peeking through.

"A sign of things to come," he thought, as he wiped his hand clean on his pants leg.

Four hours passed; Smiley's eyes were starting to tire from looking through the scope when he spotted some dust, then the muscular roan horse. Begay! Smiley's hand was sweating even more now than it was before. His whole body was drenched. He wiped another large streak of purplish-red on his pants as he wrapped his hand around his rock-hard weapon. He stretched his arm nervously, as if he were getting ready to take the mound. The moment of reckoning was near.

Begay was a quarter of mile away when he pulled on the reins and dismounted. The obedient animal stopped in its tracks on the precarious path, and waited for his master. The winds were in Smiley's favor; the horse appeared calm. After about five minutes Begay reappeared from a small cave, brushed off some fine dust, remounted his stead and started down the path directly toward Smiley. There was a large, deep alcove not twenty-five feet from Smiley's position.

He knew Begay would explore the area, focusing on what might lie inside and not on what might be ahead.

Years of hunting deer from a stand had taught Smiley the importance of stealth and patience. He controlled his breathing, trying not to make any sound; his victim was close by. His rifle was loaded, safety off, if his plan went south.

Begay pulled up on the reins. As the little horse slowed to a stop and the rider started to swing off his saddle once more, Smiley stood up and hurled the jawbreaker, hitting the horse squarely in the rump—exactly where he had aimed. The horse kicked his back legs fiercely, and then bucked straight up. Amazingly, Begay hung on to the horse's back and the reins, trying to reel in his horse, But the animal lost its footing—as Smiley had anticipated—and cartwheeled down the steep, rocky ravine, rolling twice over Begay before landing in an animal-human heap at the bottom of the incline.

Smiley's heart was pounding in his chest, and his right arm was throbbing. The monumental throw had ripped his wound wide open, coating the inside of his light windbreaker with a shower of pus and blood. He grabbed his rifle, finger on the trigger, and pointed the scope toward the mass of human and horseflesh. What he saw was pitiful. Begay wasn't moving. The horse's legs were broken and the animal was making horrific cries of pain that shocked Smiley more than Begay's lifeless body.

Satisfied his victim was immobilized, Smiley slung his gun over his shoulder, picked up the broom and shoved it into his back pocket, slowly making his way down the treacherous slope. When he arrived at the bottom, he could see Begay was not dead, but probably wished that he were. The leg still locked in the stirrup was pointing in a ninety-degree angle from his body, and bone was showing. Bright red foam was flowing from the Navajo's mouth. He was desperately trying to breathe, both lungs damaged, the shallow movements of his chest telling the story. The man was fatally injured; death would come soon.

Begay's eyes were wide open, and he stared up at the monster that had just killed his horse, himself, and, he assumed, his son.

"Why?" His words sprayed fine blood into the air.

Smiley didn't know what to say. What could he say? He had just killed a man and his beloved horse in cold blood.

"I had no choice. I'm sorry, Mr. Begay."

"You know me? Why?" Begay repeated the question, this time in more of a whisper.

A dark cloud came over Smiley as he realized whom he had metamorphosed into.

"I was forced to eliminate you so you wouldn't discover your son's body. I'm afraid you're too good a father. I'm sorry, but it couldn't be helped. You will be with your son soon. I swear he didn't suffer."

"You're the Candy Man?" Begay was trying to understand what had happened and who had mortally wounded him.

"Yes, I am the Candy Man."

Smiley turned away from the dying man, whose horse was also now in its own death throes. Smiley offered no prayers to the gods on this go-round as he began the task of wiping away any traces of his presence. The sun would be down soon. He half-heartedly searched for the jawbreaker he had thrown, but couldn't find it. It was probably lodged somewhere in the rocky terrain, or may have broken into pieces after ricocheting from the horse's rump to a rock outcropping. The murder weapon wouldn't be discovered any time soon, and the elements would wipe away all traces of the sugary treat. Only his red hand told the story, and he would soon wash away that evidence.

As Smiley worked his way back up the slope, he turned and took one final look at Begay. There was no movement; if the man weren't dead, it wouldn't be long before he passed on. Of more immediate concern was how long it would take before the body was discovered. A few days at most, Smiley figured, although the foreboding clouds might help his cause with a fall storm that would hamper all but the hardiest rescuers and wipe out any sign he had been there.

For the first time, he noticed his arm wasn't hurting as much as before the fatal throw. He gingerly removed his jacket and inspected the wound. The fastball had opened the wound and helped purge him of the infection. The injured area smelled of pus, but he would clean and look after his wound as soon as he got home—nature's way of healing, he thought.

"Everything's going to be OK, Smiley. It's time to make a new life and leave this horrific chapter behind you."

The Candy Man traversed the steep slope carefully, wiping away any possible footprints. The significant line of Begay's and his horse's fall down the cliff was the only track he wanted to remain. Once back at his boulder ambush site, he gathered his bundle and slowly headed back to his truck, using his little broom to erase any traces of his path.

Tomorrow was a new day, a fresh start. It was time to return to work. After all, he had candy to deliver. He picked up the cellophane-encased jawbreaker and stuffed it deeply into his pocket, popping the back-up weapon into his mouth.

Time to destroy the evidence, Smiley thought. He now understood that he was a cold-blooded murderer—and that his life's trajectory would never be the same.

CHAPTER 33

HERE'S MY CARD

Smiley's arm was on the mend thanks to Begay's death, the force of his throw opening the wound and allowing his body to expel the pus threatening his right arm. He decided to take a chance and make a trade with a Gallup drunk who used to sweep the grounds at the car lot. His father had decided drunks were bad for business and shooed the man away, but Smiley liked the sad little guy. He couldn't be more than thirty years old but looked closer to fifty, well along the road to self-destruction.

The Candy Man knew the drunk was constantly cycling in and out of the Indian hospital's emergency room—his severe addiction meant many accidents and infections. Antibiotics were a short-term fix for what ailed him, one that was much easier to administer than treating the underlying issue, chronic alcoholism.

The oval white pills were crumbling around the edges. It was a six-month-old prescription, but Smiley hoped the drug was still potent enough to destroy whatever bacteria were still smoldering deep in the tissue of his arm. He followed the instructions on the bottle; if it was good enough till kill gonorrhea it surely would work on a human bite. Smiley took the next day off, sleeping through it. He wanted to be fresh at work in the morning.

Mason was impressed the kid hadn't used the entire week he had been given, and thought maybe he had underestimated Smiley's dedication to the job.

The Candy Man's second stop of the day was at Toadlena, and his heart started to race as he saw a truck with a tribal sticker on the door parked in front of the post. He considered turning around and heading to his next stop, but realized that if he were seen leaving, it would look suspicious. He had to confront his demons head on—they would not be going away anytime soon.

The day was cool, the air heavy with moisture. Thankfully, he had on a light jacket that covered the underlying bandage. He loaded his work dolly with three boxes of chips and his usual assortment of candies and headed in to face the unknown.

Logan was in deep conversation with a well-dressed thirty-year-old Navajo cop whose cropped hair told the story of conformity. The officer's younger sidekick sat in the antique barbershop chair in the middle of the trading post. Half of a candy bar was hanging out of the corner of his mouth as he made notes on Logan's concerns.

Smiley followed his normal routine, not saying a word. He parked his dolly behind the hundred-year-old oak counter, making a quick count of the inventory and restocking what was needed as he listened intently to conversation between Logan and the cop.

"Mr. Logan, we are well aware of the Ricky Begay case. His father called us when his son went missing. Why do you think Mr. Begay might be in trouble too? Maybe he's on a bender—after all, his son has not been found and at this point he must know this is not a good sign. His head must be in a bad place, don't you think?"

"No, sir, he's not on any damned bender. He was searching for Ricky. Orville Begay does not touch the bottle, and he was focused on only one thing—finding his missing son. Since Ricky's disappearance, he has come in every day right at 9 a.m. to buy a sandwich, a bag of peanuts, a bottle of Coke, and one of those candies your partner is currently helping himself to. Yesterday Orville was a no show and today he's a no show. That's why I called."

"Well, maybe he went for a sing to treat his disturbed *hózhó*. That seems a reasonable possibility..." the tribal cop said, as if he knew the ways of all Navajos.

"No, Begay's not that kind of Navajo, and I would have heard about such proceedings if they happened in my valley," Logan responded, letting the man know he was no novice when it came to such sacred rituals.

Officer Tsinnigine let the white man's words slide by him and countered: "OK, so what do you think happened, Mr. Logan?"

"Well, officer, if I knew what happened I wouldn't have bothered to call you guys, would I?" Logan said in disgust.

"Listen, Mr. Logan, there is no reason to get defensive. I'm here to help," Tsinnigine said, raising his voice slightly.

Logan took it down a notch. "Officer Tsinnigine, I'm not being defensive. I'm upset and worried. This man whom I have known for damn near twenty years lost his only son to who knows what, and now he's gone missing too? Don't you find that the least bit strange?"

"Yes, in fact I do, Mr. Logan. Tell me all you know and we will see what we can find out."

Logan retold the sad story of Ricky and Orville Begay and the Indian school that put them in this place of sorrow, the younger cop furiously taking notes. A fine line of saliva dribbled out of his Big Hunk-filled mouth as he chewed vigorously on the sticky honey treat. Smiley couldn't help but notice the pattern of spittle on the sidekick's well-polished black boot tip as he listened intently to Logan describing the events as he knew them.

Smiley heard all he needed and slipped Logan an invoice to sign. The post owner didn't look up, grabbed the pen, scribbled something illegible, and kept talking to the cop. As Smiley opened the front door to escape, their conversation abruptly stopped, and Officer Tsinnigine turned to address him.

"Hey, kid, you're the Candy Man for the western part of the reservation, right?"

"Yes, sir, I am."

"Do you know Mr. Begay?"

"Which Mr. Begay? There's a lot out here," Smiley said, trying to break the tension.

The cop didn't smile. "Orville Begay. Don't you have ears? He lives not far from here and is missing."

Logan chimed in, pointing with his lips in the direction of Begay's hogan. "The guy we talked about the other day, Smiley, Ricky Begay's dad. Remember I told you he was searching for his kid?"

"Sure, sorry, that's a sad story. I never met Mr. Begay." Smiley focused on the cop's face, hearing his father's hard voice in his head: "Look a man in the eyes, boy, if you want him to believe you—or you'll never sell a damn car."

"Anything odd you've seen on your route?" the officer asked, the sidekick looking up, ready to add to the notes in his official police pad.

"Like what?" Smiley asked, fishing for information on what would be important in a possible homicide case.

"Unusual vehicle, white guy out of place, maybe someone acting odd or saying something about the missing boy?"

The cop's white guy comment matched Smiley's Begay joke. This cop was not a friend of those with white skins. He had better tread carefully.

"No, sir—can't say I have."

"OK, well, if you do, Smiley... it is Smiley?"

"Yes Earnest Smiley, but everyone just calls me Smiley."

OK, Mr. Smiley. Let me know if you see or hear anything, Here's my card."

Smiley took the officer's card, looked at it briefly, smiled politely, then headed to his truck, beads of sweat forming along his temple in the cool autumn air. Once in the vehicle, he examined the card more closely:

Lieutenant David Tsinnigine, Navajo Tribal Police

Window Rock AZ 431-5490

He slid the cheap white business card into his wallet for safekeeping. This man was potentially dangerous, and the card would remind him to stay vigilant. Smiley would rub the boy's silver ring on the card to counteract its potential power when he got back to the trailer. The young man who used to wear the same shirt for each baseball game had taken his superstitions to a new level.

The rest of the day Smiley refilled shelves in a daze. The next week might prove to be challenging. Begay's body would be found soon, and it would either be case-closed or a very long winter for the Candy Man.

Two miserable days passed before Begay's body was discovered. A group of circling vultures tipped off the cops, who recognized the real law on the rez: nature. The local radio station had scant information, but by noon the word was out: it was a tragic accident; there were no signs of foul play so far. The community had made its decision on the cause of death—a Shapeshifter—although a few were blaming the Indian school people who had taken their children away.

Lieutenant Tsinnigine, like Begay, methodically examined the entire area looking for clues; a band of rain, the remnant of the previous night's weak tropical storm, had washed away any fresh evidence. The rain had also kept predation to a minimum, limiting it to the vulture's enjoyment of the horse's abdominal cavity. The time of death appeared to be about two days earlier, correlating with Logan's account of Begay's disappearance.

Even in the wet ground, an obvious path of dislodged stones along the fall line was visible and the multiple abrasions on both rider and horse told the story of a tragic accident ending with the worst of outcomes. The victim's foot was wedged in one of the stirrups as if he were trying to either dismount or get back onto the horse at the time of their fall. Begay appeared to have miraculously ridden his tumbling mount down the slope, but with deadly consequences.

"Why the single foot in the stirrup?" Tsinnigine asked himself. "Maybe this is the reason the horse had lost its footing. The ground was dry when this happened."

No other signs of trauma were noted on either of the corpses, so it was probably an unfortunate accident. Tsinnigine understood the dangers of being alone in the desert; he hoped that Begay had not suffered. From the remains, it looked like a quick death for both animal and man.

Even so, the officer remained diligent about searching the entire area, covering a radius of a half-mile. The trail directly above the fall line, where the horse apparently had been, was of special interest. Nothing out of the ordinary was discovered other than a torn cellophane wrapper wedged in a narrow crack near two enormous boulders at the edge of the trail.

Was this a possible clue or simply trash? Discarded human detritus was not uncommon on the reservation, even in remote areas. Most residents felt Mother Earth could handle a wrapper or two.

Tsinnigine bagged and recorded the evidence, placing an "A" on a hand-drawn map of the discovery point and moving back down to the scene of the carnage for a further examination before bringing out Begay's body. The horse would be left to return to earth. It was too heavy to remove, and what relatives would want a dead horse? Traditional Navajos often killed the deceased's favorite horse and left it at the burial site, so this seemed appropriate. From what the cop understood, Orville Begay's bloodline had come to an end, assuming his son was also dead. Only one elderly aunt remained.

The horse's leather saddlebags contained Begay's soggy lunch sack, the contents exactly as described by the Toadlena Trading Post owner: a sandwich, one broken bottle of Coke, some peanuts, and an unopened Big Hunk candy bar. Also found in the saddlebags were a small folding shovel, an old, fully loaded Colt revolver, a wallet with $5 folded inside, and a worn black-and-white photo of what appeared to be his missing son in happier days standing next to the now-dead horse. Robbery seemed an unlikely motive, so the case was pushed from the criminal to the accidental category in Tsinnigine's mind.

One final look topside, approximately where the horse initiated his spiraling death fall, did uncover something odd. Wedged between two smooth stones alongside a trickle of fresh storm run-off was a round white object, not far from where Tsinnigine had discovered the wrapper. He picked up the quail egg-sized opaque ball. It was sticky to touch and smelled sweet. "A candy?" he wondered.

As he knelt on the ground trying to decode the mystery, he realized it must have been a final treat Begay was getting ready to eat, the wrapper also now making sense. He probably had a few hard candies in his bag and had eaten one or two before the accident. That the deceased liked sweets was borne out by the Big Hunk in the lunch sack and the trading post's owner, who said Begay never failed to buy a candy bar. The man clearly had a sweet tooth.

Tsinnigine bagged the evidence and would make a note of his finding to the coroner in case there was a piece of hard candy stuck in Begay's throat. It was otherwise an incidental finding, a sign of good detective work, but of little use unless the victim had choked on the sweet treat, causing him to spook his horse.

The idea that Begay choked was reasonable but unlikely; in the officer's mind this was simply an unfortunate accident. What he had not considered was the initial size of the candy. Water's powerful capacity to erode had gone unappreciated; it would be nearly sixty years before nature's forces were once again reexamined—and the finding at that time would have deadly consequences.

CHAPTER 34

SEMPER FIDELIS

Ricky Begay's bite mark left a scar on Smiley's arm that would never quite fade, a constant reminder of the evil buried deeply within the Candy Man. He had killed two people: a father and son. He could reason that Ricky's death was an accident, but how could he justify murdering a bereaved father whose only crime was trying to find a lost child? To lessen the pain of the murders that haunted him, Smiley decided to dedicate himself to being a better person and making a difference in the world—but how?

The first step was to quit working for Perry Mason. He would no longer be the Candy Man, the daily route a reminder of his darkest moments. Smiley couldn't bear passing by the monolithic cliffs where Ricky Begay's small, broken body was hidden. He was responsible for the boy's death. He had read about murderers who relished revisiting the place where they had disposed of their victims, but he was not that kind of monster.

Smiley began the road to healing by making up with his father. He had obliterated a Navajo father and son's relationship; maybe he could earn some redemption by being a decent son to his own father and letting the past go.

His father was able to convince his boss to rehire Smiley at the automobile dealership, but only if he started at the very bottom, as a gofer. This position lasted for six months. Then he graduated to repossessing cars and trucks that were two months behind in their payments. Smiley didn't relish the task of stripping struggling Navajos of their only form of transportation. He understood that by repossessing the delinquent truck he was hamstringing a family. Without a vehicle on the rez, you couldn't get food, medical help, or maintain a job. His actions as a repo man could have deadly consequences, and he felt like the grim reaper of the poor.

Smiley's father's boss was a hard man, but he had a collector's eye and was transfixed by Navajo weavings. Smiley would do his best to convince individuals who were late on their payments to trade a nice weaving or the occasional lanky steer as their remittance. There was no joy for Smiley in the destruction of a tenuous family's life. He had already accomplished this in spades, and at close range. He discovered that interacting with people in distress gave him a sense of purpose, as well as the ability to talk with them about the most horrific situations. Losing a vehicle because of poverty or addiction showed Smiley the right road toward redemption.

When given the opportunity to move into sales alongside his father, Smiley decided that being a caring repo man could make a bigger difference, one that was more fulfilling than buying himself a new car. He declined the offer to make more money in sales, a first for the Gallup dealership. His father understood his son's motivation to help and was proud of him—also a first.

Four years working car repo taught the former baseball star how to think on his feet—and that a bat could be used for things other than driving in runs. Smiley had grown even stronger. The long hours in the sun hijacking trucks and moving cattle in trade for late payments had given him the same dark complexion as his Navajo clientele.

Unfortunately, the job played out over time. There were no new challenges, and Smiley realized he had come to an impasse. He would never become a mover and shaker repossessing cars. He enrolled in community college classes and majored in political science. A steady job with good government benefits seemed like a smart choice—until the Vietnam war came knocking. The year was 1966.

Smiley joined ROTC, recognizing that the military would give him the structure he craved and help with the bills. A calculating man, Smiley weighed the risks and went with the path of least resistance. Even when it meant killing a father looking for his lost son vs. possible serious prison time, he hadn't hesitated making the most pragmatic choice.

After receiving his associate's degree, Smiley was given the opportunity to become an officer and joined the Marines as a second lieutenant. He would be a leader of men. He already knew he had the raw instincts to kill, but now it would be in the service of good rather than evil. He promised himself he would never take another's life unless it was absolutely necessary for the mission.

Smiley's athletic prowess, coupled with a brazen streak of machismo honed over the hoods of a thousand repossessed vehicles, made him the perfect military fighting machine. His helmet read "The Candy Man," a nod to his previous career. He didn't mind the reference; he had locked his evil deeds into a place where all the synapses ceased working. The sweet smell of candy was his only memory of that time.

The year was 1968, and a massive surge by the North Vietnamese known as the Tet Offensive marked a turning point in the war. Smiley was now on his second combat tour of duty and his steely demeanor had been noticed and rewarded. He was now Captain Smiley of the United States Marine Corps, flourishing in that endorphin-laced environment.

Events of May 4, 1968 would change Captain Smiley's life forever. His platoon's leader, Second Lieutenant Campos, had been killed four months earlier and Smiley took it upon himself to take over as head of the unit. After January's Tet onslaught by the Viet Cong, the forty-three men on the platoon had been cut by a fourth. But under Smiley's command, not a single additional man had been lost even as the war raged on. In the past two weeks, all hostilities from the North had halted—a possibly ominous sign.

His men were now seasoned warriors and obeyed their captain's every order. They had seen what happened if a Marine froze when they were under Lieutenant Compo's command. Many died, including the young West Point graduate himself. No fancy military training could defeat this enemy; it required a hardened man—like Smiley. The Candy Man's sharp, barking orders rang out like sirens on a streaking ambulance: pay attention now and live; falter and die.

Two tours had given Smiley a second sense of the dangers lurking in the unforgiving jungles of Southeast Asia. The men respected a captain who would command a platoon, a job that usually fell to a lower-ranking officer. But Smiley refused to lose any more of his soldiers. The brass didn't like one of their best leaders under constant fire, but knew this was a Marine who could not be suppressed. He had something to prove and fighting was the way to appease his appetite.

Smiley knew his resolve to succeed and protect his men was based on redemption, not courage or even patriotism; he must fight to pay back the gods for what he had done in a previous life. This Candy Man was different, he told himself. Wearing the name on his helmet and Begay's small silver ring with his dog tags was his way of asking for forgiveness.

The day of reckoning was a clear May morning, the air uncomfortably warm. The pesky cloud of mosquitos had abated in the last two weeks of drier weather, a rarity. Wispy clouds filled the night sky. Rain was coming in, Smiley thought. And tonight he would make a reconnaissance mission, the first in two weeks. It had been eerily quiet for too long, and it seemed like the perfect time to engage the enemy if they were indeed still around.

The unnecessary rain ponchos crackled when they were walking, so Smiley had his men remove them. They would proceed in stealth mode. Two-thirds of the platoon would break into two groups and make a square pattern, meeting three miles from their base. The remaining third would protect their well-fortified camp. They all knew the routine and no one complained: the Candy Man had their backs. The area had been cleared of land mines for the most part. Smiley figured that the biggest danger would be a well-positioned sniper—a lone gunman would be the least of their worries on this night.

Unfortunately, the second wave of the Tet Offensive started that clear night, the enemy also recognizing the opportunity presented by weather. For Smiley's platoon, the timing couldn't have been worse. A momentous VC attack split the two groups when they were as far away from each other as possible. The enemy's numbers were overwhelming, and Captain Smiley realized he had made a fatal mistake in judgment. His only hope was to regroup his men as fast as possible.

A mayday call went out from the first group of Marines, who were hopelessly pinned down and taking losses. Realizing the dire situation, Smiley had already called for air support. Leading the way from the front, Smiley somehow broke through the VC lines and reunited his panicky men; incoming fire came from all directions as he regrouped and laid out their only hope for escape. He understood the topography of the area: there was one small opening a quarter klick away where a helicopter could hover low, dropping the men into the safety of their camp where the rest of the platoon would be hunkered down in a defensive position. To survive that night would require a fast push under heavy fire to reach the hole in the jungle's canopy before the Viet Cong overran their position.

With the sound of the helicopter's rotors closing in, the men made their dash for freedom. Smiley protected the rear by picking off any VC who made their presence visible, giving his men precious time to escape. The captain understood he would die that night—a fitting end, he thought. Maybe it would finally earn him the redemption he sought from his maker, even if it meant more killing on his judgment day. The irony was not lost on the doomed Candy Man. He hoped the dog tags hanging around his neck next to a small silver Navajo ring would be given to his father with whatever remained of his body.

As the hovering helicopter filled with frantic soldiers, many seriously wounded, a second life-saving Bell AH-1 Cobra attack helicopter entered the field of battle and returned fire with its mini-guns. Smiley felt a slight glimmer of hope. Maybe he wouldn't die tonight after all.

As Smiley made a run for the rescue chopper, a searing pain sliced through both legs, crumpling him on the spot. Unable to continue and realizing his fate, he decided to make this ground his last stand and kill as many of the enemy as possible before facing his fate. But one Marine refused to leave his fallen comrade to die. Corporal Marvin Manycoats, one of two Navajos under Captain Smiley's command, jumped from the safety of the helicopter's bay and ran head first into the blistering fire, the hive of buzzing bullets whizzing past his head.

Smiley tried to wave off the undaunted fool, screaming an order to return to the helicopter now. When he realized his command would not be obeyed—this was a true Navajo brave who was not afraid to die—Smiley dragged himself onto his one semi-functioning knee and began spraying the area to cover Manycoats. Realizing their predicament, the two-man attack helicopter moved dangerously close to the ground, providing a moment of distraction that could make a difference.

A bullet hissed past Marvin's head, ripping a clean hole through his left ear. The lower part of the lobe was hanging by a single thread of cartilage. Manycoats scooped up the enormous captain as if he were no more than three sacks of Bluebird Flour—nothing he couldn't handle, the Navajo thought. He positioned the man's weight directly over his shoulders, pivoted, and sprinted for the Jolly Green Giant Helicopter.

Smiley returned fire on the enemy as Manycoats ran. Chest shots took out the first two VC that followed them. No others appeared, and they somehow made it to the helicopter intact, the green bird hovering slightly off the ground.

The VC focused their fire on the escape pod and the sound of metal pinging filled the air as bullets breached the green skin, the acrid smell of gunpowder pierced with screams of RUN, RUN! The brave men in the attack helicopter never wavered, maintaining their position between the enemy and the Jolly Green Giant. Manycoats tossed his leader into the open bay and rolled in after him. The rescue helicopter made a sharp evasive maneuver, tumbling the occupants like bowling pins, as it escaped the fire zone. The Cobra emptied its 70mm rockets, effectively ending the fight.

Five Marines had been killed. If not for Marvin Manycoats' heroic run, it would have been six.

"I gave you a direct order to leave me, Corporal Manycoats! Those orders were given to save your life and those of your comrades," Smiley yelled, spittle flying from his mouth as blood from his damaged legs sloshed back and forth on the steamy metal floor.

"Captain Smiley, a Marine never leaves a brother, especially one from the reservation. You should have given that order in Navajo. I understand that language better." Marvin smiled a large, toothy grin as a steady drip of blood puddled on the worn leather seat next to his head, the product of his semi-detached ear. Marvin's upper eyelids were twitching rapidly, the last gasp of his endorphin surge. It was a picture the Candy Man would never forget.

Then Captain Smiley, the man of steel who had never showed fear, and one of the toughest Marines in the force, broke down in inconsolable sobs. It was his last day on his tour of duty in Vietnam. Never again would Captain Smiley walk without the assistance of a cane, a constant reminder of how his life had been spared by the bravery of a young Navajo man who called him brother. The pain was almost too great to bear.

CHAPTER 35

BALANCE OF POWER

The first round of news about the discovery of the skeletal remains had flashed through the reservation—a brush fire, hot but short lived. One article even made it into the *Santa Fe Reporter.* Just a few paragraphs on the fourth page, the small-font headline read: "Navajo skeleton discovered sixty miles north of Gallup may be that of a Navajo boy who disappeared September 1961."

Both Rachael and Marvin were quoted with varying levels of accuracy, but the gist of the story was correct. Marvin's Indian school experience was not revisited; it was a subject he preferred to avoid. And he did not elaborate on why his friend had gone missing or exactly how the remains had been discovered. Manycoats understood that on the reservation a dead child, especially one who disappeared in 1961, would be of little interest to most of the affluent newspaper readers of Santa Fe or Albuquerque.

However, the single column story pinched between a large advertisement for a Ross Dress for Less spring sale and a feature about the University of Arizona recovering a Willem de Kooning painting stolen in 1985, didn't go completely unnoticed. A Santa Fe resident, a man at the height of his power, had taken notice of the article about the skeleton and made notes of the names and dates involved. The Candy Man was indeed very interested in this report.

A large puddle of sweat had expanded at the base of Earnest Smiley's exercise bike as he finished the last of his morning reading. His foot slipped violently from the harness and he lurched forward, the hard plastic pedal spinning out of control and hitting him solidly on the shin, causing him to cry out in pain.

"Goddamn it!" Smiley shook his leg vigorously to lessen the mounting pain. He reread the article, then said in a low voice, "Marvin Manycoats found Ricky Begay's body? How is this possible?" He instinctively touched his dog tags and the little silver ring under his shirt; these charms never left his body, reassuring him in periods of stress.

The Candy Man sat back on the bike seat, sweat stinging his eyes as he tried to decoded the gods' message. The man who had saved his life in Vietnam, Marvin Manycoats, could now be his undoing. This had to be more than a coincidence. The crows had come home to roost—and at the most important time in his life.

"What to do?" His mind raced as his heartbeat slowed.

"Damage control! It's been fifty years and the skeleton might not even be that of Ricky Begay. I need a reconnaissance mission to protect the people who depend on me."

Smiley picked up a landline in his huge workout room and called the one person he could count on for support, loyalty, and advice: Angel Veracruz. The Candy Man had been buried and long forgotten, but the obscure article in today's paper triggered a rebirth of Smiley's alter ego—the one he had tried so hard to destroy. The dangerous being living inside him had been re-engaged, the long-dormant evil synapses once again firing—and anyone who got in his way was a possible target.

CHAPTER 36

ROM-COMS

Four days had passed since the police recovered the remains discovered by Marvin and Rachael. Orville's Begay's grave had been exhumed and DNA tests were pending. Lieutenant Brown felt the forensic department of the tribal police was making progress.

Bloom was checking in twice a day, and Rachael continued to assure him that she was doing well and weaving. Marvin was spending evenings at Rachael's hogan. His presence seemed to help her avoid the demons bubbling close to the surface and give her a reason to focus on something other than her miscarriage. Rachael encouraged Bloom to spend time with his father, assuring him that she could handle herself. Even though Bloom was ready to come home, he was concerned enough with his father's pre-Columbian issues to want to stay in Las Cruces a bit longer. Bloom could tell that his wife was asking for space in her own way.

Marvin had decided to take a second trip to Gallup to review the police report again to make sure there was nothing they had missed. The photo of Ricky next to his favorite horse was haunting Marvin. When he looked at the image, he felt his friend was calling for his help—but he didn't know what to do.

Rachael agreed to drive. She hoped seeing Lilly Nez would be a nice distraction for her friend. Marvin shared his feelings about Lilly with Rachael, saying that he might ask the clerk out on a real date once the whole ordeal had been settled.

An unannounced Gallup visit was in order. Marvin wanted to get a better gauge on Lilly Nez's intentions toward him, hoping that an unprepared reaction to his arrival might give him a favorable nudge in her direction. As it turned out, he was not disappointed.

"Marvin Manycoats, how nice to see you. To what do I owe this visit?" Lilly asked, blinking her eyes.

Rachael, who had made a pit stop at the bathroom, rounded the corner and could see from Lilly's face that she was indeed interested.

"Well, part of the reason was to see you. Ms. Nez, and part was to look at those reports from 1961 one more time."

"Now that's what I like to hear, Hastiin Manycoats—and I'm not talking about those musty papers."

Marvin blushed and looked down at the floor. Rachael cracked a grin: Marvin did indeed like this woman.

"So can you make the time for us to get into the storage room one more time?"

"I would love to have you spend the day here, but I'm afraid the powers that be finally got around to disposing of all those old files, even if they were a few years late doing it."

"They disposed of the files? You mean they destroyed the papers we looked at?"

"I don't know if they destroyed them, but they did take them away. Officials came in two days ago and hauled off the boxes. The men told me they were cleaning out all the 50-plus-year-old dead cases."

"Do you know these men?" Rachael asked.

"That's the funny part. They didn't seem like the type to be cleaning up old files. These guys were well-dressed *bilágaanas*. I didn't really think much about it until now."

"Do you know which department they came from?"

"I don't remember. They showed me their credentials and signed in. I'm pretty sure they were from up north, Santa Fe. Wait a minute and I'll take a look."

"Yes, right here. See..." Lilly turned her logbook around to show Marvin and Rachael the official entry: removal of 1961 files, Dustin Lujan, Department of Public Safety, Santa Fe.

"I thought you said he was getting rid of all the files 50 years and older," Rachael asked, noting the discrepancy.

"Yeah. I guess I assumed that as all those files fit that classification. I didn't really notice what he wrote until now. He did take a lot of boxes. He and another man loaded them on a cart and made two trips. He signed out forty minutes after he signed in." Lilly pointed at the time stamp on the logbook.

"Did he ask any questions?" Rachael continued to press.

"He asked if the files had been touched recently, and I told him yes, there had been some activity. He pushed me for names and dates, but I told him I didn't remember who or when," Lilly said, winking at Marvin, whose face flushed red once again.

“Can we take a look at the storage room?” Rachael asked.

“I don’t see why not.”

The three went back to the area they had visited in the past; there was now a gaping hole where once there had been rows of white cardboard boxes.

“Rachael, what do you think?” Marvin asked in a low voice.

“I’m not sure, but whoever is in that department clearly knew what they were looking for. I’ve got a bad feeling that this may go deeper than we think.”

“What’s this all about, Marvin?” Lilly asked.

“Well, I can’t really say right now, but I promise you I will fill you in soon. In fact, Lilly, I would like to take you to a movie once I get my footing back. Right now, I’m having some issues with my *hózhó*. What do you say?”

It was Lilly’s turn to blush. “Of course! I’m a movie buff, and I especially like love stories. Let me know if I can help, Marvin.”

“I promise I will, Lilly.” Marvin gave his trademark grin as he and Rachael headed for the small doorway. A dark cloud of evil had moved over them, and it wasn’t clear when or if it would lift.

On the drive home, Rachael and Marvin batted around the possible reasons why the 1961 records had been removed. And why was Lujan asking if others had been nosing around? Maybe it was just the cops trying to examine the files and being overly cautious, but why would someone come from the Department of Public Safety and not the state police? The crime fell under their jurisdiction. And why did they come from Santa Fe? It didn’t make sense: this was a tribal, not a state, matter.

Rachael googled Dustin Lujan: he worked directly under a cabinet secretary, a high government post to be collecting old files. It didn't make any sense but, then, neither did a fifty-year-old child homicide.

Just when it seemed like it could not get any more bizarre, Marvin got a call from a friend he had not heard from in many years. The ring sound of "Crocodile Rock" filled the cab of the truck as Marvin answered the call.

"Yá'át' ééh."

"Marvin, is that you?" a big, booming voice asked.

"Yes, it is, Mr. Governor."

Rachael's ears perked up on hearing the word "governor." She wondered who Marvin was referring to—maybe it was a pet name for a Stone Man she didn't know. Marvin avoided Rachael's questioning eyes.

"Damn it, Marvin, it's been too long. Must be ten years."

"More like twelve. I believe you said at that time that you were testing the waters to see if you could jump from being a legislator to the head honcho of our state."

"You always did have a good memory. That's right. In fact, it was that trip to Gallup, when you met me at that rally and I introduced my war-hero buddy, that I realized I wasn't quite ready. Good thing I waited. I'm finishing up my last term as governor now, hard as it is to believe."

"What are you going to do next year? Run for president?" Marvin jested, smiling at the phone.

"Well, funny you should ask. Not president—I'm too old to win and the primaries are too far along. But I've heard talk that I could be considered for an unusual vice-presidential choice."

"Really? You're not just kidding old Marvin?"

"I'm not ribbing you; there is some serious scuttlebutt. The powers-that-be like the fact that I'm a decorated veteran and have close ties with Hispanic voters, who might be needed for the Democratic party to win the presidential election. Sounds crazy, I know. New Mexico with its few electoral votes wouldn't seem to be a smart choice for a running mate, but the party needs someone older who is seen as a strong rudder. Plus, having a significant other who is Hispanic and speaks Spanish fluently might just be the secret sauce the next administration is looking for."

"Didn't work for Jeb Bush," Marvin offered.

The governor paused, surprised by Marvin's political awareness.

"True, but that was a different time and Jeb was a Republican. The Democrats are after the all-important swing voters in Arizona, North Carolina, and Florida —and there's a hell of lot of Hispanics in those states even after the ICE raids. We don't need but a few states nowadays to win an election—and I would be vice-president, not president."

"So you want to do another Gallup stump talk and get a feel for the will of the people toward a former New Mexican governor running for vice president?" Marvin joked.

Rachael's head was cocked toward the conversation. She was having difficulty keeping her eyes on the road; it didn't sound like Marvin was talking to any Stone Man.

"Not this go-round. What I was hoping is that you could come to Santa Fe and spend a little time with me, give me a feel for the Native vote and maybe do a podcast for later distribution if this thing moves forward."

"What's a podcast?" Marvin asked.

“Same question I asked when we started one up a couple of years ago. It’s like a long-format taped radio show; it’s all the rage.”

“Format, huh?” Marvin pondered the word.

“You know, a lengthy interview where people can get a feel for the person that’s being interviewed. I’m old and this kind of media keeps me hip with the younger voters.”

“Governor, I think saying ‘hip’ probably won’t help you look young. It sounds more like you’re talking about that bad leg,” Marvin giggled.

“What can I say, Marvin? I’m an old guy trying to be relevant.”

“You think me talking on this long radio thing would be good for you? I know a lot about those days in ’Nam, some stories you might not want anyone to hear long or short.” Marvin was now smiling broadly into the phone.

“True, you don’t have to go into the weeds. And of course, I can edit as need be. It will be fun and it won’t cost you anything. You can stay with me at the governor’s mansion; I’ve got a guesthouse. Hell, you can even bring a friend.”

Marvin was trying to take in the enormity of the invitation. Yes, he had saved the man’s life, but that was years ago and now they lived in different universes.

“I can’t see why I wouldn’t want to come, governor. When do you need me to be there for that podcast thing?”

“How about the end of the week? I’ll have one of my staff get in touch with you later today. Anyone you want to bring along?”

Marvin paused for the first time in the conversation and looked at Rachael, whose eyes were still asking, ‘What’s going on?’ and said, “Yes, put down Rachael Yellowhorse for the visit with you. She’s one of my best friends.”

"Done! I'll see you in a few days. Bring a jacket—it's still plenty cold up here in Santa Fe."

The governor hung up. Soon he would know if the man who had once saved his life would now be a serious problem—or not.

CHAPTER 37

MRS. ROY BRYANT

Angel waved off the security guard as her Mercedes flew up the steep driveway to the governor's mansion. Nestled on a hill overlooking the Santa Fe basin, it had become her de facto home for governor's last term. The pair had met through mutual friends at the Santa Fe Opera's opening night. Smiley was smitten from the get-go, falling hard for the beautiful and intelligent New Mexican art dealer.

Governor Smiley proposed, but Angel had been hesitant to accept. His advanced age was a serious issue for her; she felt that he was reaching the end of his power. But, with the real possibility of a vice-presidential run, his virility returned and she was all in. Smiley recognized the flaw in Angel's character, but didn't care why she said "yes"—as long as she did.

The Democratic primary race was churning to completion and, if he were offered the number-two position on the ticket, they would announce their wedding date. Angel would be the "Second Lady" in Washington—the kind of power she had always dreamed of obtaining.

Angel was preparing for the V.P. run by donating her pre-Columbian collection to a museum in Mexico. Much of it had been illegally obtained, so it was a possible hot-button issue, plus, if managed correctly, it would be a sizable tax write-off. Dr. Bloom was the perfect person for the job, adding legitimacy to the works, and her appraiser could value the collection in the amounts she required. Her current painting inventory was relatively clean. Although she had paid cash for many of the pieces, they all had receipts. Still, if a nosy reporter dug deeply enough, the cash transactions could be problematic.

Her second cousin was the CEO of the Veracruz Company, at least in name; everyone in the organization understood that Angel was the true boss. She had carved out a niche for herself in the wake of her father's overthrow so many years ago. The Martinez alliance had remained rock solid, and gave Angel the ability to rule from afar if needed. The Martinez cartel dealt from a position of power. If anyone challenged their rule, they would act decisively—and this in turn gave Angel an upper hand in her own organization.

The Veracruz company ran seamlessly for the most part, and Angel kept out of the limelight. She didn't want or need the added exposure. She reasoned that if a reality TV show billionaire could rise to the highest power of the land, it wasn't such a stretch for the daughter of a successful cartel boss to be the wife of a vice president. On paper, she was a Latina businesswoman who had done well for herself in a highbrow profession—a perfect back-story for the Second Lady of America.

"Where's the governor?" Angel asked no one in particular as she threw her coat onto the couch for the staff to hang up. The living room was one of many in the massive hacienda-style house. The answer echoed through the chambers: "At the capitol, should be home in a few hours for dinner."

"Please take the large blanket-wrapped package in my Mercedes to the governor's bedroom. Don't unwrap the piece; it's a surprise. Tonight, we will eat on the patio and would like our privacy. Also, take down that horrible yellow painting over the bed and have someone return it to the governor's building art inventory. And leave the painting hook in place."

Angel was deciding whether to bring up the snag with the T.C. Cannon painting with Smiley. She had planned to give him the Cannon as a wedding gift, and had inscribed the back only two weeks ago, once the V.P. nomination looked imminent. The painting had been a favorite of hers, and the subject matter—candy store—fit so nicely with Smiley's backstory, which she knew.

After moving from her Palace Avenue home to the governor's mansion, Angel transferred the bulk of her painting inventory to the secure compound in Mesilla. Her days of dealing art were over.

New Mexico's capitol building also serves as an art museum, with outstanding work on every wall and rotating exhibits for the troops of tourists and art aficionados who haunted its round halls. When it came to decorating the mansion, there was plenty of free art available courtesy of the state's vast collection. The governor need only ask for what he wanted.

Angel was replacing the choices Smiley had made during his first term with her own more sophisticated taste. Their bedroom was the lone holdout. He had insisted on a god-awful painting of round hay bales, but with the T.C. Cannon as a wedding gift, the governor would acquiesce and her redecorating would be complete.

The Cannon was unwrapped and propped up against headboard of the bed, along with a dozen red roses she had picked up from her favorite street vendor off of Camino Alire. Attached to the flowers was a note that read: "You're my Candy Man. Hope you're in the mood for a tasty after-dinner treat."

On the trip to Mesilla, Angel had decided to use Dr. Benally as her operative, find out why the Bloom boys wanted information about the Cannon, then make a decision on how to proceed. She would make an unannounced visit to Benally's home soon so she could look directly into his eyes. Her father had always told her that you can tell if a man is lying to you by his eyes.

The governor showed up an hour later than expected and appeared spent. Angel could read trouble in the man's face—he wouldn't be interested in dessert tonight, tasty or not.

"Smiley, I have something that will raise your spirits. Meet me in our bedroom."

"That's good news, my dear. Today was tough. I'll explain over a bottle of the finest New Mexico wine." The two held hands like young lovers and headed to the master bedroom.

"I see my Old Yeller is gone. Is that a T.C. Cannon?"

"Yes, it is my love. In fact, it's for you—a wedding present from my collection."

"Looks like a candy store?"

"Well if the shoe fits... look on the back."

"A wedding gift to my husband, who I love more than art. Mrs. Roy Bryant"

"Ok, you've got me. Who the hell is Mrs. Roy Bryant? You?"

"Well, if you know your history, which I know you do, you will remember the civil rights case of young Emmett Till, who came from Chicago to visit his aunt in Mississippi. He went into a store to buy candy and whistled at a white woman, Mrs. Roy Bryant, whose husband owned the store."

"I do remember that pivotal moment. Roy Bryant and his half-brother shot the poor kid, destroyed his face, and the boy's mother in Chicago had the body displayed in an open casket to show everyone what these men they had done." Smiley was trying to understand the story and how the name might be connected to him.

"Well, my love, the inscription is my way of saying I've got your back always—no matter what."

Smiley didn't like being compared the murderous child killer and bigot Roy Bryant by his fiancée, but assumed it was an expression of Angel's twisted code of honor toward her husband to-be. She was the only one who knew the true story of the Candy Man.

Smiley had shared his horrific story one night after drinking too much wine, crying at some points; the burden had become too much for one man to bear. Angel took it in stride and did not judge him, saying only, "You did what you had to—and look how far you have come. It helped make you who you are."

Smiley loved her more than his own life after this show of faith, so he assumed the inscription came from a place of loyalty. "Well, you're right. I am the Candy Man—but I hope you don't think I'm in the same lane as Emmett Till's murderers."

"Oh, Smiley, it was my way of saying we are in this world together. I'll be your wife soon and I will take your past indiscretions to my grave. I love you and I wanted you to have this painting. I'm Mrs. Roy Bryant—not you—and believe me, I have my own dark secrets."

"Your timing couldn't be better then, Mrs. Bryant, as it looks like my secret may be about to resurface." Smiley pulled a folded-up section of the *Santa Fe New Mexican* newspaper from his back pocket and flipped it onto the bed next to the Cannon.

Angel first read the small article about a stolen De Kooning painting being recovered—the lost piece that had propelled her to get art degree had finally resurfaced. Then, in disbelief, she saw the article Smiley was referring to: Marvin Manycoats had discovered the remains of a young boy and the missing persons case was being reopened.

Smiley told Angel his plan: he had arranged a meeting at the mansion with Marvin for a visit and possible podcast. Keep your friends close and your enemies closer, his alcoholic father used to tell him. The premise was that Manycoats would be helping him with the V.P. run. The topic of the skeleton would come up organically, and he hoped he could push Marvin to forget old scars and look to the future.

Both newspaper articles rocked Angel's world. Could the simultaneous recovery of the De Kooning painting and the skeleton be connected in some cosmic way? She realized her best-laid plans could be at risk. If need be, she would take care of any problems that Manycoats might present. Maybe recovering the De Kooning painting that had set her on her course as an art dealer was a message from the gods telling her to do whatever she must, to stay faithful to her chosen path. She was indeed the real Roy Bryant—and no one would get in the way of Smiley's vice presidency.

A stolen T.C. Cannon painting was now playing second fiddle to a child and father's murder. The De Kooning was once again talking to her.

CHAPTER 38

BABY TRAIN

Rachael uncharacteristically paced the kitchen. Bloom's nightly phone call would come soon. The day had been filled with firsts: Marvin was a friend of the governor of New Mexico and she had been invited to meet the man at the mansion.

She realized she was longing for Bloom's touch as much as his voice. A rendezvous in Santa Fe in two days-time was needed, and the Inn of the Anasazi was the answer. The hotel was above their pay grade, but Rachael was ready to get back on the baby train. It was off-season at the hotel, and the rates were as low as they ever would be for a four-star hotel. It would be a well-needed mini vacation for both. The governor had invited Marvin to spend the night in the mansion's guest quarters to give them extra time to talk about old times, and Marvin had accepted the generous invitation.

Rachael knocked over one of her metal kitchen chairs in a rush to grab the phone she had left near a boiling pot of pintos. The chair crashed to the floor. Rachael listened for kid noises, heard none, and answered the phone.

"Hi, honey. How is my favorite boyfriend?" Bloom could hear the warm affection that had returned to his wife's voice.

"Someone is doing better. I'm surprised it took two rings for you to pick up." Charles smiled on the other end, knowing his wife anticipated his nightly call.

Rachael's voice was full of excitement as she recapped the day's events. She and Marvin were invited to Santa Fe for a Friday visit with the governor, and afterwards she wanted to meet him at the Inn of the Anasazi. Rachael reasoned that spending the money was a business expense as Bloom could check on the gallery while they were in town. Then both of them could visit the rental house in La Cienega for a quick look-see and to check on the pastures for her sheep; after all, they would be moving there shortly.

Bloom was excited to hear Rachael's enthusiasm as she described a night alone. His father had decided to turn in the completed pre-Columbian report with its empty appraised-value columns, and the Veracruz group had approved the final version. Bloom was ready to come home and suggested that his father ask them to mail him the check—but the Trust insisted on giving it to him in person on Monday morning. His father asked Charles to come with him to the compound and wanted to plan a celebratory lunch after getting the payment—his treat. Bloom wasn't sure a celebration was in order, but his father seemed satisfied, and that was what was important. Bloom realized his dad was aging quickly, and that this might be his last significant archaeology job. The lunch was a kind of retirement party for the older man, something more important than getting a paycheck or a free meal.

Charles definitely could use the quick trip to Santa Fe and back. He would meet his wife Friday and come back to Las Cruces on Sunday. Marvin could take his own vehicle so Bloom could pick up Rachael in Santa Fe. She could drive south with him and accompany him to the celebratory lunch. Rachael's neighbor, Mrs. Bennally, would love to have the kids for the weekend.

Bloom was smiling on the other end of the phone, seeing all the pieces coming together, when the tone of the call changed as Rachael filled him in on the other events of the day: Police reports from 1961 had been hauled off from Gallup to Santa Fe under odd circumstances.

"Isn't it possible this is simply part of the investigation?" Bloom asked.

"Well, we considered that, so I called Gallup and talked to officer Brown. He said he had not given the orders to have the boxes picked up and didn't have any idea of what was going on. And listen to this: Brown said the skeleton's DNA matched Orville Begay's—it is Ricky!"

"I'll be damned. Marvin was right! How's he's faring?" Bloom asked.

"Surprisingly well. Finding his friend helped ease his mind, and so did the governor's invitation. The real question for me is how his friend's body ended up in that man-made grave. Did his father bury his son and then die by suicide? Was it just bad luck? Or were more sinister forces at work?"

"Well, my gut says those fifty-year-old records disappearing is a huge coincidence. Maybe someone is trying to shut down this investigation pronto," Bloom reasoned.

"But why? There are only a couple of Navajos interested in finding out the real story, so there's not much pressure there—and I would think it's an impossible case to solve."

"That could be the answer, Rach. If the records are destroyed, which they could be legally after so much time, it would be easier to simply close the case and save on manpower and the bad press about a young

Navajo boy's disappearance in the desert so long ago—plus no one likes the thought of some Shapeshifter out there terrorizing the rez, regardless of when the death occurred."

"So what are our options other than letting the cops do their job and seeing what shakes out?" Rachael asked.

"Well, we might have a little time after your big-wig meeting with the governor and before we check into the Inn of the Anasazi to do some investigating of our own. We can start with Mr. Lujan."

"As long as there is plenty of hotel time... I'm ready to start trying again," Rachael giggled.

"Me too, my love, me too."

CHAPTER 39

FULL CIRCLE

A day had passed since Angel learned she would be hosting Marvin Manycoats and his Navajo guest at the mansion. An itinerary was set for them for Friday:

> 10:30-11:30 a.m. Tour of the state capitol building and the art
>
> 11:30 a.m.–12 p.m. Meet at the governor's office
>
> 12-1 p.m. Free time
>
> 1-2:30 p.m. Late lunch with the governor at the mansion

The VIP tour of the capitol building and the governor's mansion originated from a most unlikely source: Marvin Manycoats. Rachael always knew Marvin was a special man; now she wondered how deep his talents really ran.

Willy and Sam got an early breakfast and were dropped off at Mrs. Bennally's house, who would take care of them until Rachael and Charles returned around five on Monday. March weather is iffy in Northern New Mexico, and Mrs. Bennally was fine if it took them a little longer to return; she loved having the children around, as her own grown daughter no longer lived with her.

The morning air in Toadlena was a brisk 25 degrees, but the warm sun and cloudless sky made it feel much warmer. Marvin seemed to be in a good mood. Amazingly, this was his first trip ever to Santa Fe and it came with a personal meeting with the state's governor. Rachael tried not to show her excitement. Santa Fe was no big deal—it was her home in many ways—but today felt very different.

The route north they chose was I-40. It was not as scenic a drive as traversing the Bisti Badlands and dropping down through O'Keeffe country, but they didn't want to take the chance of being late; the interstate was the more prudent route when a weak cold front was threatening the northern half of the state. The road's white mesa and the atavistic cliff-dwelling communities sprinkled along the vistas were today's backdrop for conversation.

"Marvin, are you excited to see the governor?"

"Well, yes, but I don't think of him as the governor. He's my captain or the Candy Man in my mind. I never got used to the governor mantle, but I'm proud of his accomplishments."

"I get 'captain' from his ranking in the Marines, but what does 'Candy Man' mean?"

"A long time ago Earnest Smiley delivered candy and chips to the trading posts. He grew up in Gallup and was a teenager when he made the reservation route his livelihood. I didn't remember him as a person then, but that old beat-up candy truck I remember plenty well."

"So he delivered treats when you were a kid, and then you end up in the same platoon?"

"Sounds crazy when you say it out loud, but it's true. I saved his life during a firefight in Vietnam. Worlds have a way of coming full circle, I guess."

"You never talk about Vietnam or your medals. Is it too painful?"

"Medals don't matter. Lots of guys got medals for doing nothing, and lots didn't get any for saving lives. I don't like my mind to go there. With this memory of mine, it's better if I focus on the present."

Rachael had never considered those ramifications of photographic recall. For the first time, she could see the negative side of the gift and changed the topic.

"I don't remember hearing about Governor Smiley working on the reservation."

"Yeah. He never really tried to make it part of his backstory. I figured he was embarrassed to have been a candy truck driver."

"If you ask me, Marvin, we need more politicians who did drive trucks."

"I'm not a fan of any politicians," Marvin said, "New Mexican or tribal. Both those groups allowed Indian kids to be shipped away to boarding schools."

Rachael could feel Marvin going down the rabbit hole that led to the death of his best friend and changed the topic."

"I can't believe you have never been to Santa Fe. It's our capital."

"No, Window Rock is OUR capital."

"I stand corrected. Santa Fe is the capital of New Mexico."

"Rachael, I've always wanted to go to Indian Market to see all the great weavings, jewelry, and art made by our nation's many tribes. Visiting Santa Fe scratches that itch. So does seeing the Candy Man, or should I say governor. He did pretty doggone well for a kid from Gallup."

"Marvin, this summer you can be our guest during Indian Market. We are renting a big house in La Cienega. I imagine Bloom will want to put you to work at the gallery."

"Sounds fun, even the work part."

Both laughed and thought about their lives as they crossed the open vista toward a destiny neither could imagine. Life was about to prove Marvin right—and expose the underbelly of how the real world worked.

Rachael helped Marvin navigate the many narrow, one-way streets of Santa Fe before miraculously emerging in front of the huge New Mexico state house. Large sculptures by noted Native artists Allan Houser and Doug Hyde graced the front of the building, a statement of the importance of the Native voice in New Mexico. Caches of dirty snow piled in small recesses behind clumps of piñon pines signaled that winter had not quite finished with the City Different.

Marvin's truck found a parking place right next to the building—a sign of a good day in the making. A young Puebloan man with a dark, moon-shaped face and comforting smile was anxiously waiting for them at the information booth.

"Welcome, Marvin and Rachael. The governor sends his best," Ray Lovato chirped in a higher-pitched voice than expected. Marvin returned the smile and stuck out a limp hand to shake, wondering how this person recognized them. After introductions were complete, the two were whisked on their art tour.

The cavernous building was laid out in a circular format with four floors of office space and a centrally located semicircular assembly room where the legislators met. Art filled every wall. Contemporary, Hispanic, and Native artists were represented, filling the space with sculpture, painting, ceramic, and fiber art from a variety of periods. It was a true museum experience. The quality and breadth of the artwork surprised Rachael, who had never been inside this hidden gem of a building.

Lovato described each work's meaning, the rationale for its inclusion in the collection, and why the artist was important. The vetting was a stringent process, and once a piece was part of the museum's holdings it would never be sold—a treasure for all New Mexicans to see when visiting their government's headquarters.

A side hallway on the third floor held BUFFALO WHO WOULDN'T DIE, a large, impressive mural by the famed Santa Clara painter Pablita Velarde, an accompanying bronze sculpture of the artist bringing home the gravitas of the painting. Rachael's eyes worked their way down the length of the horizontal canvas, then froze in disbelief. In an acrylic case near the emergency exit door was a small, fine tapestry, a Toadlena/Two Grey Hills weaving. The bronze tag read "Rachael Yellowhorse (1979-)."

The weaving was tiny in size, but dynamic in composition and warp count—a true tapestry of over 80 wefts/inch. She remembered Bloom selling it to a New Mexico collector a few years back on an opening night the day before Indian Market, but she didn't remember the details. Opening nights in the third week of August were always pandemonium. The older man's smiling face as he shook her hand was the only memory she could muster. The weaving's inclusion among the capitol art works caught Rachael off guard; her eyes filled with tears, knowing she was a part of this important collection, her first museum representation to her knowledge.

"This is an amazing example of Spider Woman's gifts by the talented young Diné artist Rachael Yellowhorse. Descended from a long line of well-respected weavers, she is the sister of the great Willard Yellowhorse, whose work hangs in the Museum of Modern Art in New York City. Rachael and her deceased brother were both graduates of IAIA."

The tour guide's eyes gleamed in excitement as he discussed the weaving in front of its maker. Clearly this twenty-year-old Puebloan didn't understand the nuances of discussing the names of the dead with a Navajo.

"Not that young, I'm afraid—and my late brother is the real artist in the family," Rachael said as her lost baby flashed through her mind. The bronze tag on the acrylic case drove home her mortality: her name, birth year, and no death date made her lifecycle clear.

"I'm with a star," Marvin teased, breaking into Rachael's reflection.

"No great star, Marvin. I'm the guest and you're the governor's friend. What do you say we keep moving?"

Rachael backed away from the claustrophobic hallway, flicking her tears aside. The two men followed her cue and continued the tour. The contemporary art suddenly stopped and a new form of imagery lined the walls—old paintings and photographs of past governors and crazy-quilt images of the members of the legislature arranged by year.

Marvin stopped at the 25th legislature of 1961-62. "I remember this year too well," he said. "1961 was when these public officials sent me and my friend to Indian school, or at least me. He died trying to avoid the bilagáana's rules. I don't see any Native faces on that wall."

"Not only are they not Native, they are all men, except for one. That lady must have been one tough person to make it in that environment." Rachael pointed out the outlier woman as Marvin walked the gauntlet of legislative years.

"Here's the 1967-8 class photo. That's the year I nearly died twice in Vietnam, and the reason I'm here today. Same white men, different faces."

"Though one lone woman manages to remain," Rachael observed, touching the face of the woman with blond short hair, glasses, and pearls in the Vietnam-era photograph. Marvin, things have changed now. Look at this more recent photo; at least a third of this class is women and lots are people of color. We have made progress and none of the women are wearing pearls."

"I guess that's true—and even more importantly, our guide is Native!" Marvin ribbed Lovato, who was looking at his feet during the intense discussion of Native perceptions of right and wrong.

They passed by numerous small offices with dozens of legislators' names on the walls. Rachael scanned the names, looking for one in particular, which she found in Room 413: Dustin Lujan, Department of Public Safety. The man who had taken the records from Gallup was located only a few doors away from the governor's office. Rachael would be back to investigate, but for now they were being ushered in to see the governor. The Candy Man was waiting.

CHAPTER 40

THE GOVERNOR'S OFFICE

Gold embossed letters stenciled on top of a Greek-style parapet read, "Office of the Governor." The tour guide said his good-byes and left his guests to enter the chamber of the most powerful person in New Mexico, Governor Earnest Smiley.

A three-foot carved emblem of the Great Seal of New Mexico with eagle and arrow motifs dominated the back of a dark wooden wall. An equally impressive oak desk was populated with two large computers and a single individual manning a multitude of phones. The receptionist's swale of coifed gray hair played well against his requisite dark blue suit and red tie. He was juggling a phone in each hand and signaled with his head to have a seat.

Marvin and Rachael sat quietly, waiting for the surreal scene to play out.

"Sorry to keep you. I'm assuming you are Mr. Manycoats and Ms. Yellowhorse?"

"That would be us," Marvin said confidently, unfazed by the power of the office.

"The governor will be right with you. He had a meeting that ran late and hopefully he's catching up on paperwork. I'm afraid this can be a demanding job."

A large oak door was flung open and a tall, muscular man who looked much younger than his age walked out, supporting himself with a metal cane whose round silver top was embossed with the state's Zia symbol.

"Marvin, it's been too damn long. Hell, you haven't aged at all since the last time I saw you—and this must be the great weaver Rachael Yellowhorse. My staff tells me we have one of your pieces hanging in the roundhouse museum." Rachael blushed as the governor embraced his old friend and stuck a large hand out to her.

"Well, captain, I can't say you look the same, but I do see you got a fancier cane."

"Yeah, my fiancée bought me an art cane, said I need to upgrade the old cottonwood one that I got out at Hopiland when I ran for congress."

"How's your leg?" Marvin asked.

"A little worse, I'm afraid. The docs say I need a knee operation, but with all the hubbub of me angling for the vice-presidency, I can't afford to look more of an invalid than I already do."

Rachael looked at Marvin; she had not been aware of the political possibilities the governor was entertaining.

"Please come in to the office and have a seat. We need to catch up."

Followed by Marvin, Rachael entered the spacious office. A huge hand-wrought desk dominated the room. Hundreds of photos were spaced around the walls, and a tasteful Fritz Scholder painting of what appeared to be a medicine man hung behind the desk.

"Well, captain, what is it you want me to do on this podcast deal?"

"Things have gotten a bit backed up, so I'm not going to have time to do the podcast with you today, but I hoped we could chat and I could lay the groundwork for an episode if I get the nomination."

Marvin was relieved that he didn't have to do a radio show right then.

"Tell me, Rachael, how do you know Marvin?"

"Well, we are both from the Toadlena basin. In fact, our family homes aren't more than six miles apart as the crow flies."

"Tell me what's going on in Marvin Manycoats life. I understand you're in the archaeology profession these days?" The governor put the question to Marvin in a joking way, but was deadly serious about the answers he was looking for.

"Not archeology, more detective work I guess. I'm trying to find out what happened to a childhood friend who disappeared in 1961 and whose body was recently discovered."

"Shit, Marvin, that sounds pretty serious."

"I'm afraid so. I hope we get some answers soon," Marvin said.

Rachael jumped in: "We are currently waiting on the final forensic reports."

"We could use some help, captain."

"How can I help, Marvin? I'll do what I can."

"There were a significant number of Gallup police files from 1961 that were taken to be destroyed because the case is fifty years old. The timing seems odd since this case has just become active again. A man in the Department of Public Safety, a Dustin Lujan, picked them up last week. If you could find out why he took the files it would be helpful. We're worried there maybe information in those old records that could be important in solving this old missing-person case. It's still not clear if it was an accident or something worse."

"I know Lujan, and I'll see what I can find out. What do you think is going on, Marvin?" Smiley asked with a piercing stare.

"Captain, I honestly don't have a clue. Part of me wants my friend's death to be an accident, but another part of my brain says something's out of place—but I don't know what."

"Well, if you figure it out let me know. I've been looking to return a small favor—you know, the one where you saved my life. Hell, look at these platoon photos, Marvin. Can you believe how young, dumb, and full of you-know-what we were?"

Marvin leaned down. There was an old Polaroid on the desk of the men in the platoon, all with their shirts off, pointing their guns to the sky. Captain Smiley's gun was across his chest, a cigar clenched in his mouth.

The Navajo brought one of the photos closer to his face, apologizing that he needed glasses. The men's faces and arms were deeply tanned; the rest of their bodies were ghostly white. There was a scar on Smiley's arm that he had never noticed before. What was it about that scar? Marvin couldn't put a finger on it. It was probably no big deal; rural kids get lots of scratches and most don't receive proper treatment.

Marvin's thoughts were broken by the sound of the telephone.

"Sorry, guys. I've got to take this call. You've got a free hour I believe, so go wander around and help yourself to coffee or Sanka. My assistant Vivian will meet you at the front desk at 1 for a tour of the mansion. You're staying the night, aren't you Marvin?"

"Yes, captain, if you don't mind a lowly sergeant in your quarters."

"Hell, Marvin, if things go right, we might have you as the next head of the Department of Interior." Marvin smiled widely at the absurdity.

As Marvin and Rachael showed themselves out, it looked like Marvin's world was about to change in ways he could never have imagined.

CHAPTER 41

DEAD EYES

Rachael and Marvin decided to revisit Dustin Lujan's office before they headed down to the front desk. Mary Lou, a plump Hispanic woman in her mid-fifties whose dress was the height of fashion in 1985, looked at the two visitors' paper nametags and greeted them by name. Rachael took charge, saying that they had just finished visiting with the governor and had a couple of quick questions if Mr. Lujan were available.

The receptionist made a call to Lujan and asked her visitors to have a seat. Ten minutes passed before the large oak door opened and a well-dressed man appeared. His blue suit and red tie made him look more FBI than Department of Public Safety; his sharp eyes and tight lips identified him as a man with a background in security.

"Hello, I'm Dustin Lujan. Mary Lou says you had a meeting with our esteemed governor today and had a question?"

"That's correct, Mr. Lujan. We appreciate you taking the time to meet with us unannounced. This is Marvin Manycoats, who is an old Marine buddy of the governor, and I'm Rachael Yellowhorse, a close friend of Mr. Manycoats." Marvin smiled when Rachael said "close friend."

"Nice to meet you both. What would you like to know about the Department of Public safety? Have you had a problem with identity theft? We get a lot of those questions."

"Not exactly...." Rachael said.

"What we were wondering is why all the old police records from 1961 were removed from the Gallup holding area," Marvin said bluntly, bypassing Rachael's more gentle approach. Lujan's facial expression didn't change, but his gaze shifted from Rachael to Marvin as he replied.

"I don't understand your question, Mr. Manycoats."

"Well, Mr. Lujan, you drove down to Gallup a few days ago and hauled away all the 1961 police records. Are those to be destroyed? Or are they being examined to see what might be in there regarding Orville's and Ricky Begay's deaths?"

"How do you know about this, Mr. Manycoats?" Lujan asked, his unblinking eyes now locked with Marvin's.

"Because, Mr. Lujan, I went down to take a look at the records for myself and apparently you had already removed them," Marvin replied, equally stone-faced.

"Huh, interesting. Well, I'm afraid I'm not at liberty to discuss this, but I can assure you it's procedural. Nothing to be concerned about."

Rachael decided it was her turn to join the conversation: "Mr. Lujan, when would we be able to get an answer to this question? Our biggest concern is that the Ricky and Orville Begay cases are being fully investigated."

"I'll personally make sure you and Marvin are notified when I have more information that I can share. Just leave your contact information with Mary Lou."

"Thank you, Mr. Lujan. We had also asked the governor about looking into this, and he said he would get back to us as well—so it sounds like we have all the bases covered. I'll let the governor know we talked when we see him for lunch at the mansion," Rachael said, letting Lujan know they were not only visitors but also friends of the governor.

"Perfect. If that was all you needed, I've got paperwork piling up today. It's Friday, and everyone likes to hit the road early. Give Governor Smiley my best." Lujan turned smartly and went back into his office.

Rachael peered into the office as he closed the door. White cardboard boxes were stacked in a corner—the ones from 1961. It seemed like everyone had a lot of paperwork to deal with today.

* * * *

The encounter with Lujan was disconcerting. Rachael and Marvin walked out quietly and instinctively headed for higher ground, exiting the capitol and finding the nearest bench.

"What did you think of Lujan's answers, Rachael?"

"Honestly? It seems like he's hiding something, but I'm not sure what," Rachael replied.

"I've met men like Lujan, a practiced smile with nothing behind the eyes. He's not going to keep us in any loop," Marvin continued. "I don't know what the true story might be, but I will ask the captain tonight."

"Be careful, Marvin. Men like Lujan might have the governor's ear and their own power base to protect. You might have saved the governor's life at one time, but power has a way of corrupting."

"I will. Don't worry about this old man getting into trouble. How about you show me that Plaza I've heard so much about. Do we have time to walk there?"

"Sure, it's five minutes away so we have time if we hurry. Let's splurge on a piece of coconut-cream pie at the Plaza Café and watch the tourists wander by—though on a cold day like today, the flow may be a bit light."

"There's so many tourists that you can watch them, like sheep going to the pen?" Marvin asked incredulously.

"It's Santa Fe," Rachael countered. "Home of the Jackalope and tourists from Texas who keep the gallery doors open. There are always tourists here, whether it's cold, warm, raining, or snowing."

"Even watching sheep is fun with a piece of coconut-cream pie. Let's go!" Marvin joked, trying to keep his mind off Lujan's true intentions in his friend's case.

CHAPTER 42

LUNCH IS SERVED

Rachael gave Marvin a quick tour of the Plaza, its leafless cottonwood trees, and its trampled brown grass. Marvin was amazed by the Palace of the Governors, which Rachael told him was built in 1610. The array of Pueblo artisans selling beneath the portal seemed like a job he would have enjoyed if he were a silversmith—and he wondered if his father would have agreed. He wandered through a dozen booths before he found the perfect piece, a plain silver bracelet with thunderbird designs that he bought from an elderly Santo Domingo silversmith—a hospitality gift for his old friend, the captain.

Rachael enjoyed watching Marvin go from vendor to vendor, laughing and smiling before pulling out his wallet and counting out $50, then shaking the artist's hand. Other than their uneasiness with Lujan, the Santa Fe trip had been good for both of them. She was ready for lunch and could feel Bloom's presence nearby. Charles had texted her saying he had made it to Santa Fe safely and was working at the gallery. Bloom, like everyone else in town, had some paperwork to finish and asked if Marvin could drop her off at the gallery after lunch.

Rachael also had work she wanted to do—but none of it involved paperwork.

Marvin's Ford truck followed a black government vehicle carrying the governor up the winding Mansion Road on the north side of Santa Fe. The high mesa overlooking Santa Fe and the Jemez Basin was pockmarked with massive, gated Santa Fe-style haciendas hidden behind rows of neatly trimmed piñon pines and transplanted aspens.

A guard at the mansion waved Marvin's truck through the front gate, and they parked up front, next to a new Ford pickup. The hacienda was a tribute to Puebloan architecture. The exterior featured an expansive front yard, the now-dormant grass awaiting the summer's entertainment schedule. Inside, an expansive ceiling of pine vigas was interspersed with hand hewn wooden slats, and the slick, cream-colored plaster walls were hung with works by early Taos and Santa Fe artists.

"Come on in, Marvin, and look around. This is the public's home—I'm just the current renter. Can I get you a drink? It's got be 5 o'clock back in D.C."

"Is that your new truck out front?" Marvin asked.

"Yes, sir. I like to escape from the circus of handlers on the weekends, and the only way to do that is if I have my own transportation. Now how about that drink?"

"We're not drinkers, I'm afraid. Too many issues for our people," Rachael said matter-of-factly.

"Rachael, I grew up in Gallup and do understand the problems alcohol can cause," Smiley replied. "How about we get you a Coke instead?"

"I'll take one," Marvin said.

"Make that two," Rachael agreed.

"We are waiting on Angel, my significant other, before we start our late lunch. She should be here shortly. How about a tour of the place while we're waiting?"

"That would great," Marvin and Rachael said in unison.

The governor walked around the living room talking about the art and WPA furniture before heading back to the master bedroom.

"I don't let too many people back into my private area," he said, "but I've got a special painting that I think you both will love to see."

Smiley flung open both of the double doors, exposing an expansive bedroom with a large T.C. Cannon painting hung directly over the bed. "What do you think?"

Rachael's mouth fell open as she tried to decipher the meaning of the display. How had the painting gotten from a storage unit in Mesilla to the governor's mansion?

Marvin, who did not know about the T.C. Cannon thread, spoke first. "Great image, captain. Who is the artist?"

Before the governor could answer, Rachael said, "T.C. Cannon."

"That's correct, Rachael. I figured you would recognize the artist's work. Pretty amazing piece, isn't it?"

"I have never seen this image before," Rachael said, hoping she sounded convincing, "and I agree it's a great painting."

"I don't know if it's been shown much. It is a wedding gift from my wife-to-be, the best present I have ever received—other than maybe being elected governor by the fine people of New Mexico."

"Your fiancée has great taste," Rachael said, fishing for information.

"Yes, she does. She has her own private art business and she knows her stuff. She picked out most of the paintings in the mansion. I'm trying to learn as much as I can from her."

Angel Veracruz walked into the room as the governor was speaking. "Are you talking about me behind my back again, my love?"

"Yes, I am. I was just telling Rachael how much I admire your ability when it comes to art, and how you gave me the best present I've ever received."

Angel hadn't considered the possibility that anyone other than the governor and the mansion staff would be seeing her Cannon.

"Oh, that's enough about me, Smiley. Let's go eat—I'm starving."

As the four walked out the room, Rachael took one last glance at the Cannon—a look that did not go unnoticed by Angel Veracruz. Nothing got by Angel, who was herself a master of the composed facial expression.

✱ ✱ ✱ ✱

A spread of blue corn tamales, Christmas-style chicken enchiladas, steaming fresh pinto beans, and a large stack of corn tortillas covered a seven-foot long Sabino hardwood table. All ate heartily; small talk dominated the meal, revolving around the issues of living on a reservation, New Mexico politics, and the upcoming nuptials. Angel listened, occasionally interjecting bits of information, but letting the governor drive the conversation. Then he switched gears.

"So, Marvin, Dustin Lujan called me before I left the building and said you and Rachael dropped by his office and are concerned about the Begay case?"

Both Smiley's and Angel's eyes locked on Marvin's face.

"Yes, we stopped by. The police boxes from 1961 were taken from the storage area in Gallup and I wanted to make sure they were removed for the right reasons," Marvin said.

"What does 'the right reasons' mean?" the governor asked.

Rachael jumped into the fray. "Governor Smiley, we are concerned that the case is active, but of such an age that the police might not want the publicity or simply don't want to deal with it. All the victims' relatives are dead and the only people left alive who care about this case are Marvin and me."

"I don't think that's true, Rachael. I care," Governor Smiley said empathetically. It was clear why he had become top dog in New Mexico politics—his smile seemed genuine.

"Well, I'm happy to hear that, governor. Hopefully you can find out why those files were removed," Rachael continued.

"I'm happy to talk to Mr. Lujan. As I said in my office, I'll look into it further and let you know what I find. Now who is ready for dessert? We've got hot sopapillas and plenty of organic honey to go around."

Angel had lost her appetite; there was something in that Navajo woman's voice that said, "I will never give up until we have answers." Her investigation into Rachael Yellowhorse, Marvin Manycoats, and Charles and James Bloom would begin in earnest tomorrow; no one was going to get in her way to the vice-presidency.

CHAPTER 43

ANGEL IS NO ANGEL

The last time Bloom had been in Santa Fe was over the holidays, and he was disappointed to see the same paintings hanging in his gallery as when he had left. He realized the state of affairs was his own fault: Dr. J, his only employee, was older and shouldn't be climbing a ladder—and any change to the exhibit was a decision he should have made before leaving at Christmas.

Bloom couldn't help but be a bit jealous. Rachael was eating lunch with the governor and he was snacking on peppered turkey jerky. Even though he had grown up in the state, he had never met a New Mexico governor. He had once been invited to the mansion to celebrate a lifetime achievement award for one of his artists, but the party was so large and hectic no formal introductions were made. Who would have thought that meeting a sitting governor would require a connection to Marvin Manycoats?

Most art exhibits take immense effort and planning, but occasionally a gallerist can throw together something of quality in short order. Today was one of those days. Bloom called the new show "Rite of Spring" and pulled paintings from his art bins that fit the general concept: an abstract dusting of snow on cubist adobe forms, a flower garden lined with shovels painted in Wayne Thiebaud's pie style, and a large Yébîchai dance painting he had on consignment from the acclaimed Navajo painter Tony Abeyta. The Abeyta, with its strong imagery, he placed in center of the room and built the exhibit around the piece, adding some additional paintings that implied "spring" to fill in the remainder of his main wall. He was amazed at how different the gallery felt with a fresh-up that showcased the Abeyta in different surroundings.

Bloom ordered a rush exhibit title for the main wall that would be delivered in the morning. He would hang it above the Abeyta painting before he left town. He wrote a two-paragraph description of the show and composed an email blast that would drop automatically on Monday, promoting a Friday opening. He would also send a small write-up to the *Santa Fean* and to the *New Mexican's Pasatiempo* magazine for the next week's art walk. He hoped a sale or two before spring actually arrived would pay the hotel room bill he would get next month.

Getting back into the gallery gave Bloom a sense of purpose he had not felt in a long time. The thought of the child that would never be kept drifting in and out of his consciousness, as if they were expecting a newborn in late summer—and he wondered if his wife were having a similar issue. He couldn't wait to see Rachael in a few hours. A quick call to the Inn of the Anasazi set everything up for an early check-in; tonight would mark a new beginning.

* * * *

Angel overheard Rachael ask Marvin if he could drop her off at the gallery.

"What gallery are you going to?" Angel inquired.

"Bloom's on Canyon Road—that's my husband's and my gallery. He deals in contemporary Native arts."

Angel was dumbfounded: the man who she had assumed had taken photos of her T.C. Cannon—and possibly all of her art—was the husband of Rachael Yellowhorse. Could this be a set-up? All she could muster was, "Yes, I've heard of the place."

As Angel tried to fit the pieces of the puzzle together, Marvin said, "I'll take you, Rachael."

Angel knew she needed more information and inserted herself back into the conversation. "Marvin, you don't need to go. I've got some chores downtown and I'm sure you boys have old war stories to tell."

The governor sensed his fiancée's concern and chimed in: "Marvin, how about I show you the guest house? It's pretty sweet."

"Well, you know I like sweets. Is that OK with you, Rachael?"

"Not a problem. I'll see you back at Toadlena."

"You never know, Rachael, I might never come home. This fancy living is something I could get used to," Marvin said, his humor returning. The trip had revived his spirits.

Angel and Rachael climbed into a bright red Mercedes sedan, and Angel immediately began her interrogation: "Rachael, Bloom's has been around a long time, hasn't it?"

"Yes, nearly 25 years."

"Native American art—it's mainly contemporary imagery, isn't it?" Angel asked.

"That's correct, mostly the contemporary Native masters. But lately we've been handling traditional artists, too—weavers and silversmiths."

"That makes sense, seeing as you're a weaver," Angel said.

"And it helps pay the light bill," Rachael teased, underplaying her importance as an artist.

"That's a great T.C. Cannon in our bedroom, don't you think?"

"It's amazing. I graduated from IAIA and I've always been a Cannon fan, but I've never seen that image before." Rachael was also looking for answers.

"Yes, it's an old family picture. We don't lend work from our private collection—too many prying eyes, I'm afraid."

"Did your family get it from T.C. Cannon?"

"Yes, directly, years ago, long before my time."

There was a pregnant pause as the women sized each other up.

"What's the story with this 1961 case?" Angel asked as she turned off Paseo de Peralta and headed up Canyon Road.

"Marvin was just a kid when his best friend disappeared in the desert and was never heard of again. Marvin decided it was time to put the issue to bed and started looking for his friend's remains—which he and I actually found."

"My god. How in the world did you do that?"

"Long story short, we did some research in the old police records and used some of Marvin's own ideas about the disappearance—and he found the boy's remains. It's not clear how his friend ended up in that grave, which is why he's so concerned about the police records being removed."

"I understand. You seem to be his best friend. Is it just you and Marvin who are trying to solve this case?"

Angel pulled into the gravel lot in front of Bloom's and parked next to a four-wheel-drive Ford truck whose wheel wells were splashed with a residue of red rez mud. She turned to Rachael to better gauge her reaction.

"I'm afraid so, Angel. Marvin has no one, and this little boy's death is a deep wound he has to try to heal. Maybe some kind of closure can be achieved—that's why the police taking the case seriously is so important to him, to both of us."

"I see. Well, I hope you both find the resolution you seek. I'll make sure the governor knows the whole story."

Rachael thanked Angel for the lunch and headed into see Bloom, whom she was missing terribly.

Angel pretended to check her phone while she remained parked in the lot, watching Rachael as she embraced her husband. The weaver seemed genuinely happy.

"Enjoy your happiness while you can, my dear Rachael Yellowhorse." Angel spun her wheels as she pulled out, sending the gravel flying. She was on a mission and time was not on her side. She, too, was seeking closure—but of an entirely different kind.

CHAPTER 44

KEEPING POWER

The hug between husband and wife after a nearly two-week separation was gasoline on a hot fire. The Anasazi Hotel was calling, but Rachael had been so upset by seeing the T.C. Cannon in the governor's mansion that she was distracted from her husband's passion.

Rachael shared her and Marvin's discussion with Lujan with Bloom, as well as the shock of seeing the Cannon painting in Smiley's bedroom. She also told Angel's story of the piece being in the family forever and of getting it directly from the artist. Dr. Benny Benally had told her the painting had been on T.C.'s easel a few days before his death. And what about that odd inscription on the back?

"Bloom, I know you're ready to have some us time, and I am too, more than you know, but I'm a bit freaked out. Why is that T.C. Cannon painting in the governor's home—a gift from Angel no less. What the hell is going on?"

"Remember I told you I saw government cars at the Mesilla compound? I'm assuming that must be Angel's place. In fact, it has to be. The paperwork for my father's consulting job was from the Veracruz Trust—and that's her name, right? Angel Veracruz?"

"I'm not sure, Bloom. She was only introduced to me as Angel, the governor's fiancée."

"It's Veracruz, I'm sure. That woman is a private art dealer. I've heard her name before—top-notch contemporary and deceased artwork. Her rep is that of a big buyer, lots of cash, big name clients—and I can tell you after seeing that vault that she has more than lots of cash. There's a fortune in there."

"What does that inscription mean? Who is Mrs. Roy Bryant?" Rachael asked.

"No idea. Let's Google it and see what comes up."

Bloom typed his query into the desk computer as Rachael stood over him. The first listing was for a PBS site that read: "Roy and Carolyn Bryant and J. W. Milam will always be linked to the 1955 murder of Emmett Till."

"A monster from the Civil Rights era? I don't get it. What does that have to do with a gift? It makes no sense," Rachael puzzled.

"I agree, no sense whatsoever. Maybe your Benny Benally has some insight into it. Why don't you give him a call," Bloom suggested.

Rachael dialed the professor's phone number—no answer—so she left a message asking Benally to call her, saying it was important.

"Hopefully he will call me back, but if he doesn't, I remember where he used to live. I'll bet he hasn't moved; we could drop by on the way out of town."

"Perfect. I have a sign that needs to be hung for my new "Rite of Spring" exhibit in the morning. How do you like the idea?" Bloom asked, opening his arms to encompass his hastily hung show.

"Lovely exhibit. I didn't realize you had planned a new spring show. It's all nicely placed and I like the concept."

"Yeah, I didn't know I was going to do it either...." Bloom smiled at Rachael, who understood that her husband had come up with the exhibit on the fly.

"OK, Mr. Creativity. Are you ready for some other type of spontaneous activity?"

"That would be affirmative. Since you've done the leg work with Lujan, let's go see how firm the mattresses in a really expensive hotel are."

As Bloom and Rachael headed outside, her phone rang: it was the professor returning her call. Rachael asked Benally if he knew the meaning of the inscription on the painting's reverse. He said didn't have any knowledge of it, and hadn't discovered any additional information since they last spoke. When Rachael told him she was in town for the day and was hoping to see him, he invited the couple to come to his home. Rachael accepted and they headed to the south side of Santa Fe. It was only 3 p.m.; they could be back at the hotel in time for happy hour—with or without drinks.

"Bloom, I know you don't want to go to Benally's house, but I need to ask him about Angel Veracruz and I prefer to do that in person so I can get a better read on what he has to say."

"Rachael, you have become the detective in our family. What exactly are you expecting this retired professor to know or say? Do you think he's hiding something?"

"No, not exactly, but my gut says there is more to this story than meets the eye, starting with that odd inscription—and why is the painting now hanging in the governor's mansion?"

"You know, we could check-in to our lovely hotel room first; it's just a mile away from here...."

"I know, Bloom. We will make the Benally trip really quick. We don't need to rush; we have the whole night," Rachael said, her eyes promising Bloom it would be worth the wait.

"Well it's your loss; let's go...."

Rachael and Bloom walked out of the gallery holding hands. He opened her door and she hopped into Bloom's mud-caked truck. Rachael snuggled up to her husband, gently placing a hand on his knee as they made their way toward Zia Street. She was content to be back home with the one she loved.

It was obvious that Benally had gotten old. The front yard was overgrown and it took him a few minutes to answer the door. Still, Rachael was pleased to see her mentor; it had been fifteen years since they last met. His mind seemed like it was still sharp, but his body was clearly failing.

The paintings in the house were hung salon-style, and a variety of sculptures dotted the sparse furnishings. Most of the art employed Native themes, representing years of student work from IAIA. The art tour began as soon as they entered the house, with Benally pointing out pieces and giving an encyclopedic dissertation on the artist's work and progress.

"How about this piece, Rachael," Benally asked, pointing to a small sculpture.

"My god, I had forgotten about that piece. I was mad at the world when I made that thing, not long after my brother's death in New York City."

Rachael picked up the sculpture and examined her workmanship. The piece was a composite of three unrelated objects: the top was an ice pick inserted into a hatchet handle, its base stuck into a large plastic apple.

"You presented this sculpture to me after I gave you an A even though you had missed a week of school."

"I felt bad for missing so many classes, and you still gave me an A. It was the least I could do for you—and, as you know it's not a great piece of art. C work at best I would say."

"Well, I love it. In fact, Rachael, you and your brother were very much alike, both extremely talented artists. Do you ever miss making sculpture?"

"That's a wonderful compliment, Dr. Benally. I don't miss making three-dimensional objects. Spider Woman called me and I found my true creative space."

"I'm happy for you, Rachael—and from what I've heard, your weavings are magnificent."

Rachael blushed, not knowing how to answer, so Bloom spoke up. "Yes, they are amazing. We have a waiting list for her pieces, but I do agree with you that she is the one who is amazing."

"Professor Benally," Rachael asked to move the conversation away from herself, "I have a question about the T.C. Cannon we talked about earlier."

"What's your question, Rachael?"

"The Cannon is hanging in the governor's mansion as we speak. Do you know how it got there?"

"I thought it was in Las Cruces...."

"It was, and now it's in the governor's bedroom."

"How do you know that, Rachael?"

"I saw it about two hours ago."

"Wow, you're moving in some powerful circles. I'm not sure what to say."

Rachael dismissed the professor's compliment and asked another question: "Do you know Angel Veracruz?"

"Yes, she's an art dealer. I see where you going with this. I read in the papers that she's marrying our governor."

"Correct. She's also the owner of the Cannon. She gave it to the governor as a wedding gift, and told me it was an old family piece purchased directly from the artist. How could it have come from the artist if you saw it on his easel right before he died?"

Benally paused, then said, "I guess they must have purchased it the week of his death."

It was Rachael's turn to think a while before she asked, "What do you think about that inscription? I looked it up on Google and a PBS website said that Mrs. Roy Bryant was the woman Emmett Till whistled at, an act that got him killed in 1955. Are you familiar with the story?"

"I remember that horrific moment in history quite well. The boy went into a grocery store to get some candy after working in the fields. He was from Chicago and apparently made some of offensive remark to the owner's wife, which the white men didn't take kindly. You know back in the fifties people treated us Navajos like second-class citizens too. I was told more than once to go back to my own country—can you imagine?"

"Why would Angel put that inscription on the back if it relates to Till? I don't get it...."

"Sorry, I don't know. I would guess that it's not actually related to that event."

"It just seems like there's more to this—but maybe I'm overthinking the whole thing."

"I think you're probably right that it's much ado about nothing. That inscription might relate to something entirely different. Maybe they bought the piece from the estate or Cannon's New York gallery and the family history is a little off. It's not really our business, is it Rachael?"

"Your probably right, professor," Rachael said as the three sat down and Benally regaled Bloom with stories about what Rachael Yellowhorse was like when she was twenty years old. Bloom had not heard any of these stories before and was entranced.

Rachael and Bloom said their good-byes to Benally and headed to the Inn of the Anasazi.

After they left, Benally sat down in a worn recliner, its blue color faded to a steel gray, and pulled a book of photos from a side table. He rifled through its contents until he found what he was looking for: a Polaroid from the 1990s that was yellowing at the edges—a photo of the Cannon painting when it was hanging on his living room wall, with Rachael Yellowhorse's small abstract sculpture sitting on a table beneath it. The world certainly was an unbroken circle of connectivity.

Benally removed the photo from the book and tossed it into the fireplace. He would destroy the last vestiges of his connection with the Cannon tonight; there was no sense taking any chances.

Angel considered the implications of the drama unfolding before her. It was a horror show running on a continuous loop, and she was one of the main actors.

Marvin and Rachael had found Begay's remains and reviewed the Gallup police records that were now safely in her husband's possession, so there were at least two meddlers looking for answers.

Charles Bloom and his father had been hired to do a pre-Columbian appraisal and had taken photos of who-knows-what while they were working. They had asked questions about her T.C. Cannon, which Rachael now knew had been moved from her protected vault to the governor's bedroom—something that would have raised serious questions in that smart woman's mind. The consequences could be huge. Was it all a set-up to destroy her husband's nomination for vice-president?

Rachael mentioned that she had been an IAIA student, and Benally had said the person with the T.C. Cannon photos was an old student. Bloom must have sent his wife the images—maybe of more than just the Cannon, possibly her entire painting inventory. If her staff was dumb enough to hire a gallery owner's father to do an appraisal, anything was possible. This could be a problem. Many paintings had been paid for with cartel money; at least two were stolen and were being stashed in the vault for a yearly fee.

The man most invested in the murder investigation, Marvin Manycoats, was staying in their home. Loose ends needed to be tied up and disposed of in such a way that no one could ever discover a motive or any remains—unlike those of Ricky Begay.

There were many people involved and their stories would be messy to unravel, but she had dealt with messes before, and business was business. She would need to discuss all the pieces of the puzzle with Smiley soon, and she hoped he would agree with the way she planned to solve the problem. There were really no other options if they hoped to achieve the power she had long desired.

CHAPTER 45

AN AX TO GRIND

Angel made a detour before heading home. One part of the puzzle needed to be put together first: Benally. The professor's south-side home was nestled at the end of a long dirt driveway near Zia Road. Large, scraggly junipers marked the entrance, the trees' dead branches telling the story of an old man living alone.

The car crept down the roadway. The roundabout in front of the house was devoid of cars, and she parked there, leaving the motor running. Angel didn't bother to ring the doorbell, twisting the doorknob instead. The door was unlocked, and she walked in quietly, a small revolver nuzzled in her gloved right hand.

Benally was bent over a teepee of kindling wood in the fireplace, blowing on it weakly to start a flame. He stumbled backward in surprise when he saw Angel with the gun in her hand. Trying to right himself, he instead fell hard to the ground, knocking over the small table displaying the Yellowhorse sculpture. Its plastic apple base rolled to Angel's feet.

Angel picked up the sculpture with a gloved hand. Its weight could be useful.

"Interesting work. Who is the artist?" She smiled at Benally, who was still sprawled on the ground.

Stammering, he said, "Rachael Yellowhorse."

"Are you kidding me?" Angel asked, a look of disbelief flooding her face. Everything was coming together.

"No, I'm not. It's Rachael Yellowhorse."

"You two are friends?"

"I guess you could say that."

"When was the last time you saw Ms. Yellowhorse, professor?" Angel stepped closer, the small gun acting like a metronome as she spoke.

Benally paused, afraid to answer, then slowly said, "She and her husband were here not more than thirty minutes ago. I was getting ready to call you. Please don't point that gun at me...."

Angel used the toe of her boot to nudge the man in the thigh. She then saw the Polaroid starting to burn in the fireplace. She walked past Benally and used a hand-wrought fire tool to fish the photo out. The image of the Cannon painting that had once hung on Benally's wall was still intact.

"Why are you burning a Polaroid of my Cannon? And why was Rachael Yellowhorse here thirty minutes ago?"

"Well, she wanted to know about the inscription on the back of the painting and was curious about how the painting ended up at the governor's mansion."

"And the Polaroid?"

"It was the only evidence that the Cannon had once been in my possession. I figured Rachael might be onto something so I wanted to get rid it."

"So you did know about the inscription—but you didn't share that tidbit of information with me."

"I know, I'm sorry. I didn't know what it meant, and I didn't think much about it."

"Sure you did, professor. It was leverage, and I would have done the same thing. Did you figure out the inscription?"

"I looked on the computer and the only reference I could find was about the murder of Emmett Till. I assume that Ms. Roy Bryant is a reference to you?"

"Correct. It's my little inside joke to my husband-to-be. Did you know that there is a commemorative sign where Till's body was found in Mississippi, and that every year some rednecks shoot up that sign and it has to be replaced?"

"Doesn't surprise me. I guess racism runs deep in some places in America," Benally gasped as he worked himself up to a sitting position with his hands outstretched in a triangle in front of him as he tried to pull more air into his damaged lungs.

"I think, professor, that it's not so much about racism but power. Those good old boys shoot the memorial sign out as a warning to everyone in that area, telling them they are still in charge, so keep your mouths shut. If you betray or harm us, we will seek revenge. Nothing is sacred—not even a child."

Benally's legs began to visibly shake, seeing this evil side of Angel. His breathing grew more rapid as his fear increased.

"You should be afraid, Professor Benally. I'm not a person to be trifled with, so tell me everything that happened during that visit from start to finish, and don't leave out anything."

The old man retold the entire story while still sitting on the ground, Angel imposing her will on him.

"Nothing else?"

"That's everything, I swear. Please put the gun away."

"Do you think Ms. Yellowhorse and her husband were satisfied with your explanation?"

"Yes, I do. You don't have anything to worry about. She trusts me and the husband seemed fine too."

"OK, let me help you get up."

As Benally put his weight on the couch to push himself up from the floor, Angel stepped closer and, in a single motion, thrust the ice pick on Rachael's sculpture deeply into the professor's chest, pushing him back to the floor. The sharp metal blade passed between the man's seventh and eight ribs, burying the ice pick up to the hatchet handle and piercing the old man's left lung and racing heart.

Benally knew he was mortally wounded as the pools of blood pumped into his thoracic cavity. "Why?" he asked, looking up at Angel in disbelief.

"Don't blame me. Rachael Yellowhorse did this to you. We have an ax to grind, you might say. The fact you tried to get rid of that Polaroid told me you were scared—and I don't trust scared."

Angel was grinning about her sculpture pun as she picked up Benally's cell phone and placed it on a table a distance away from her victim.

She then stuffed the remains of the Polaroid into her coat pocket and left the gasping man to bleed out. She would dump her burner phone on the way home.

One down, three to go: the pieces of the puzzle were coming together nicely.

CHAPTER 46

BARBED WIRE CUTS DEEP

When Angel arrived back at the mansion, Marvin and Smiley were in deep conversation. Marvin, who rarely drank, was sipping on an icy Negro Modelo. Angel decided to let the boys have their fun before she broke them up: she and Smiley had decisions to make.

"Angel, come see this," Smiley yelled, his right arm raised high in the air. "Marvin bought this lovely Indian bracelet for me this afternoon from under the portal. It's a great fit; it's hard to find big bracelets like this."

"I was hoping it was too big for you so I could keep it for myself," Marvin teased.

"It's a wonderful keepsake of this special day," Angel said as she retired to the back bedroom. Arrangements for tomorrow needed fine-tuning.

Marvin was admiring the bracelet when he noticed the scar on Smiley's arm that he had seen in the photo in the governor's office.

"Captain, what is that scar from? A love kiss from the war?"

"No, that kiss gave me this beautiful cane." Smiley tapped the tip on the floor for emphasis. "That little sweetie on my arm was a cut from going over barbed wire as a kid. I pushed down with my hand and the wire slipped and boomeranged onto my forearm, leaving a jagged scar. I learned to use gloves and wear long sleeves when working with barbed wire from then on."

Marvin's memory clicked on the words "long sleeves," remembering that even in Nam the captain wore long sleeves, something he had never thought about until that moment.

Marvin pulled up his jeans to expose a long cut on his calf. "Cut me like a knife. Barbed wire went right through my best jeans. Needed stitches, but I was dumb and didn't show my dad, figured he would get mad. Lucky I didn't die of tetanus. The gaping wound that resulted, which I lovingly call my Ziploc bag, is the reminder to be smarter next time. Looks like you did the same by the size of that scar."

The governor, who wanted to move on from this subject, said, "Yep, that's right. Not enough money for doctors, and at that age, we didn't worry about scars."

"Well, at least you had a good paying job delivering candy. We Navajo got paid half the salary for twice the work."

"That job paid OK. I wasn't getting rich, but the free candy was a bonus."

The thought of free candy jogged Marvin's subconscious. "Captain, I think you might have delivered candy when I was a kid. Were you working on the rez in 1961?"

"I don't remember the dates—it was a long time ago. But I do remember I worked for a little over a year for old man Perry out of Gallup. He was a piece of work."

"I never met old man Perry, but sure did like his candy," Marvin said, then pushed on.

"That skeleton I discovered last week, well they found a candy wrapper near where my friend's dad died. Do you think that has anything to do with the case?"

"I wouldn't know, Marvin. It seems pretty unlikely. A candy wrapper could blow in on the wind from anywhere—or maybe the man just liked candy. As much candy as I delivered, it was clear Navajos like sweets."

"True enough," Marvin said, unleashing a half-smile.

"I would guess that it's pretty unlikely there's any hidden meaning to the wrapper—just trash blowing in the wind."

Marvin thought about the captain's words, then decided to pull the jawbreaker out of his medicine pouch. He was keeping his friend close to him by carrying Ricky's photo on his phone, and the candy had taken on a power he could not explain.

"What about this?" Marvin asked, as he laid the opaque cellophane wrapper and purple jawbreaker dusted in corn pollen on the table.

Smiley froze. He didn't know what to say. Was Marvin testing him? Did he somehow know the backstory? "What this?" he asked nervously.

"I found this candy near my friend's body in the crypt. I can't figure out why this would be in the grave and why there was the empty wrapper near his father, who also died suddenly. Seems like some kind of a connection to me, not wind."

"Hum, hard to say. It is odd, but maybe your friend simply liked candy."

"No, it's not like that. His skeleton was in a fetal position and had no clothes, like he had been stripped of his earthly goods. It was more like the wrapper was a fetish for the afterlife."

"Marvin, I'm sure the police will get to the bottom of this. You should give them that jawbreaker; it could be important evidence."

"Probably. Rachael said the same thing, but I'm hesitant. I know it's important and I don't trust the police much."

"I will take it to the head of the New Mexico State Police. You can trust me to give it to him personally. You won't get in trouble, I promise."

Marvin considered his words and pushed the candy toward his old Marine buddy, leaving a fine yellow trail. "OK, give it to them, and let them know I think there is a connection. They can call me and I'll fill them in on where exactly I found it."

"That's the correct move, Marvin," Smiley said, smiling at his friend as he raked the candy into his palm. "Why don't we get to bed? We can talk tomorrow."

"It has been a long day, captain. I appreciate you inviting me up here to the mansion; it was a great day too."

"Marvin, that's what friends are for."

* * * *

Angel didn't waste time telling Smiley about what had transpired with Rachael and the T.C. Cannon painting as soon as he came to bed. She left out the killing of Benally for the moment. The less he knew, the better; he might not understand her reasoning. Smiley, in turn, filled Angel in on his conversation with Marvin, his questions about the scar, and his passing along of the candy evidence.

"He found the jawbreaker at the grave, right?"

"The Begay kid had stolen a bunch of candy. I thought I retrieved all of it but one piece must have escaped me. I was pretty shook up, as you can imagine."

"Where is the jawbreaker?" Angel asked.

Smiley grinned and stuck out his purple-tinged tongue.

"You ate it?"

"Well, I was curious if it would taste as good as they did when I was as a kid."

"Did it?"

"Not really. I tossed the wrapper in the trash."

"Smart. Misplaced evidence. It happens," Angel said, seeing a new side of her husband-to-be.

"Angel, we have the old police records and there is no evidence in them to implicate me. Can't we just let this run its course?"

"My dear Mr. Vice President—if that is a title you ever want to hear—we cannot take a chance on this running its so-called course. This tragedy started in 1961 and it's time to tie up all the loose ends. I know you love your buddy, but if I don't take some drastic measures, and soon, you're not only looking at losing all your power, but also at the possibility of going to jail for the rest of your life."

Smiley took this in as if he were sitting in a trance, not saying a word for two solid minutes. Finally, he asked, grim-faced, "What do we need to do?"

"Nothing. It's what I have to do—the less you know the better. Dustin will help me do what's necessary; you just keep playing the host. Tomorrow I'm going to take Marvin down to the ranch. You need to finish that podcast, remember? I need you to ask Marvin to do this for you."

"True, we do need the content and the compound has the recording room if I remember correctly." The governor's mind had taken a turn, and he was playing along as if this were a normal conversation about a scheduled event for his soon-to-be deceased friend.

"I'll have him follow me down to the compound, and I'll get Bloom and his wife to come down too," Angel said.

"How are you going to do that?"

"Mr. Vice President, better I keep the details to myself while you follow your own script."

"How the hell did it come to this?" Smiley exploded.

"You killed two people, darling, that's how. Shit happens in life—believe me, I know," Angel said as she pivoted to the bathroom to get undressed. The governor's mess would soon be cleaned up and everyone would come out smelling better—well, almost everyone.

CHAPTER 47

PAYBACK

Sleep was scarce in the mansion that night. The governor's mind was preoccupied with what his fiancée was planning. Marvin—the man who had saved his life, a complete innocent like Ricky Begay and his faithful father—would soon be toast.

Smiley was a lot like Angel, but she knew her heart and embraced her dark side with gusto when required. The new silver bracelet adorning his right arm would be another reminder of his crimes, like Ricky Begay's small ring hanging around his neck. Both were a memorial to what true power requires, the collateral damage of politics.

In the guesthouse, Marvin's mind was also in turmoil. Buried memories had been reactivated by shared war stories, and he found himself back in the jungle saving his friend's life. Bullet's whizzing, the smell of gun powder, then a flashback to Ricky Begay's skeleton, a frozen scream dominating his dreams. No sound came from the open mouth, but the meaning was clear: "Look at me. It's me—I'm talking to you. You must listen or die."

Marvin woke up in a cold sweat in the oversized bed, plush white sheets tangled around his body. The thin mattress on his metal army cot was nowhere to be found. The expensive, very firm mattress in the guesthouse, made sleep difficult and the beer filled his bladder. As he found the nearby toilet he relived the nightmare: what was Ricky trying to tell him? There was something hidden in his usually infallible memory—but what?

Marvin placed the fluffy blanket on the ground, rolling up in it like a battered corndog, and made his balled-up coat the pillow. He needed a sing. His *hózhó* was off balance and Ricky's *chindi* were overpowering his waking world. He hoped they would soon bring answers about the death and he would sleep again.

Little could Marvin have imagined that his world was about to implode and the answers he desperately sought would be freely available. A river of emotions was raging toward him, and the hard male rains that were normally life-giving could instead sweep all in their path to their deaths.

The die was cast. Angel had assembled all the pieces of the puzzle and the picture was ready to complete. Her plan required good timing and a smidgen of luck, but, if all went well, their problems would disappear and the jigsaw could once again be put back in its box, this time for eternity.

Step one was get the three loose ends—Dr. Bloom, his nosy art dealer son, and his smart wife Rachael—rounded up.

Angel sent her goon squad to the old professor's home at 8 a.m. James let them in the door as if they were the best of friends: he thought they were bringing him his check early.

The thugs quickly subdued him and took control of his phone and computer. Gutierrez texted Charles Bloom from his father's phone saying that he was having some difficulties with the appraisal and that he needed his help today. He apologized because he knew he was with Rachael. If Charles could come to his house, he would be waiting for them.

Bloom texted back: "What's up?" and Gutierrez responded, "Can't talk now. I'll see you this afternoon. Let me know if I can expect you. Love, your father."

Bloom then called—no answer. He texted again and then called his dad's landline—no answer on either phone. Then his father texted back: "Not good with this phone texting; home phone broken. See you soon. Thanks for your help—I need you, Son. Father."

"Rachael, I don't know what's going on, but clearly there is something wrong. My dad's having problems using the new phone I gave him and he says the home phone is broken. Maybe his blood pressure is up. That pre-Columbian appraisal was fishy and could be weighing on his mind."

"Why don't you call Angel? Rachael suggested. "That compound has to be her place. The Cannon painting was in the storage unit and now it's in the governor's mansion, a wedding gift."

"Sure. I have her number in my contacts. I'll just call and say, 'Hey, I happen to know that you own that compound because I took photos of the off-limits Cannon last week—and by the way, who is Mrs. Roy Bryant?'"

"You don't have to be condescending, Charles Bloom. I'm trying to help. How about this: we don't have to stay a second night at the Anasazi. We can save some money, and I want to see this so-called compound."

"OK. I'll text my dad to tell him we're on the way. If we check out by 11 a.m. we can be in Cruces by 3 p.m. I want every second of the time due us in this hotel. It's beyond our budget even in the off-season—and that bed is wonderful," Charles said.

"Yes, it is!"

Holding hands, their family bond reignited, they strolled across the historic Plaza like tourists heading for an inexpensive breakfast at the Plaza Café. The great people-watching, the hottest green chile in Santa Fe, and a plate of huevos rancheros and fresh tortillas would start the day off right.

* * * *

The governor asked Marvin if he would accompany his fiancée to their get-away compound in Las Cruces to record the podcast. He told Marvin he could spend the night there if he wanted, promising plenty of food and all the pecans he could pick.

Marvin could do the math and a bag of pecans at this time of year was gold; it was hard to believe they hadn't all been picked. A sack of fresh pecans would pay for his food, gas, and a week's worth of ice cream bars. Marvin agreed to go and texted Rachael that the governor needed him to do the podcast after all, but down in Las Cruces. He might not be home for a few days, so she shouldn't count on him for any dinners until mid-week. He was surprised when Rachael texted back that she and Bloom were also on their way to Las Cruces to see Bloom's father. She asked him to give them a call if he spent the night down there. Maybe there was a dinner in his future after all.

The light-blocking shades in the guesthouse had done a number on Marvin's circadian rhythm, so he woke up late the next morning. The governor insisted on showing him the property and taking another trip down memory lane, so it was looking like he would be spending the night in Mesilla—his actual destination—a small town adjacent to Las Cruces. Over brunch Smiley explained that Angel had to leave early and didn't want to wake him, so, if he didn't mind, Dustin Lujan would accompany Marvin to the compound. The Department of Public

Safety head had some work to do in Las Cruces and would catch a ride back to Santa Fe with Ms. Veracruz the next day.

Marvin wasn't that happy about going to Mesilla with Lujan; he had thought the purpose of the trip was to accompany Angel so he could record the podcast—whatever that was. The change in plans seemed a bit odd but it was not alarming. The drive south with Lujan might be uncomfortable, but it would give Marvin time to soften the man up as to why the police records had been removed to Santa Fe.

The trip from Santa Fe to Las Cruces transverses the complete topography of New Mexico, from its snow-peaked mountains to bosque forests of cottonwoods, from dry mesas to large tracts of irrigated farmlands. Interstate 25 had little traffic in March, but watching the huge flocks of Sandhill cranes feeding along the Río Grande made the time pass easily.

Lujan was a man of few words. He answered Marvin's questions monosyllabically, keeping to "yes" and "no" for the most part. Marvin massaged the conversation the best he could, trying to figure out the relationship between state employee, the governor, and Angel. Apparently, Lujan had been a friend of Smiley's since the man first ran for Congress. Lujan insisted he had not heard of Marvin until last week, and he declined to answer questions about the records he had removed from the Gallup town hall. The conversation soon faded into silence, with only the sound of some 1970s popular music filling the cab. Marvin surmised Lujan was a loyal "yes" man to his governor, and if Smiley asked for the records to be looked into, Lujan would not destroy them.

After four hours of driving, they arrived in Las Cruces. Marvin's truck continued west on I-110, then turned south onto the Mesilla exit just as Sammy Davis Jr.'s voice filled the air, repeating over and over, "The Candy Man knows...." It was an upbeat song Marvin had first heard when he twenty-three. He had listened to it many times since, but this time the lyrics hit a nerve, a dark one, leading Marvin to consider the other side of the coin: what if it was the governor, the Candy Man, who wanted the records expunged? Then what? And why? He had asked for the jawbreaker and Marvin had given it to him!

As he drove past the 1852 Basilica of San Albino in Old Town Mesilla, Marvin's mind started to spin wildly. He had never considered this possibility before. Why was Ricky talking to him? What was it he wanted to tell him? A shiver ran down Marvin's spine as memories and facts rose into his consciousness and became clear. The former Marine was having a come to Jesus moment as Lujan pointed past an old adobe to a road lined with cottonwood trees and surrounded by a huge grove of pecans.

"Take that road." Lujan ordered, but Marvin drove on by.

"No, that road, that was the road," Lujan commanded.

"Oh, sorry. Let me turn it around." Marvin kept going until he came to an isolated dirt road and parked the car.

"Why are you parking the truck? The road is back there, along the cottonwoods."

"I know, but before I go there, I have a few questions."

"What questions?" Lujan's voice turned harsh.

"How long have you known the Candy Man?" Marvin no longer called Smiley the governor.

"You mean the governor?"

"No, I mean the Candy Man. I think you know who I'm talking about."

"I told you: I've known him since he first ran for Congress nearly thirty years ago."

"Why, Mr. Lujan, are you doing his dirty work for him?"

"What the hell are you talking about?" Lujan asked, his anger flaring.

"I'm talking about taking police evidence in a double murder so you could destroy it. That's right, isn't it? Murders?"

"You're out of your mind. I don't know what you're talking about, Manycoats, but accusing a sitting governor of a capital crime can get you in a lot of hot water."

Lujan watched Marvin's face for a reaction, but the Navajo didn't flinch. Then Lujan reached for his pocket, but Marvin was expecting a move and grabbed the man's hand. Years of chopping and loading firewood and working heavy construction had given Marvin's wrist the strength of an arm wrestler. His elbow struck Lujan in the jaw as he wrenched the gun from his grip, pointing it at the man.

"What are you doing? You know you just assaulted the head of the Public Safety Department. You're screwing with the wrong person."

"You may think so, but I don't. I believe I just saved my life, and now you're going to start talking. I may be old, but you can tell I'm strong. I'm a Marine with two Purple Hearts, so I know how to use this gun and I am not afraid to do it."

"What's going on here?" Marvin demanded again. Lujan still didn't answer.

"Let me fill you in, Mr. Lujan. As it so happens, I have a great memory and thanks to Mr. Sammy Davis Jr., the fog of childhood has lifted and I now remember what was going on fifty years ago.

"Governor Smiley, as I'm sure you know, was called the Candy Man because he delivered candy on the rez. I remember the truck, but until this moment I didn't remember seeing our governor when I was a kid. Now his face has been unmasked. He was the deliveryman who served both me and my deceased friend. You know how I know this?"

"I don't have a clue what you're talking about," Lujan sneered.

"There is a scar on the Candy Man's arm, the same arm that's wearing a bracelet I gave him last night. It's a very jagged scar. He says it's from barbed wire, but I know barbed wire slices like a knife, cuts clean. No, this scar looks like something entirely different. It's teeth marks, Ricky Begay's teeth marks."

"My god, you've gone mad, Manycoats. Give me that gun now, before it's too late."

"Too late—that's funny. I think there is something dangerous in that compound and you're supposed to be delivering me up on a plate to get rid of a problem—just like you were doing with those police records. That's why the governor's fiancée isn't here, but you are. How did Ricky Begay's bite mark get on the Candy Man's arm?"

Lujan didn't respond.

"You're a man of few words, so I will tell you. For some reason, my friend clamped down on the Candy Man's arm, making a very deep, serious wound. Then my friend ends up in a Navajo grave. Only a person with intimate knowledge of the rez could bury someone like that—maybe a man who had driven hundreds of miles on the rez delivering candy, one who understands the culture."

"I don't know how you came up with this cockamamie fantasy to explain your friend's death," Lujan blustered, "but to try to implicate an honorable governor who may be the next vice president of the United States of America is insane. This is very dangerous talk."

"I think it's the vice presidency that has the Candy Man spooked. The governor wants that position and I found the body at the worst possible time for him. I don't know if Smiley killed my friend or not. That's something we are going to have to find out—but not at some compound of your choosing."

"Marvin, you don't know the powers that are working here. You and the governor are friends, and connected in ways few could understand. Let this Begay case go away quietly and you and your friends could find yourself very wealthy. The vice president has the power and the ear of the president, and that power could be yours too."

"And what about Ricky and Orville Begay? What power do they have lying in their graves?"

"Let them go. They are dead and no one cares but you. Be smart. We can work a deal. If you don't cooperate, I can't help your friends."

"What does that mean?" Marvin yelled.

Lujan pulled out his phone and showed the photo to Marvin. The Eagle has landed; all is in order. One small step for man, one giant step for the governor.

"Charles Bloom, James Bloom, and Rachael are our guests at the compound, and without your cooperation they will be permanent guests. It's in your hands."

"That road you wanted me to turn onto—does that go to the compound?"

"Yes, it's right there. You can hang onto the gun. I'll drive us in and we can work this out the smart way."

"Isn't there a road that would let us come in the back way, through this pecan grove, so I can check out the situation on my own terms?"

"There is only one road. The trees we're parked under are at the rear of the compound; they block anyone from coming or going. The front gate is open now and remember—you can hang on to the gun."

"Put your hands on the dashboard!" Marvin ordered as he opened the driver's door and slid out of the seat. Lujan did as ordered.

"OK, now slide over toward me."

"This is a smart move, Marvin, you will see."

"Now step out of my truck S-L-0-W-L-Y."

"What?"

"I'm the one with the pistol, and I can assure you the safety is off. Don't mess with this old Marine." Marvin waved the gun at Lujan. "Do as I say and take off your shoes and socks."

Lujan got out of the truck and did as he was told.

"Now lay face down on the ground and put your hands in your back pockets—or you'll end up like my friends did when the Viet Cong captured them. It wasn't pretty."

Lujan complied. Marvin watched him carefully as he opened the back of his truck and removed two rolls of duct tape that he kept there for an emergency—which this certainly was. He taped the man's hands and legs tightly together, then rolled him over and taped his eyes, then started to cover Lujan's mouth.

"Marvin, think about what you're doing. You're out-gunned in the compound. There are German Shepherds there and professional killers. I am your only chance. Don't throw your life away!"

"Where will I find my friends?"

No answer from Lujan.

"You want me put a sock in your mouth, then tape over your mouth and nose with only two little holes for air? I can do that, but if I do it will take all your effort to breathe. You will last maybe thirty minutes before your body gives out. It's a slow, horrible death, Mr. Lujan. You're the one who is throwing your life away, Viet Cong style."

"There is a surgical room at the far end of the compound. They will probably be in there," Lujan volunteered.

"Smart move, Mr. Lujan. Looks like you're going to miss out on the kind of torture my Marine brothers suffered.

"Here's what's going to happen: I'm going to put you into my truck and cover you with a tarp. Don't make any noise. If I get caught, I'll tell them where you are, and if I get killed, someone will find you. It doesn't look like it will be too cold tonight, so you won't freeze. If I do make it—well, at this point you haven't done anything that would get you thrown into your own jail. I'd say your best hope is that I succeed or that they don't kill me—so wish me luck!"

Marvin tossed the man into the back of the truck like he was another load of firewood, and tied a tarp over the top to hide his package. He left the tailgate slightly ajar so his prisoner could eventually escape if he didn't return. He figured it would take Lujan a while to get out, and by that time he would have succeeded or failed in saving his friends.

Empty potato sacks meant to hold pecans were duct-taped around Marvin's arms and legs to provide a protective sheath in case the dogs attacked. The wrappings allowed him to retain mobility; he could penguin-run if need be. It felt awkward, but functional. Marvin loved dogs: they had never frightened him, but this was different—these animals were killing machines. He would use the gun as a last resort, but only if he were cornered.

Mentally and physically prepared, Marvin was ready to begin his reconnaissance mission. He was back in Nam heading for his destiny, running not through a tropical jungle but through a grove of New Mexican pecans trees. Payback had begun.

CHAPTER 48

OLD MAN

Angel's two men were waiting, guns drawn, inside Dr. James Bloom's house when Charles and Rachael used their key and strolled through the front door saying, "We're here, Dad."

A large man stepped from the shadows and pointed a gun at them. Charles recognized him from the compound and knew this was serious trouble, but it was too late. The door was shut behind them and two guns were pointed at their faces.

The word "father" in that last text echoed in Bloom's mind. His father always referred to himself as "dad." How could he have been so foolish?

Rachael and Bloom were frisked and told to lie face down on the ground with their hands behind their backs. Then hands and legs were then bound with heavy-duty duct tape. Their pleas for information were meet with, "Shut up and do as we say and no one will get hurt." They were rolled over like well-cooked ears of corn on a grill and roughly gagged with a pair of Dr. Bloom's brown socks.

Two industrial-sized duffel bags with wheels were pulled up next to each of them, as if they were being checked for size. Rachael was crying, her head bent to the side. She was looking over at her husband, who was trying to communicate his love with his eyes. Rachael, then Bloom, were manhandled into the bags as if they were old rugs going to the dump.

"No noise, you two, or one of my boys will use his steel-tipped boot to give you something to cry about." The tattooed man lifted up his boot to emphasize his words.

The thugs zipped up the bags, transferred them into the back of a large black Escalade, and headed for the compound. The look of terror on Rachael's face before they zipped up the bag was devastating to Bloom; her muffled cries were tearing at his heart.

The fifteen-minute drive to the compound felt like an hour. Bloom's mind was awash in what-ifs—what could he use as a weapon, what were his options, what had happened to his dad? He remembered the back of the compound well. There was one weapon there, a pre-Columbian ceremonial golden spear. He remembered photographing it and where it was located. If he could somehow get free, maybe he could take at least one of these bastards out, maybe get a gun. He now knew what the surgical suite was used for, and it wasn't animals—it was human beings.

The vehicle's back door opened and the bags were lifted out, rolled into the back storage area, and parked there for what seemed like an hour. Rachael's crying had stopped, but Bloom could hear other voices nearby and he thought he could smell the odor of blood. This was not the first time this storage bag had held a human body, he thought, wondering if the last person was still alive.

The bags were finally opened and blinding lights greeted the hostages. The fresh air was welcome as Bloom was starting to think about suffocating. But what he and Rachael saw was anything but comforting.

They were lying in the art storage room next to three people with guns by their sides—a large man he assumed was the Gutierrez his dad had talked about, the man with finger tattoos who worked the front entrance, and Angel Veracruz.

Angel spoke, her voice harsh and definitive: "Cut off the tape and remove the gags." The tattooed man pulled out a switchblade and with two clean cuts freed each of the prisoners. Then he ripped the socks out of their mouths. Both Charles and Rachael gasped for air as they rubbed their wrists.

"Sorry to say this isn't quite the governor's mansion, Ms. Yellowhorse. It's my house, and my rules. I'm in charge here, not the governor, so you might as well get comfortable; this could take a while."

"Why are you doing this to us?" Rachael pleaded in a halting voice. She was trying to get her breath back as she pulled of the last of the tape from her wrists. In the dark bag she had envisioned her children's faces and wondered if she would see her recently deceased baby in the afterworld. Who would take care of them? Marvin? Now she was free, even if for a moment, and not dead yet.

Bloom looked over at Rachael and gave her a wink to say, "It's OK, stay strong," as he too removed the last of his bonds.

"You can thank your husband for part of this unfortunate situation and your nosy friend Marvin Manycoats for the rest. He will be joining us soon." Rachael's thoughts about Marvin raising her kids faded away.

"But why? A Navajo boy who has been dead for fifty years and a T.C. Cannon painting? What's the connection?"

"Well, the Cannon is mine fair and square, though the late Dr. Benally did take some liberties in how he obtained the piece."

"You killed Professor Benally?"

"No, actually you did." Angel smiled.

"What does that mean? I killed him?"

"Apparently when you were at his home, you got enraged and shoved your sculpture into his chest. My understanding is that you and Bloom were there. I'm sure your fingerprints are all over the place and phone records will collaborate your visit. A young weaver like yourself has strong arms and the angle of the sculpture will point to a person shorter than me."

"That's insane. No one will believe that story: the professor was a friend of mine."

"Well, you won't be there to defend yourself, and I will have some nice evidence concocted by our dear friend and supporter Mr. Lujan to point to you. The police will buy it. After all, you and your husband will have a truck full of stolen art—my art. I believe it will look like a murder suicide; it happens all the time."

"I looked up Mrs. Roy Bryant," Charles said, looking for any kind of leverage. "She was the wife of the monster that killed Emmett Till. So is the governor Ricky Begay's killer?"

"That's quite good, Charles Bloom. I heard you were a decent art dealer and now I can see why. Too bad you play by the rules; you could have been quite something. In fact, instead of this Navajo, maybe you and I could have been an item," Angel taunted.

"Angel, you must have had a horrible childhood to have come out this damaged," Rachael said, her courage returning.

Angel walked over to Rachael and slapped her with the back of her gloved hand, hard enough to leave a red mark.

"Be careful how you talk to me, Ms. Yellowhorse. Death can come fast or slow, and I can easily put those bonds back on you—much tighter this go around." Angel stepped back and readjusted her glove.

"Your father-in-law is in our surgical unit now. He's not so lucky. I'm afraid when he finds out you're dead, he will simply disappear. He was so distraught. There are lots of holes out on the desert; our holdings are vast."

Bloom cringed thinking of what they might be doing to his father at that very moment.

"My dad knows nothing. I took the photo of the Cannon out of interest in the painting. No other photos of paintings were taken, I swear. It was me, only me. Please leave my dad out of this. You can look at my phone, pull the sim card, do whatever analysis you want—there was nothing but the Cannon."

"I believe it was you, Charles Bloom, but a little pain is good to loosen the lips. Let's make sure your story holds water, or when Mr. Manycoats shows up, we may have to turn up the heat, so to speak. Your good friend should be here any minute."

"How can you want to kill the man that saved your husband? How can a governor, a man of the people, allow such a horrific act?" Rachael asked, her jaw swelling from Angel's blow.

"The Candy Man is a lovely person, but he's old and he doesn't rule this roost. I'm in charge here and no one is getting in my way, especially some old Marine buddy. Smiley is going to be the vice president of the United States regardless of any stupid murders in his past. If we're lucky, he may even be president.

"I'm here to clean this mess up, and you've unfortunately stepped into the middle of a big pile. Now let's see how your father-in-law is progressing."

Angel turned her back to the hostages to go into the surgical unit when a voice came over the intercom: it was Governor Smiley.

"An old man, huh?"

For the first time, Angel was thrown off balance. Smiley had followed her down to the compound in his truck and was listening in on the conversation from the front desk. There was a reckoning in the making.

CHAPTER 49

COMBAT MODE

The sun would be down in a few hours. Dead leaves and a scattering of pecan nuts covered the ground. Emerging spring grasses damped the noise of his footsteps as Marvin worked his way closer to the storage unit. He could see the back of the compound. There was a wire fence he would need to scale—hopefully it wasn't electrified—and then he would have to avoid the dogs. His plan was straightforward: get into the compound, then use whatever means necessary to save his friends. He was nineteen again, in full combat mode, all of his senses full-on.

Marvin gingerly placed a hand on the top wire of the fence, awaiting a shock—nothing. He did a roll over the barbed wire, his potato-sack armor making the task easy. No dogs, no people. Marvin slid down the metal fence and worked his way to the adobe wall. Then he peered around the corner: there were no windows and only one entrance to the storage unit. Marvin steadied his nerves, ready to make a dash for the door, when a huge man accompanied by a barking dog appeared with none other than the governor in tow.

"Go on back to the front and take that damned yapping dog," Smiley ordered.

"Sorry, Mr. Governor. The dog is upset. Maybe he smells our guests."

The governor opened the door and walked in as the man went back to the security gate.

Marvin ran over to the door and peered inside. He could see a cavernous building with rows of ceramics lined up in cases that had been stacked like dominos. The governor's cane made a tapping sound with each step he took. Marvin entered the room as the sound faded away and Smiley headed toward the back of the room. He shut the door behind him and followed the sound of distant voices. Marvin slid behind the last row of ceramics; he had a partial view of the room from there, and turned his good right ear toward the conversation.

"Angel, what the hell do you mean you're in charge?"

"Smiley, don't get your tit in a wringer. I'm simply having a conversation with our guests and, as I told you, this is MY operation. By coming here, you have opened yourself up to a huge liability. I told you let me take care of this. Don't you think people are going to start asking where the hell the governor is? You're not from Virginia, and you're not going on some walkabout to see your girlfriend in Brazil.

"Screw the governorship and even the vice presidency. This shit has gone too far. I'm not that guy, not any more. I can't be a part of this. You must stop, Angel!"

"Ha! You have to be kidding me! It's a little late to become the all-mighty righteous governor, don't you think, my love? Smiley, you're a murderer. I'm a murderer. We are cut from the same ungodly cloth. We want power and power can bring good along with it. These people are simply obstacles that must be overcome, as unpleasant as that may be."

Smiley's legs felt weak; he didn't know what to do in this situation. He had made an awful choice once before, but what could he do now?

"Gutierrez, take the governor back to his car and drive him home. I have work to do."

The large man put his hand on Smiley's arm and escorted him out the room, the tattooed man staying to watch the captives.

"Now let's see how the doctor is coming with your father. Watch them closely and shoot them in the head if they try anything, Raoul."

The large man nodded, his EWMN tattooed hand tightly gripping the gun trained on the Charles and Rachael as Angel went into the surgical suite.

As Marvin watched the drama unfold, he knew he must now act one-on-one. He slipped out from behind the cases and worked his way behind the guard.

Bloom's and Rachael's eyes were locked on each other, saying their goodbyes, when Marvin spoke: "Drop the gun!"

The man spun and fired wildly. Marvin fired a single shot, hitting the man in the head. The thug dropped to the floor, dead. Rachael and Bloom saw Angel coming out of the other room followed by a man in a translucent, blood-splattered plastic cloak, a stainless-steel scalpel in his hand.

Marvin, who had his back to Angel, felt a searing pain in his head as she clobbered the base of his skull with her gun butt, the same way she had seen her father and brother do many times. Marvin dropped hard to his knees, his head spinning and vision blurred. Angel frantically scanned the room as she picked up Raoul's gun. Both Rachael and Bloom had sprinted away, in opposite directions, during the melee.

Bloom told Rachael to hide as he went for the spear, which he found; it had not been moved. Then he headed back to face Angel, wielding an ancient spear against two guns, when a huge crash filled the room. Rachael had made a super-human effort to push over two cases of artifacts. The metal frames cascaded in a domino-style, landing against the adjacent wall and pinning the scalpel-wielding man against the surgical suite door. The door slammed shut and the man's ribs broke in tandem with the shattering ceramic vessels.

As Angel reflexively jumped to one side of the oncoming vessels, one of the guns fell from her left hand. The gun in her right gun was still poised for action, her eyes wide open looking for targets. "Give up, and I'll spare you a horrible death. Otherwise prepare to be dissected alive—and not by a professional!" she screamed.

Marvin had lifted himself up to his knees. His eyes were clearing and he could once again see Angel. Rachael was directly in her line of fire, so he jumped up and yelled, "Shoot me." Angel smiled wickedly as she took aim when the governor pushed through the door, yelling, "Angel, stop this madness," as he placed himself in front of Marvin.

"It's too late, Smiley. The puzzle must be completed. All of them must die."

The governor, reverting to his high-school baseball days, instinctively hurled his cane at Angel's hand just as she pulled the trigger. The hit redirected her aim, the single bullet ricocheting off the hard-packed adobe wall. The errant shot did find a victim—but it was not Marvin Manycoats. Instead the bullet penetrated Smiley's neck, piecing his carotid artery.

The silver tip of the walking cane shattered Angel's hand, and she toppled to the ground in agony. As the shock passed, she began searching with her uninjured arm for one of the guns.

Rachael, a basketball star in her own rights in high school, took two large leaps forward and pounced on her assailant's good hand, which had just secured a weapon. Rachael's weight crushed Angel's arm in two places, as the weaver simultaneously gave Angel a full elbow to the temple, which laid her out, unconscious.

"Mrs. Roy Bryant, child killer, you are the lowest form of a human being. Don't you ever screw with an angry mom," Rachael yelled, her chest heaving from the adrenaline surge.

Bloom clutched his golden spear, waiting for the second round of attacks, when he realized the fray was finished. He ran to the front of the room and slid the large wooden stick through the metal holders of the front door, securing the room from the inside. Dogs barking and men yelling could be heard bearing down from the outside.

Marvin, his head clearing, crawled next to Governor Smiley, whose body was soaked by an already thinning gush of bright red blood.

"Marvin, I'm sorry. I'm truly sorry for everything. I'm not a bad man. Please forgive me." Tears streamed down both men's faces as the governor's life started to slip into another dimension.

"I forgive you, captain," Marvin whispered, "but you must find those you have wronged and confess your horrible deeds. Enter the afterworld with an open heart. Share your story and maybe you will find the solace you so desperately seek, for redemption and compassion are the true sweets of life that have so long escaped you, my dear, lost Candy Man. A new journey driven by forces out of our control begins now, and you must plead with the Holy Ones for guidance and mercy to have chance to reach eternal peace.

CHAPTER 50

THE AFTERMATH

Bloom used Marvin's phone to call the Las Cruces sheriff's office, bypassing the Mesilla police department that he feared might be compromised by the Veracruz machine. Bloom yelled a warning through the secure door that the governor was dead, and that swarms of police were en route. Gutierrez made a unilateral decision: he gathered his remaining men and canines, cleaned out the safe, and abandoned their dethroned queen, all of it disappearing into the ether of Juarez, Mexico.

The "surgeon," a sadistic two-time felon, did survive Rachael's destructive pre-Columbian dominos. He was uncooperative and was currently being held in the Las Cruces jail on charges of attempted murder and parole violation.

Dr. James Bloom survived his ordeal with a severely bruised torso, an amputated index finger, and the trauma of torture that only time, therapy, and family could repair.

Las Cruces Memorial's excellent hand surgeon reconstructed and reattached the index finger, which was an important part of the healing process for all involved. Within weeks Dr. Bloom was joking that he had begged his tormentor to please spare his right hand, which he needed for the bowling league.

Governor Smiley's death at the hands of his fiancée was national news that trended number one for a short time on Twitter. The headlines in three regional papers read:

> "Santa Fe art dealer pleads insanity after murdering governor"
>
> "Retired art professor stabbed to death over rare painting; governor heart-broken"
>
> "Governor's fiancée axed over shady art dealings"

Angel was awaiting trial in jail, having been deemed a flight risk after pleading insanity. The T.C. Cannon inscription was her alibi: surely no sane person would associate herself with the killer of Emmett Tills. A partially burnt Polaroid was found in her purse, an image of the Cannon painting hanging on Benally's wall with the murder weapon, Rachael's sculpture, sitting in front of it. It was damning evidence.

Angel's entire art inventory, including the Cannon, was confiscated and put under title review. Unfortunately, Angel never saw the results. Shortly after her bail was denied, the Martinez family's jail operatives interceded. There could be no snitches; killing a governor was too big a risk to their operation. Angel's petite body, dressed in an oversized orange NMCD prison jumpsuit, with two short arm casts, was discovered hanging from a long bar, her neck looped in her bed sheets.

The morning headlines in Santa Fe read: "Angel of death commits suicide, her final flight" in large type. No questions were asked by the police, and the coroner ruled it suicide by strangulation.

The press tried in vain to interview Marvin Manycoats, looking for that next headline: "Ex-Marine hero trying to save governor for a second time." Marvin refused to be a part of the circus, knowing the mob of reporters would spin whatever he said to sell papers, not to tell the truth. He had nothing to say and he was no hero.

The murders of Ricky Begay and his father Orville by Governor Smiley were never mentioned to the police. Before the cops arrived at the compound, everyone involved decided to leave Ricky Begay out of the story if possible. They figured the police would soon lose interest in the case if no one were insisting they follow-up. In Marvin's mind, the case was closed and it was up to the *chindi* of Governor Smiley to make amends and determine his everlasting punishment.

Smiley's portrait would remain on the walls of the capital building, his dignity spared. He was buried on a high point of the military cemetery on the north end of Santa Fe, overlooking the snow-capped Sangre de Cristo Mountains.

Marvin was invited to the state funeral, but avoided the public event knowing he had nothing to say. The governor's military dog tags, the small silver ring, and the Indian bracelet on his right arm now positioned for eternity told the story. Marvin felt the man had tried to follow the light when confronted with right and wrong, and his life's good deeds should be left to stand on those merits. A cane thrown to save a life had sealed the governor's fate; the circle of life and death had been completed.

Rachael was convinced her lost child made the destruction of the evil Angel Veracruz possible. She was able to release her soul's grief and could once again focus on bringing a new life into the world. She and Bloom planned to work in great earnest over their summer in Santa Fe to bring that goal to fruition.

The police found Dustin Lujan early the next morning, a mile from the compound. He was hopping, barefoot, along a dirt road, his bonds intact. Lujan was told of the governor's death and went with a story he had concocted while lying in the truck bed. He didn't recognize his assailants because his eyes were taped. They were most likely cartel men. He also denied any knowledge of what had gone on inside the compound. He was an innocent person, lucky to be alive, who had come to the area to look for the governor.

The papers were reporting that the New Mexico Democratic Party was considering Dustin Lujan an excellent candidate to run for the vacant governor's office—his platform, stronger border security for the state.

Marvin's use of deadly force was ruled self-defense and no charges were brought against him. He decided to let the Holy Ones and the people of New Mexico decide Lujan's fate. The truth would never be believed in a court of law, and Marvin was convinced the political court of the afterlife already had Dustin's number—666.

On a bright afternoon in early April, when the first cottonwoods' tender sprouts of green announced the regeneration of life, Marvin Manycoats, Rachael Yellowhorse, Charles Bloom, Dr. James Bloom, and the residents of the Toadlena Basin attended the burial of Ricky Begay next to his beloved father. The locals chipped in for a marble headstone and an oak coffin, a statement of the community's support for one of their own, no matter how long ago he might have passed.

Marvin brought his own offering of deep respect for his departed friend—a Purple Heart lined in gold with a bust of George Washington under a shield of three red stars—that he pinned on coffin's plush interior.

This farewell gift, one of the two Purple Hearts he had won in the jungles of Vietnam saving a captain who wasn't deserving of such raw youthful courage, had found its proper recipient. In Marvin's mind, the true hero was a boy of eleven, slight of build, with a strong sense of right and wrong—a boy who had been prematurely removed from Mother Earth's loving embrace.

A special arrangement was made with the Toadlena cemetery to allow a rusty blue metal chair to be positioned near the Begays' headstones as a permanent memorial. The chair's embrace was no longer meant for rambunctious boys, but for the contemplation of an old man, a retreat where one could rest, rock gently in the desert winds, and remember the importance of life-long connections. Marvin now had a place where he could once again talk to his childhood playmate. It was a fitting home for a good friend who refused to be forced from the Dinétah, and whose courageous actions spoke of his loyalty to a people and their land.

The End

GLOSSARY

Acequia: A community-maintained irrigation ditch; developed first by indigenous tribes in the arid Southwest, then popularized by colonists who brought the Moorish agricultural tradition from Spain

Adobe: Refers to both bricks made from sundried clay and buildings constructed from the mud bricks; adobe has been in use in the Southwest since the 16th century

Anasazi/Old Ones: Ancestral Puebloans who occupied the Four Corners region of the United States; commonly defined as "ancient people," the Navajo word translates as "enemy ancestors"

Arroyo: The Spanish word for "brook," an arroyo is a dry creek created by fast-flowing water that fills up when there is a downpour

Atlantis: A legendary lost island with an advanced civilization popularized by the 5th century Greek philosopher Plato; its actual existence is the subject of ongoing debates

Big Hunk candy: A chewy, honey-sweetened peanut-nougat bar introduced to the U.S. in the 1950s by the Annabelle Candy Company

Bilagáana/bilágaanas: White man/men or white woman/women

Bosque Redondo: The internment camp at Fort Sumner, NM, at the end of the Navajos' Long Walk: after systematic destruction of their Canyon de Chelly homeland by Kit Carson in 1864, surviving Navajo were force-marched more than 300 miles across New Mexico to the Bosque Redondo (*Hwéeldi* in Navajo) where more than 8,000 were imprisoned until May 1868, when they were allowed to return to their homeland

Canyon de Chelly: A deep sandstone canyon on Navajo Nation land near Chinle, AZ, inhabited first by prehistoric peoples, followed by the Ancestral Puebloans, and now the Navajo, who have lived and farmed in the water-rich canyon for more than 300 years

Canyon Road: A half-mile long art gallery- and boutique-lined street in Santa Fe that hosts an annual Christmas Eve farolito walk popular with both locals and visitors

Casita: The name for a small house (often a guesthouse) in the Southwest

Chindi: The ghost left behind when a person dies; the Navajo believe *chindi* should be avoided because they are often "unbalanced," or malevolent, and can negatively affect the living

Chuska Mountains: A heavily forested mountain range towering almost 10,000 feet above the San Juan Basin, the Chuskas lie within the Navajo Nation near Gallup and Toadlena

Colima dogs: Playful Pre-Columbian ceramic depictions of pot-bellied, short-legged dogs; crafted between 250 BCE and 200 CE in what is now the state of Colima in western Mexico

COPD: Chronic Obstructive Pulmonary Disease refers to several conditions—including emphysema and chronic bronchitis—that obstruct airflow from the lungs, becoming more severe over time

Diné: Translating as "The People," it is the name the Navajo use to refer to themselves and their language

Dinétah: The traditional homeland of the Navajo people, the Dinétah is bounded by Blanca Peak to the east, Mount Taylor to the south, the San Francisco Peaks to the west, and Hesperus Peak to the north

El Niño rains: El Niño and La Niña are oscillating points in the Pacific Ocean that affect rainfall in the U.S. over a three- to seven-year cycle. El Niño, the "male" rain, usually brings more than the average rainfall to the southwest

Fritz Scholder: An enrolled member of the California Mission Luiseno tribe, Scholder (1937-2005) is credited with radically changing ideas of who "Indian artists" were and what kind of work they produced; a major influence on Native artists, he taught at IAIA from its founding until 1969

Gallup, NM: A small town in McKinley County, NM, on the edge of the Navajo Nation; according to the 2000 U.S. Census, more than 30 percent of the population is American Indian

Hastiin: A title of respect for men, it's the Navajo equivalent of "Mr."

"Hi Yo Silver, Away!" Although most people think "Hi-Hi Silver, Away!" was the command the Lone Ranger gave his trusty steed as they moved into their next adventure, the opening for both the radio and TV series actually said, "Hi Yo Silver, Away"

Historic Toadlena Trading Post: Founded in 1909, the Toadlena post is the historic home of the Two Grey Hills style of Navajo weaving; closed by its last owner in 1996, rug trader Mark Winter negotiated a lease with the tribe and reopened the carefully renovated post in 1997; it continues to provide goods and services to local families and Winter purchases their rugs, and sells them along with jewelry and other handcrafts to visitors

Hogan: A traditional eight-sided Navajo dwelling with a center hole to allow smoke from the fire at the center of the floor to escape and a doorway that faces east so the family can greet and be blessed by the morning sun

Hóhzó: One of the most important concepts in the Navajo belief system, *hózhó* refers to the beauty, order, and balance that are at the core of a healthy and happy life

Holy Ones/Holy People: Key figures in the Navajo creation story, the Holy People taught the Diné how to live in balance on the earth, and are believed to have the power to help or harm humans

Hopi/Hopis: A Pueblo Indian tribe based in twelve villages on three mesa tops in northeastern Arizona; once an enemy of the Navajo, the tribe's land now sits in the middle of the Navajo reservation, fueling a long-running land dispute created by a Congressional order in the 1800s

Huevos rancheros: "Ranch eggs" served in the style of rural Mexico usually consist of fried eggs layered on corn or flour tortillas; they may or may not be sided with refried beans and/or rice. "Christmas style" refers to a topping of both red and green chile particularly popular in Santa Fe and other parts of New Mexico

IAIA/Institute of American Indian Arts: Originally founded as a high school in 1962 on the campus of the Santa Fe Indian School, IAIA became one of three Congressionally chartered colleges in the United States in 1986, charged with "the study, preservation, and dissemination of traditional and contemporary expressions of Native American language, literature, history, oral traditions, and the visual and performing arts." Many of the United State's most popular and highly regarded contemporary American Indian artists are IAIA alumni or former faculty. The school now offers associate, bachelor, and graduate degrees to Native students

ICE: Immigration and Customs Enforcement is a federal agency created in 2003 through a merger of segments of the U.S. Customs Service and the Immigration and Naturalization Service. The agency is charged with enforcing more than 400 federal statutes related to immigration, terrorism, and the illegal movement of people and trade

Jackalope: A mythical jackrabbit with antelope horns, Jackalope is also the name of a chain of shops in Santa Fe and Albuquerque that sell furniture, pottery, rugs, plants, and gifts from around the world

Jean-Michel Basquiat: A New York City-based American Neo-Expressionist painter of Haitian and Puerto Rican descent, Jean-Michel Basquiat (1960-1988) achieved fame in the 1970s and '80s. In 2017, a 1982 painting of a skull sold for $110.5 million at a Sotheby's auction, setting records for the highest price for a work by an American artist; for an artwork created after 1980; and for a work by an African American artist

Jolly Green Giant helicopter: The U.S. Air Force developed the Sikorsky HH-3E helicopter, nicknamed the "Jolly Green Giant," to perform combat search and rescue downed airmen and wounded soldiers during the Vietnam War

Josephina's: Situated in an adobe house on the historic Mesilla Plaza, the café has been serving the local community for three generations; it's a real bricks-and-mortar restaurant as well as a favorite of the fictional Bloom men

La Cienega: A spring and associated marsh that supplies water to El Rancho de las Golondrinas and the Santa Fe River Canyon; La Cienega is also the name of a small, census-designated place that is part of the Santa Fe, New Mexico, Metropolitan Statistical Area. Charles and Rachael rent a house here when they are living and working in Santa Fe

Las Cruces, NM: Colonized by the Spanish in 1598, Las Cruces had been under the serial control of Spain, Mexico, and the Republic of Texas until the Treaty of Guadalupe Hidalgo established the United States as owner of the territory in 1848. Laid out in 1849 by the U.S. Army, Las Cruces is now the second largest city in New Mexico, with a population of about 101,712

Lotaburger: Founded in 1952, Blake's Lotaburger is a fast food chain with about eighty locations in New Mexico, Texas, and Arizona; a favorite stop of Charles Bloom, its claim to fame includes being named "The World's Best Green Chile Cheeseburger" by *National Geographic Magazine*

Medellín Cartel: A powerful Colombian drug cartel originating in the city of Medellín, Colombia, founded and led by Pablo Escobar and Gustavo Gaviria, the organization originally smuggled contraband before turning to cocaine in 1979. At the height of its power, the cartel supplied 90 percent of the cocaine that entered the United States. Gaviria was assassinated in 1990, Escobar in 1993

Mesilla, NM: Also known as La Mesilla and Old Mesilla, Mesilla is a charming small town in Doña Ana County, New Mexico, built around a historic plaza facing the San Albino Basilica; part of the Las Cruces Metropolitan Statistical Area, it is often mistaken as a part of the larger city

Mule: A courier who smuggles contraband across a border is known as a mule, taking the name from the sturdy pack animal. The use of mules protects members of criminal organizations from personal exposure and arrest

Nasazi: What the Navajo call the Anasazi, or Ancient Puebloans, who lived in the Four Corners region of the Southwest

Navajo Police Department: The largest tribal law enforcement agency in the United States, the Navajo Police Department (formerly known as the Navajo Tribal Police) serves a population of more than 178,000 with only eight response districts scattered over 27,000 square miles

Nayarit warriors: Pottery figures of male warriors, often depicted wearing armor and a helmet and holding a club, are classic artifacts of the Protoclassic Period (100 BCE–250 CE) of the Nayarit culture of west-central Mexico

Olmec/Olmecs: The earliest known major Mesoamerican civilization, the Olmecs occupied what are now the Mexican states of Veracruz and Tabasco from 1200 BCE to c. 400 BCE; considered the forerunners of all Mesoamerican cultures (including the Maya and Aztecs), the Olmecs are known for 17 huge stone heads, possible likenesses of Olmec rulers

Petroglyphs: Prehistoric rock pictures, symbols, and designs carved or pecked (but not painted) on rock surfaces by indigenous peoples 5,000 to 10,000 years ago

Piñon: A small, low-growing pine tree with edible seeds (piñon, or pine, nuts) that are an important, high protein staple for Native people from the southwestern United States to northern Mexico

Pre-Columbian: Pre-Columbian art designates work created by the indigenous peoples of Mesoamerica and the Andean region between 2 BCE and the arrival of Christopher Columbus in 1492, when the native cultures were conquered by the Europeans; artifacts of the period include terra cotta pottery, textiles, featherwork, stone, and gold and silver works

Protohistoric: A branch of study focused on the transition period between prehistory and the earliest recorded history—the period just before a culture's recorded history begins

Rez: Slang for a North American Indian reservation

Shapeshifter/Skinwalker: In Navajo culture, a witch who has the ability to turn him- or herself into an animal is known as a shapeshifter or skinwalker

Shiprock: Called Tsé Bit'a'í—winged rock or rock with wings—by the Navajo, the volcanic remnant is extremely important to the tribe's history, mythology and religion; its Anglo name refers to its resemblance to a nineteenth-century clipper ship. The town named for the formation is home to about 8,000 people, the largest settlement in the Navajo Nation

Shrek: The title character in a 2001 American computer-animated film, the word Shrek has come to designate an ugly person—possibly a nod to the German actor Max Schreck, who played a very ugly vampire in *Nosferatu*

Slot canyon: Long, narrow, deep channels with high, steep walls. Slot canyons are carved into sedimentary rock by rushing streams; they can be dangerous places, subject to flash flooding

Spider Woman: In Navajo legend, Spider Woman wove the web that helped create the universe; she also taught Navajo women how to weave the tribe's distinctive textiles, guiding and inspiring them with her song

Stone Man: Gallup, New Mexico, near the Navajo Reservation, is home base for an exclusive group of turquoise dealers known as stone men; see the fourth book in the Charles Bloom Murder Mystery series for more information

Tsénaajin and Tsénaajin Yázhí: The Two Grey Hills —two mesas located east of the Historic Toadlena Trading Post

VC: The Viet Cong, also known as the National Liberation Front of South Vietnam, was the guerrilla force that fought against the governments of South Vietnam and the United States, eventually winning the Vietnam War

White Shell Mother/Woman: White Shell Woman appears in the creation stories of several Native American tribes. In the Navajo creation story, she is Yoolgai asdzáá, the sister of Changing Woman. Her twin sons are among the most important beings in Navajo cosmology

Willem de Kooning: Born in the Netherlands, the Abstract Expressionist painter Willem de Kooning (1904-1997) is considered one of America's—and the twentieth century's—most influential artists

Window Rock: Window Rock (in the Navajo language Tségháhoodzání), named for a prominent window-shaped sandstone formation popular with tourists, is the capital and governmental seat of the Navajo Nation. The Navajo Nation Council, Navajo Nation Supreme Court, and the offices of the tribe's president and vice president are located there, as are the Navajo Nation Museum and the Navajo Nation Code Talkers World War II memorial

Yá' át' ééh: The traditional Navajo greeting, it translates literally as "It is good"

Yébîchai: Navajo Holy People associated with the forces of nature like wind, rain, snow; embodied in sand paintings during the Nightway healing ceremony

Zia: The Zia sun symbol—a circle with lines radiating in four directions—has represented the state of New Mexico on flags, license plates, and other paraphernalia for close to a century. Originating on the Zia Pueblo in the year 1200, the tribe says the sacred symbol has been illegally usurped by the state and other entities. In 2000, tribal officials asked the state to pay them $74 million for the continued use of the Zia; the NM Legislature did not give the pueblo any money, but did acknowledge that the state had been appropriating the image without permission since 1925

Photography courtesy Mark Sublette, unless otherwise noted

Page 1: *Mesillas Adobes*, NM

Page 6: *Tucson Adobe, To Mrs. Bandwell* by Maynard Dixon (1875-1946), July 1907, Oil on Canvas Board, 7.5" x 7.5" Courtesy Maynard Dixon Museum, Tucson, AZ

Page 11: Navajo Late Classic Third Phase Chiefs Blanket c. 1875-1880, 53" x 64" Courtesy Mark Sublette Medicine Man Gallery, Tucson, AZ

Page 19: *Navajo Hogan*, NM

Page 25: *Historic Toadlena Trading Post*, NM

Page 31: *On the Way to Las Cruces*, NM

Page 38: *Josefina's Old Gate Cafe Sign*, Mesilla, NM, Photographed by Teresa Melendez

Page 46: *Self Portrait* by T.C. Cannon (1946-1978), 1977, Ink on Paper, 11.5" x 8" Courtesy Mark Sublette Medicine Man Gallery, Tucson, AZ

Page 53: Navajo Two Grey Hills Bear Clan Rug c. 1930s, 72" x 52" Courtesy Mark Sublette Medicine Man Gallery, Tucson, AZ

Page 64: Navajo Silver Beaded Necklace c. 1940s, 23" Courtesy Mark Sublette Medicine Man Gallery, Tucson, AZ

Page 72: *3:33 iPhone Screenshot*

Page 79: *United States Post Office, Mesilla, NM 88046*

Page 86: *Crevice*, NM

Page 93: *The Blue Chair* by Josh Elliott, 2015, Oil on Masonite, 24" x 36" Courtesy Mark Sublette Medicine Man Gallery, Tucson, AZ

Page 103: *Black Ice*, NM

Page 108: *Near Ancient Toadlena Mesa*, NM

Page 114: *Sheep Pens Out of Rock*, NM

Page 126: Pre-Columbian Pottery, Nayarit Sitting Figurine and Colima Dog Figurine, c. 100 BCE - 250 CE

Page 130: *Winter Afternoon, Canyon Road* by Sheldon Parsons (1866-1943) c. 1943, Oil on Board, 24" x 35.75" Courtesy Mark Sublette Medicine Man Gallery, Tucson, AZ

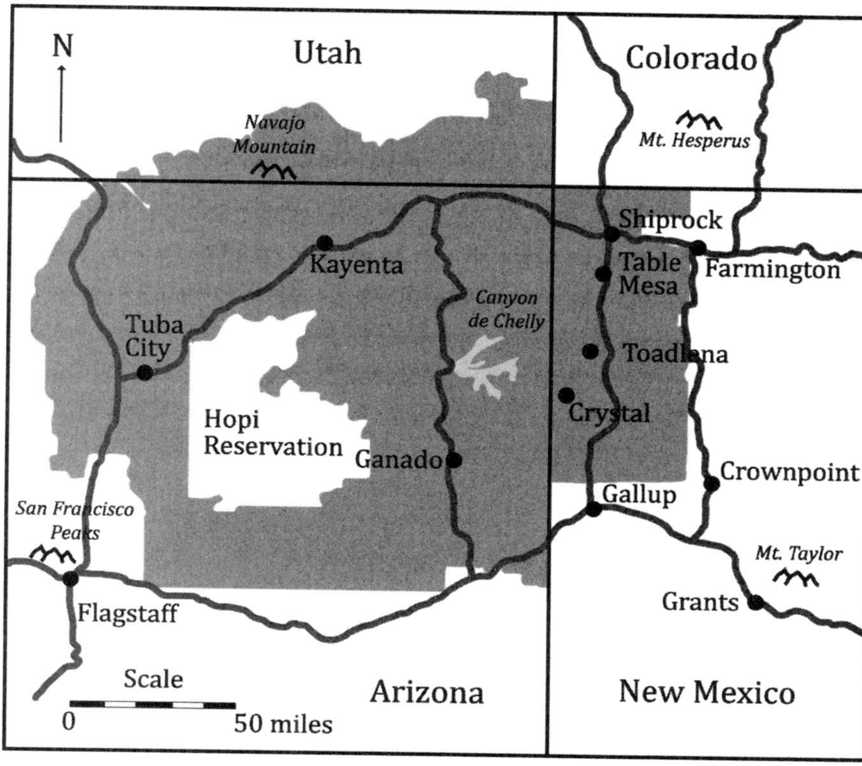
N
Utah
Colorado
Navajo Mountain
Mt. Hesperus
Shiprock
Kayenta
Farmington
Table Mesa
Canyon de Chelly
Tuba City
Toadlena
Crystal
Hopi Reservation
Ganado
Crownpoint
Gallup
San Francisco Peaks
Mt. Taylor
Grants
Flagstaff
Scale
0
50 miles
Arizona
New Mexico